MYSTERY
KEEPING BAD COM

WITHDRAWN

Fran Varady knows that making friends with down-and-out 'Alkie' Albie Smith on Marylebone Station is not a wise move. But Fran, who knows what it's like not to have the money for a cup of tea, is a soft touch. Albie, though, has a disturbing tale to tell—he claims he's witnessed the violent abduction of a young girl, in a distinctively marked blue Cortina. So vivid is Albie's tale that Fran overcomes her reluctance and reports the crime to the police, only to be sent away with a flea in her ear. But when Fran spots a blue Cortina with a white scrape, she is suspicious—and her suspicious are confirmed when she is warned off by her sparring partner Sergeant Parry, and then approached by a self-styled friend of her father, distraught over the kidnapping of his daughter. Then, days later, 'Alkie' Albie is found dead . . .

W9-BUH-429

KEEPING BAD COMPANY

Ann Granger

Thorndike Press
Thorndike, Maine USA

This Large Print edition is published by Thorndike Press, USA.

Published in 1999 in the U.S. by arrangement with Blake Friedmann Literary Agency Ltd.

U.S. Softcover ISBN 0–7862–1590–9 (General Series Edition)

The text of this Large Print edition is unabridged.
Other aspects of the book may vary from the original edition.

Set in 16 pt. New Times Roman.

Printed in Great Britain on acid-free paper.

Library of Congress Cataloging-in-Publication Data

Granger, Ann.
      Keeping bad company / Ann Granger.
         p.   cm.
     ISBN 0–7862–1590–9 (lg. print : sc : alk. paper)
     1. Large type books.   I. Title.
   [PR6057.R259K44   1999]
   823'.914—dc21   98–29750

To friend and fellow writer
Angela Arney

CHAPTER ONE

I was sitting on one of those red metal benches on Marylebone Station concourse when I first met up with Alkie Albie Smith. Not that Alkie Albie would have been my choice of companion. A cup of coffee brought about our acquaintance.

I was miserably aware how cold it was that morning. I wasn't wearing my usual jeans, but a daft mini skirt and useless tights which wouldn't have kept out the mildest breeze, let alone the draught straight from Siberia that cut through the open-arched station entry to whistle around my ankles.

I was waiting for the train from High Wycombe to arrive, and for Ganesh Patel, who'd be on it. Just for the purpose, all the trains were running late. To fight off the cold, I'd bought coffee from the Quick Snack stall, and settled down to wait. The coffee was in one of those green-with-white-polka-dot polystyrene beakers and scalding hot, so I put it on the vacant seat beside me until it cooled down. A simple thing like that can cause so much trouble. If I'd kept hold of the beaker. If I'd worn warmer clothing. If the train hadn't been running late. When all these things come together and then events turn out as they do, you have to believe in Fate—or Sod's Law, as

1

you may prefer to term it.

Ganesh, by the way, is a friend of mine. His family used to run the greengrocery that stood on the corner of the street in which was the house where I shared a squat. Redevelopment flattened our whole area and displaced us all. We straggled away like a bunch of refugees carrying our belongings to find somewhere else and start all over again. I had less to lose than the Patels. I'm an aspiring actress who has yet to get her Equity card and hasn't done anything yet but street theatre. But what little the squat was it had been a roof over my head, and then it wasn't there, captured by the council after a long, spirited and ultimately doomed defence.

Yet others fared worse. The Patels lost their shop, which was their livelihood, and the flat over it, which was their home. That's to say they pretty well lost everything. Compensation doesn't necessarily make that good. How do you compensate someone for years of hard work? For their plans and dreams for the future?

They hadn't been able to find another similar place to rent—or which they could afford to rent—in London and had moved out to High Wycombe. There they could stay with their married daughter, Usha, and her husband, Jay, while they searched for premises they could afford. That's why Ganesh was coming in on that particular train. He'd been

2

to see how they were getting on.

Ganesh wasn't living in High Wycombe, as there wasn't room for him. He was lodging with and working for Uncle Hari. Working for Hari had advantages and a rather greater number of disadvantages. The big advantage was that Hari's newsagent's and tobacconist's shop was just round the corner from where I lived. I'd just moved into a basement flat in Camden, of which I'll tell you more in a minute. The move was thanks to an old fellow called Alastair Monkton for whom I'd done some detective work. (And done it, I may say modestly, rather well.)

It was a bit of luck for me, having Ganesh nearby. Ganesh thinks clearly in straight lines. Sometimes it's irritating, but sometimes it helps. At least I knew he was there. I could count on Ganesh and we all need someone we can count on. It was good for him, too, because the job was cleaner and easier than the greengrocery—no hauling sacks of spuds and crates of fruit and veg around—and his family hadn't to worry about him.

But on the other hand, Uncle Hari was by way of a grade-one neurotic, one of those people who live on their nerves. Everyone who came into his shop was, in his mind, a potential shoplifter, which meant that after they'd left, he'd rush to count the remaining stock of Mars bars and peanut brittle. If anyone bought a magazine, he leafed through it suspiciously to

3

make sure the customer hadn't slipped another mag inside it. Either that or he worried that some juvenile had got hold of one of the adult mags on the top shelf. If the customer asked for a packet of ciggies from the shelves behind his counter, Hari's head swivelled like an owl's, right round, to make sure the customer hadn't palmed something from the counter while his back was turned.

He was, in fact, the most worried man I'd ever met. He worried about everything, not just the business overheads and rates and things like that. He worried about the state of the pavement outside the store and the unreliability of the streetlighting and lack of litter baskets. He fretted about his health, Ganesh's health, my health, anyone's health . . . Chiefly, however, he lived in fear of some unpleasant surprise being sprung on him.

He did have reason for this. Ganesh told me Hari had had a traumatic experience that had marked him for life. A kid had come into the shop one day and bought twenty cigarettes. He was a big tough-looking kid, perhaps not quite sixteen, but big enough to be sixteen. Anyway, as Hari tried to explain to the magistrates, he was the sort of kid who, if he'd been refused the cigarettes, would've come back that night with his mates and kicked in the windows. So Hari sold them to him.

Only moments later, when he'd hardly had time to put the money in the till, a woman

4

representing some trading standards agency rushed in, yelling at him for selling cigarettes to an underage customer. She was followed by a guy with a camera and another with sound equipment. The whole thing had been a setup by one of those TV programmes which like to make sure the consumer is being protected, or getting his rights. Never mind protecting poor Hari against that element of local youth which didn't care about anyone's rights. Hari found himself star of a show he hadn't volunteered to be in. He nearly had a nervous breakdown and was still swallowing a fearsome array of herbal remedy pills, all supposed to enable you to Cope.

Now he worried every time he sold a packet of ciggies to anyone who didn't qualify for a bus pass, and worried more when he didn't sell any, because business was down. Chief among his current crop of obsessions were: that the traffic going past the shop was shaking the foundations of a very old building; that the air pollution was bad for his sinus problems; that the new council parking regulations had put double yellow lines outside, which put people off pulling in to the kerb and nipping in to buy something.

Ganesh is a practical sort of person but even he was getting jumpy, being with Uncle Hari all the time. The way things were going, he would be trying the herbal pills soon. Visiting his parents that day would have given him a break, though not exactly a restful one. But even a change of problems is something, and the way life goes, sometimes it's the best you can hope for.

The display screens above the access to the platforms flickered and informed us that the delay, which was due to a unit failure at Wembley, was likely to last another half-hour. I wasn't going to sit there for thirty minutes more slowly petrifying. I'd take my drink and find somewhere warmer. So I reached for it and that's when I became aware that I had company.

The immediate impression was of a looming presence, hovering over me, and a whiff of sour booze dregs. There he was, no more than an arm's length away, with his eyes fixed on my coffee. He was wondering whether it belonged to me or whether some traveller had abandoned it to sprint for a train. He reached out tentatively and asked, 'That yours, dear?'

I told him it was and snatched it up protectively. Disappointment crumpled his face, which was already creased in folds like a bulldog's. He was a good sixty-five, or so I judged, with long greasy grey hair and pepper-and-salt stubble on his chin. He wore a tattered, dirty army greatcoat teamed oddly with clean, newish, stone-washed jeans. Some charity that hands out clothes to the homeless had probably given him those. It was a pity they hadn't also given him a pair of trainers as

6

the ones he was wearing were about to fall apart. Inside all these clothes he was so thin he looked as if the keen breeze might bowl him over and back down the escalators to the tube, up which I guessed he'd just come.

Partly to get rid of him and partly because often enough myself I've not had the price of a cuppa, I took pity on him. I fished out a fifty-pence piece and told him to go and buy himself a coffee.

He brightened up. 'Thanks very much, dear!' He grabbed the money and padded off in a curiously light-footed way, actually making, rather to my surprise, for the coffee stall. I'd have guessed he'd have put my contribution towards something in a bottle, but it was a cold day.

I know I should have ignored him, but when have I ever acted wisely? I soon knew I'd been unwise on this occasion, because, having got his coffee, he came back and chummily sat down beside me.

'You're a good girl,' he said. 'Pity there ain't more like you.'

That was a first. I don't remember getting such generous, unqualified approval, not since Dad and Grandma Varady died. My mother walked out on us when I was only a kid, so I was brought up by my father and Hungarian Grandma Varady. They were the best family anyone could have asked for, so I didn't miss my mum. Things started to go wrong, as far as

I was concerned, my first day at primary school. There was a mishap with the fingerpaint and the teacher stood over me— like a twenty-foot-tall ogre in a fairytale— shaking her finger and intoning, 'I see you're going to be a naughty little girl, Francesca Varady!'

She must have been a witch because that really put the kibosh on it. I never did get the hang of pleasing adults. After that, it was downhill all the way until the fatal day, just before I was sixteen, when I was asked to leave the private dayschool I attended.

That school was a meeting place for upwardly mobile entrepreneurial types and downwardly sliding impoverished professionals clinging on by their fingertips. The two groups collided there via their daughters. One group of pupils was collected by sharp-faced, bottle-blonde mothers driving flash cars. The other set of girls was collected by plain, vague women in sagging skirts, driving old motors. Occasionally, when it was raining hard, one of the first group would let down the car window and bawl at me as I stood at the bus stop, 'Jump in, love, and I'll run you home!' The others never offered me a lift and acted as if I were contagious.

I couldn't blame them. The fact was, I belonged to neither group. They didn't know what to make of me. I didn't have a mother in skin-tight designer wear nor in a Barbour. I had Grandma Varady, who'd turn up on Open Day in a rusty black velvet dress and a crooked wig. They treated me like a freak so I began to behave like one and it stuck. My family had slaved and saved to send me to that school. I wasn't sorry to leave it but I was desperately sorry for Dad and Grandma, who sacrificed so much for me. I was also sorry I dropped out of the Dramatic Arts course at the local college which followed my swift removal from school. I did seem to fit in there. But my leaving was due to circumstances beyond my control, as they say: Grandma dying about a year after Dad died, and my becoming homeless and all the rest of it. One day I'll make it as an actress, you see if I don't.

In the meantime, even the approval of an old wino like my companion rang comfortingly on the ear. So easily are we flattered.

I said, 'Thanks.'

He was prising the plastic lid off the beaker and he had a touch of the shakes, so I added a warning that he should take care. I doubt he had much sensation left in his fingers, which were white beneath the dirt, due to lack of circulation, and tipped with ochre-coloured overgrown nails.

'It's all right, dear,' he said. 'What's your name, then?'

'Fran,' I told him.

'I'm Albert Antony Smith,' he announced with something of a flourish. 'Otherwise

9

known as Alkie Albie. They call me that but it ain't true. Slander, that's what it is. I like a drink like anyone does, don't they? Dare say you like a drink, glass of wine, mebbe?' He belched and I was engulfed in a souvenir of his last encounter with the grape.

I shifted smartly along the metal bench and told him that yes, I liked a glass of wine, but this wasn't one of the occasions and if he thought I was going to buy him anything alcoholic, he could forget it. The coffee was as far as it went and he should make the most of it.

His crinkled, grey-stubbled face was a mesh of open-pored skin dotted with blackheads, which gave the impression he looked at you through a spotted veil, like the ones on hats worn by forties film actresses. These damaged features took on a shocked expression. He denied vehemently that he'd had any such idea in mind.

Then he slurped up the boiling coffee in a way that suggested he couldn't have much sensation left in his mouth either. I sipped mine cautiously and it was still almost unbearably hot. Why do they do that—serve it so hot? They know you're waiting for a train and have only got so much time to drink the stuff.

'I've been down the tube,' he said, confirming my guess. He indicated the entry to the Underground a little way off, by the ticket

10

windows. 'It's nice and warm down there. I spend most of the day down the tube this time of year, till the transport coppers throw me out. They're miserable buggers, them coppers. I sleep rough mostly, in doorways and such. Bloody cold it is, too.'

I knew that. But I said nothing because I didn't want to encourage him, though I'd left it a bit late for that and he didn't need encouragement anyway.

He rubbed his nose on his sleeve and snorted noisily. 'Cold gets you terrible on the chest.'

'Have you tried the Salvation Army hostels?' I asked.

'I never go to hostels 'less I has to,' he said. 'They're very keen on baths in them places. Don't do you no good, bathing. Washes away the natural oils.' Slurp. Sniff. Snort. 'You got a job, dear? Or you on the dole?'

'I haven't got a job at the moment,' I said. 'I was waitressing but the cafe burnt down.'

'Shame,' he sympathised. 'Protection geezers, was it?'

'No, just the chip pan.'

'Nasty,' he said.

'I want to be an actress,' I told him, though goodness knows why. Perhaps to stop him sniffing.

'They always want girls in them bars in Soho. Bit of waitressing, bit of stripping. Do all right.'

'Acting, Albie!' I snapped. 'A-C-T-I-N-G, all right?'

'A thespian!' he said grandly. 'I know what that is. I ain't ignorant. Ter be or not ter be, that's the ticket!'

'That is the *question*, Albie!' I wasn't sure why I was bothering but I sensed there was a good-natured sociability under all that grime. It made me feel I couldn't just tell the poor old devil to push off.

'I had an act once.' He leaned back on the metal bench and gazed dreamily at the Quick Snack stall. People had cleared away from all around us and we sat there together in cosy isolation.

I thought he'd got a pretty good one now, considering how easily he'd conned me out of a cup of coffee. But his next words cut me down to size.

'I was on the halls,' he said. 'Don't have variety no more. All that tellyvision, that's what killed it. We had some marvellous acts on the halls.'

'Go on, Albie.' I was surprised and really interested. Poor old fellow. He'd been someone once. Just shows you shouldn't judge. And, oh God, look at him now. Was I going to end up like that? As a bag lady, mad as a hatter, and with all my belongings in a couple of sacks?

'I had some poodles,' he said. 'They're very intelligent, are poodles. They learn very quick.

12

Three of 'em I had. Mimi, Chou-Chou and Fifi. They done tricks, you know. You wouldn't think how clever they were. They played football, walked on their hind legs, played dead. Mimi pushed Fifi along in a little cart, done up like a nursemaid in a frilly cap and Fifi with a kid's bonnet on. But Chou-Chou, he was the smartest. He could count numbers and read 'em. I'd hold up a card and he'd bark the right number of times. I had to give him a bit of signal, of course, but the audience never saw it. He was the best dog I ever had, Chou-Chou, and dead easy to train. He was very partial to a glass of stout. He'd have done anything for a nip of stout, would old Chou-Chou.'

'I'd have liked to have seen the act,' I said honestly. I didn't ask what happened to kill it off because I didn't want to know. Perhaps it had just been the down-turn in the variety scene, but I guess the bottle had done it. Albie'd shown up once too often, too drunk to do the act, or made a fool of himself on stage and that had been it. I wondered what happened to Mimi, Chou-Chou and Fifi.

As if he could read my mind, he added. 'I couldn't feed 'em, after that. I couldn't feed meself. They was clever little dawgs. Woman took them as said she could find 'em homes. I hope she found 'em good homes. I asked her to try and keep 'em together. They were used to being together. But I reckon she split 'em up. No one would want all three of them.

Reckon they pined.'

Not only the poodles had pined, I thought.

He seemed to pull himself together with an effort. 'What else you do, then?' he asked. 'When you're resting, as we sez in the business?' Clearly he now saw us as fellow professionals.

'I look into things for people. I'm a sort of enquiry agent—unofficial.' I tried not to sound self-conscious.

He put down his beaker and stared at me. 'What, a private eye, like?'

'Not a proper one. No office or anything. I'd have to keep books and pay tax and stuff if I set up properly. I'm unofficial. Anything legal.'

'Are you now . . .' he said very slowly and, when I thought about it later, very seriously.

I should have got up and run then, but I didn't.

'You any good at it?'

'Not bad,' I said with just a twinge of conscience because I'd only had one case. But I'd managed it pretty well, so my failure rate was nil and there's not many detectives can say that, can they?

He was quiet for quite a while and I was just grateful for it. A few people had come through the gates from the platforms and it looked as if a train was in. They must have fixed the broken-down train or shunted it away.

'You see funny things when you sleep rough, like I do.'

14

'What?' I was watching for Ganesh and only half heard Albie.

He obliged by repeating it. 'Only I keep my head down. I don't want no trouble. It's like anyone what's out and about at night, on the streets. You see a lot of things and you say nothing. Fellows what work on the dustcarts, going round the restaurants and so on, clearing away, early hours of the morning—they see all sorts, but they never say anything. That way, no one bothers the dustmen and it's the only way they can work safe, see?'

He peered into the bottom of his empty cup but I wasn't obliging with another fifty-pence piece. I'd just got my giro but it didn't stretch to supporting Albie as well as me in the style to which we had the misfortune to be accustomed.

But he had other things on his mind. 'I saw something the other night, though, and it's been really buggin' me ever since. I saw a girl. Nice young girl, she was, not a tart. She wore jeans and a little denim jacket over a big knitted sweater. She had long fair hair with one of them things what keeps it tidy.'

He put his hand to his head and drew a line from ear to ear over the top of his skull, meaning, I supposed, an Alice band. I knew about them. The daughters of the mothers with the baggy skirts had been keen on them.

'About your age, mebbe a year or two younger. Not very old. Pretty. Running like the

15

clappers. She had a good turn of speed, too.'

'Running for the last train,' I said idly. I don't know why, perhaps because we were in a station.

'Naw . . . I told you. I was in the porch, over at St Agatha's church. You know St Agatha's?'

I did know it. It was a quarter of a mile or so from where I lived, a red-brick Gothic lookalike with wire over all the windows to protect them from missiles, like stones or Molotov cocktails. Churches attract that kind of attention these days.

'She wasn't running for no train. She was running from two fellers. Only they was in a car, so it didn't do her no good. They come screeching round the corner, pulls up by my porch. Out jumps these two blokes and grabs the girl. She starts kicking and yelling, but one of 'em put a hand over her mouth. They shove her in the car and whoosh, off they go.'

This story was beginning to worry me, always supposing that he hadn't simply made it up. But it had a ring of truth about it. I thought of a possible explanation, not nice, but possible.

'St Agatha's runs a refuge,' I said. 'For battered wives and so on. She might've come from there, or been on her way there, and her husband, or boyfriend, and one of his friends grabbed her.'

'She didn't look like no battered wife,' Albie said. 'She looked like one of the Sloanes, what

16

they call 'em. I seen it clear. Right by me. Only they didn't see me. I squeezed in the back of the porch, outa the streetlight.' He paused. 'They weren't no amateurs,' he said. 'They were heavies. They weren't no husband or boyfriend. They knew what they were about. He'd got a bit of a cloth in his hand.'

'Who had?' I was getting more and more worried. At this rate I'd be needing some of Hari's pills.

'One of the fellers. He put it over her face. It smelled, like a horspital. I could smell it, even from where I was. She stopped kicking, sagged a bit, and he shoved her in the back of the car. She went in limp and just lay there on the back seat in a heap. I could just see her shoulder in that woolly sweater. Knockout drops.'

'Did you report this, Albie?'

'Course I didn't!' He sounded reproachful as if I'd suggested something mildly indecent. 'Think I want my head bashed in? They'd come looking for me, they would, them fellers. I'd be a witness. I see their faces and their motor. It was blue, or I think it was. The lamplight plays tricks with colours. It was an old model, Cortina. It'd got a bit of damage along one side, a white scrape, like he'd had a run-in with a white car and it'd left its mark, know what I mean?'

I knew what he meant. I also reflected that the fact he'd noticed so much was remarkable.

17

However, on the whole, I thought so many details made it unlikely he was making it all up.

'Albie, you're saying you witnessed a serious crime! That girl could be in real danger. You ought—'

'Fran?'

I'd been so engrossed with Albie's story that I'd failed to see that Ganesh had arrived. He was standing in front of me, hands shoved in the pockets of his black leather jacket, and frowning. The wind whipped up his long black hair. He took a hand from his pocket to point at Albie and asked, 'What does *he* want?'

'Who's this, then?' asked Albie, and it was clear he was offended. 'Friend of yours?'

'Yes, I was waiting—' But I didn't get any further.

Albie got up. 'Ta for the coffee, ducks.' He began to pad away in that surprisingly nimble way he had.

'Wait, Albie!' I called.

But he'd gone, through the main arch and out into the road.

'For goodness' sake, Fran!' (I could see Ganesh hadn't come back from High Wycombe in the merriest of moods.) 'What do you want to sit talking to him for?'

'He's a witness!' I exclaimed, jumping up.

'To what? How to live on an exclusive diet of whisky?' Ganesh asked, making an impatient move towards the exit.

'To a kidnapping!' I shouted and it was then,

as the words left my mouth, that I fully realised what I'd said.

Ganesh was staring at me. With more than a touch of despair I repeated, 'He witnessed a kidnapping, Gan, and I'm the only person he's told or is ever likely to tell about it.'

Ganesh dropped his holdall to the ground and made a violent gesture of dismissal. 'Why must you always do this, Fran?'

'Do what?' I babbled, taken aback by the vehemence in his voice. Ganesh gets sarcastic and he gets censorious but he doesn't generally lose his cool.

'Mix in such bad company!' he retorted. 'You know it always brings you trouble!'

CHAPTER TWO

Before I go any further, I ought to explain that, despite what you may be thinking, life wasn't going too badly for me at that time. At least I had a decent place to live and that was definitely an improvement on my previous situation.

Immediately before moving into my present flat I'd been living in short-term council accommodation in a tower block. The lets were short term because the whole building was scheduled to come down. Half of it already stood empty, boarded up and vandalised. Drug addicts broke in and indulged their various habits and insalubrious ways. Kids sniffed glue and various down-and-outs dossed. The council cleared them out at intervals and boarded the flats up again. Back came the junkies the next night and so it went on, with the occasional suicide plunging past the window on his way from the roof, muggers lurking in the entry hall, and Leslie, the neighbourhood pyromaniac, sneaking round trying to start his fires.

People like me were moved in there because the council had nowhere else to put us, or that it wanted to put us. We had low or nonexistent priority on the housing list and we were desperate enough to be prepared to put up with the squalor and the danger. It wasn't the first such place I'd lived in. I'd been vandalised out of an earlier one. That second one was even grottier than the first one, something I wouldn't have considered possible. But it's a fact that no matter how bad things are, they can always get worse. Beggars can't be choosers, they say, and I bet 'they' are comfortably housed.

There's only so long anyone can stand living like that and I'd got to the point where I was considering asking Leslie if I could borrow his matches. Things Had To Change. But if I walked out, the council would have said I'd made myself homeless intentionally, and they were under no further obligation towards me.

I'd have been prepared to settle for almost anything else. I had been enquiring without much hope about a place in another squat when Alastair Monkton got in touch.

The last time I'd seen Alastair he'd promised to see what he could do to help. I'd taken it as his polite way of saying farewell, like people you hear bawling 'we must have lunch' at someone they clearly mean to avoid like the plague.

But Alastair had come up trumps, being a gent of the old school, man of his word, etc., etc. Besides which, since I'd almost got killed trying to help *him* out, he owed me a favour. He told me about his friend in Camden. She was a retired lady librarian by the name of Daphne Knowles, whose house had a basement flat that she was willing to let to the right person.

I foresaw a problem in that. As you'll have gathered, few people would consider me 'the right person' for anything, much less to have lodging under the same roof. Any lady librarian of advanced years, and certainly any known to Alastair, would, I imagined, be rather fussy about the company she kept and fussier still who lived in her basement flat. I knew Alastair had put in a good word for me, but I wasn't counting on it being enough.

Still, worrying what she might think of me was jumping the gun. Without money one can do nothing and I had to establish my financial

21

position before I approached the librarian. Without much optimism. I set out for the council's benefits office. If I could at least persuade the woman I'd be able to pay the rent, it'd be something. Though what poor old Alastair and the lady librarian might consider a reasonable rent, would probably fall way outside my budget. I was undergoing one of my frequent jobless spells.

It was a quiet morning when I got to the benefits office, just a student with his head in a book, an out-of-work dancer, and a man with a cardboard box on his knees. The box was bound with string and had airholes punched in it. From time to time, a scrabbling sound came from inside it.

The student's number was called first, so off he went and I sat talking to the dancer who'd been out of work because of medical problems. She had consequently got behind with the rent and received notice to quit. She told me all about her stress fractures and asked me whether I thought she ought to accept a job she'd been offered abroad.

'Some of these overseas dancing jobs are a bit dodgy,' she explained. 'When you get there, the sort of dancing they want isn't the sort of thing I trained for.'

I commiserated, knowing how hard it is to get a living from the performing arts, but suggested she check out the job offer carefully.

The student had gone off in a huff. It was

the dancer's turn at the counter and that left me with the man with the cardboard box. By now, he was talking to it in a furtive whisper. I had to ask what was in it. I'm human.

He was happy enough to untie the string and open it up. It turned out to contain a large white Angora rabbit with pink eyes. It wouldn't have surprised me if the box had been completely empty or held an old boot, because you meet a lot of people like that out on the streets.

'I've got to leave the place we've living at,' he explained. 'It's got a rule, no animals. Plain stupid, I call it. I mean, it's not like a rabbit is a dog, is it? Winston's got his own little hutch and everything. I keep him clean. He don't smell. Cats is worse than rabbits. Cats go roaming around. Winston don't do that. But the landlord's downright unreasonable. He reckons if he lets me keep Winston there, next thing he'll have to allow pet snakes and things what more rightly oughta be in the zoo. So we've got to go. I mean, I couldn't part with Winston. He's all I've got.'

Winston twitched his nose and crouched quivering in his box. He looked like a nice enough rabbit, as they go, but it was a depressing thought that anyone could be left with no living friend but a rabbit. Whenever I get too smug about my own lack of strings attached, I try to remember people I've met like this.

The man leaned towards me, his face creased in worry. 'I never leave him behind when I go out. I always bring him with me in his box like this. He don't mind. He's used to it. There's people living where I am now that I wouldn't trust if I left Winston all alone. When I came back, I'd find the kids had got him out of his hutch, taken him round the back somewhere, and chucked him to a couple of dogs for a bit of fun. I've seen a couple of dogs with a good grip, one either end, tug a small creature like Winston here, clear in two. 'Course, that'd be if someone else hadn't turned him into rissoles first.'

I said sincerely that I hoped he found them both somewhere else safer to live.

After this, it was my turn at the counter.

I explained I'd been told of a vacant flat. Before committing myself, I needed to know what kind of help I might hope for with the rent, being out of work.

After I'd answered all the questions—and there were a lot of them—about my personal circumstances and where the flat was and what it was like (which I didn't yet know), there was good news and bad news.

The good news was that I would probably qualify for maximum benefit. The bad news, before I got too euphoric, was that in my case this would be based on what the council considered a reasonable rent for the sort of accommodation suitable for me in the area where I intended to live. Here we hit a snag. The accommodation the Rent Officer seemed likely to consider suitable for me was probably something a little bigger than Winston's hutch. Since Daphne's flat was likely to be quite a bit roomier, and was located in an area where vacant bedsits were as rare as hen's teeth, and landlords could name their price, whatever I got by way of benefit wouldn't nearly pay the rent. I'd have to find the difference myself.

'Or find a cheaper place,' suggested the woman behind the counter, smiling kindly at me.

It was much as I'd expected and I couldn't grumble. But it did seem that even going to view the flat would be a wasted journey. I went all the same, because I felt I owed it to Alastair.

I must say the first view of the area served to confirm my fears that I'd be considered the wrong person. It was depressingly genteel. Coming from where I was living, it was like being beamed down to another planet. The house itself was tall and narrow in a long curving terrace of such houses, all white-washed, with freshly painted doors and sparkling windows. One flight of steep steps ran from pavement to front door and another down into the basement. The road seemed unnaturally quiet. One or two householders had put shrubs in ornamental containers outside their doors.

That sort of thing wasn't recommended on the balconies of my tower block. The tub and plant would disappear inside five minutes, very likely pitched over in a lighthearted attempt to brain someone on the ground below. What I saw in Daphne's street was life, all right, but not as I knew it.

One oddity struck me. At intervals along the pavement, before each house, was a round brass disc like a small manhole cover. Before Daphne's house the brass disc had been replaced by a circle of opaque toughened glass similar to the glass skylight in subterranean public toilets. Strange.

Before I announced myself, I crept down into the basement and took a look around. The entrance area was cramped because part of it was taken up with a newly constructed wall which ran between the house and the pavement above. I couldn't see the purpose of this and it had me puzzled. There was a window by the front door and taking a look through it I saw a large room brighter than many basements because additional light was admitted through a window at the far end, which appeared to be an outlet on the garden. It was furnished with quite decent furniture. Through a half-open door, I glimpsed a kitchenette. Even this first sight revealed the place to be clean, newly decorated and highly desirable. I was amazed it was still empty.

I was already certain I wasn't the sort of

person who got to live in flats like this, even with the council's help. Daphne Knowles would probably press an alarm button or something the moment she set eyes on me. I might find a job, at some future date, that would pay a decent wage and enable me completely to transform myself and my lifestyle, but as of that moment I had neither job nor money and this place was right out of my league.

I'd come this far and Alastair would be asking Miss Knowles whether I'd been in touch, so I climbed back up both flights of steps, and rang her doorbell.

After a moment I heard a regular padding footfall. The door opened and there stood a tall, very thin woman with wiry grey hair. She was wearing jogging pants and a sweatshirt. On her feet were brightly patterned Fair Isle socks with soft leather soles attached. I was prepared for her to say, 'Go away, I don't give at the door!' But she didn't.

'Hullo,' she said cheerfully.

'I'm Fran Varady,' I introduced myself. 'Alastair sent me.'

'Of course you are,' she replied. 'Do come in.'

She shut the front door behind us and set off ahead of me down the hall at a brisk pace. I scurried along behind her, trying to get a look at the place as I went.

What I saw only convinced me more that I

had no chance. The house oozed respectability. The furniture was old but polished and probably valuable. We were talking antiques here. Narrow stairs with carved wooden balusters ran up to unseen regions. The stair wall was lined with early French fashion prints. There was a lingering smell of coffee brewed fresh at breakfast time, lavender wax and fresh flowers.

We arrived in a large, airy sitting room overlooking a scrap of garden. The sun beamed in and lit up the spines of rows and rows of books. This was a librarian's home, all right. There was a table by the window and on it, a cumbersome old-fashioned manual typewriter. A sheet of paper was sticking out of the top and a pile of other paper was stacked beside it. It seemed I'd interrupted her at work. That would probably also count against me.

Daphne Knowles seated herself in a cane-framed rocking chair upholstered with bright green and pink flowered cretonne, and indicated I should take a seat on the sofa. I sank down into feather cushions and sprawled there, trapped, and feeling at a considerable disadvantage. Daphne, beaming at me, began to tip back and forth in her cane rocker, which groaned a teeth-grinding protest.

'So you're Alastair's girl!' she observed.

For one dreadful moment I thought there had been a mix-up, and she imagined I was

Alastair's granddaughter, who was dead. I tried to lean forward as I hastened to explain, 'No, I'm only Fran who—'

'Yes, yes, I know that.'

She waved a hand at me and I sank back again. Getting out of this kind of sofa was always more difficult than collapsing down on it. I couldn't get leverage from my legs and it was a question of grabbing the arms and hauling oneself up and out.

'It was such a sad business, but life does go on. I'm a firm believer in reincarnation.' The rocker creaked and I could see why she preferred it to this sofa or either of the matching armchairs.

'I've a friend who believes in that,' I told her.

She leaned forward, serious. 'It isn't the dead, you see, who have the problem. The problem is for the living who have to go on, well, living when they've lost a dear one. I've told Alastair he mustn't worry about Theresa but he took it all very hard.' She sighed, then perked up. 'He tells me you want to be an actress.'

'It's what I dream about.' I added apologetically, 'We all dream about something. I did start a drama course, but I had to drop out.'

'Ah, yes,' she said and her eyes drifted towards the typewriter. I wondered whether it was in order to ask what she was working on.

29

Before I had a chance, she asked, 'Would you like to see the flat?'

Jangling a bunch of keys she led me out of the house and down to the basement steps.

'As you see,' she said. 'It's completely separate down here, quite self-contained. There's no longer any communication through from my place. It's been bricked up.' She unlocked the front door and we went in.

She seemed to think I'd want to look around by myself, so she stayed by the door and waited.

I could see now that the furniture consisted of a pine rustic-style table and four chairs, and a large old-fashioned sofa covered in blue rep. There was a small television set on a low pine occasional table. The floor was newly carpeted wall to wall in dove grey.

I opened a door and found a small bathroom, also newly equipped. I inspected the kitchenette glimpsed from outside. Like the main room, it had a small window admitting light from the garden. It would be at ground level outside, but here it was halfway up the wall. There was a dinky little cooker and a fridge.

She must be asking the earth for this place. I was grateful to Alastair, but he just didn't realise. I knew I could never afford it.

Out of curiosity, I went back to the main room and asked, 'Where does the new brickwork you can see from outside come in?'

'It's a corridor leading to the bedroom.' Daphne led me to a door to the left of the basement window. She opened it and sure enough, the new brick wall outside created a narrow corridor inside that led into a small square windowless room. Windowless, that was, in the normal sense. Light permeated through from a round skylight above and I realised that we stood beneath the pavement. Eureka!

'Victorian coal cellar,' explained Daphne. 'These houses had all the mod cons of their day. The coal was tipped down a chute through one of the brass manholes you probably saw in the pavement as you came along here. Straight into the cellar, no need for the coalman to invade the house. Most houses still use the cellars as junk rooms. One or two, like this one, have made an access from the basement flat. Previously the only access was in the well of the building, completely detached from the house.'

She switched on the light. A pine bedstead and wardrobe more or less filled the space. It gave you an odd sort of feeling in there and wouldn't do if you were at all claustrophobic. It was reinforced by the sound of footsteps passing over our heads. I wondered if this might be a bargaining point when it came to fixing the rent. Not everyone would fancy the setup.

'No one can see through the glass,' Daphne

31

said reassuringly, perhaps thinking my silence meant I was worrying about that. 'And not many people go past. It's a very quiet street.'

It was confession time. I owned up. 'It's all very nice, but I couldn't afford it. I'm sorry. Thank you for taking time to show me around.'

She put her head on one side like a tall thin bird. 'If you really like it, and it would suit you,' she said delicately, 'we can discuss mutually convenient terms.'

My heart hopped. I sternly ordered it to calm down and not start getting excited about what wasn't going to happen.

Daphne led me back to the sitting room and we both sat down on the blue rep sofa.

'I should explain,' she began. 'I'm seventy-one now.'

I expressed surprise because she didn't look it. She waved my words away.

'My friends and relations, who mean well but *will* interfere, say I oughtn't to live quite alone. I can't see why not. I'm perfectly fit and not a bit gaga. They keep nagging at me. So I had the basement flat done up and the cellar turned into extra living space and joined on as you saw. I was playing for time with the alterations. I didn't really intend to let it. I hate the thought of strangers living in my house, even detached strangers down here. But eventually the work was finished and then they all began asking, when was I going to advertise the flat?

'Never, was what I told them. I'd wait until someone was recommended to me. So then they began recommending people and none of them was at all *sympathique*, as the French say. There was absolutely no rapport between us. My family said it didn't matter because I needn't ever see the tenants. But then, what was the point of them being down here? The idea was, if there was an emergency, I could get hold of someone quickly. But if there's an emergency you don't want to get hold of people you don't like, do you? So I kept making excuses not to let.'

She paused to look at me anxiously, her eyes asking whether I understood. I told her I did. It was her privacy and her independence all those well-meaning people were intent on chipping away at. Knowing how much I valued my independence, I knew exactly how she felt. I tried to explain this.

She beamed and nodded enthusiastically. 'I thought you'd understand. Alastair was pretty sure you'd be just the person but I was cautious. I wanted to wait and see. But I think you are *sympathique* and so, if the flat would suit you, we can fix a rent you can pay.'

I was in no position to turn the offer down. Besides which, it was far and away the best offer I was likely to get, probably in my entire life. I had a couple of qualms, I admit. One was that nothing comes without a price tag of some sort. It doesn't have to be money. The other

33

doubt had to do with that strange little bedroom under the pavement. But I could worry about all that later. I told her the flat would suit me fine.

*   *   *

'Sure he saw a kidnapping,' said Ganesh. 'He also saw pink snakes, giant pandas and little men in green jackets playing fiddles.'

Ganesh can be difficult and he was being particularly so right now. We'd gone straight to my new flat from the station and had argued all the way there. Now we were sitting over plates of reheated dal and still arguing. (I'm not a cook. Ganesh had brought the dal from High Wycombe in a plastic tub.) Not only the dal had been rehashed. We were picking over Alkie Albie's story for the umpteenth time.

'I believe him,' I said. 'Mostly because of the details, like the bit about the cloth with the knock-out drops on it.'

Gan put down his fork. 'Oh, come on, anyone could make that up!'

'And the Alice band.'

'The what?'

I explained what an Alice band was. 'He could have described her any way he liked, but a detail like that isn't something he'd imagine. He saw her. Besides, because he's down and out doesn't mean he isn't perfectly capable of observation.'

34

Gan pushed his plate away. 'You think I don't know anything about that old fellow, don't you? You're wrong. He's always around this part of town. You happen not to have run into him before. Let me tell you, you got him on a good day. He goes past the shop. Usually he's roaring drunk and the drunker he gets, the more aggressive he gets. He staggers along shaking his fist and leaping in front of perfect strangers, offering to fight them. Hari runs and shuts the door in case he tries to come in the shop.'

'I don't know why Hari even tries to run that shop,' I said, nettled. 'He doesn't trust anyone who goes in it. He's getting an ulcer. Why doesn't he go into another line of business which wouldn't attract the kids? We need a dry-cleaner's around here.'

Ganesh's face lit up. 'You and I could—'

'No, we couldn't, Gan!'

'It's a decent business.'

'I can't stand the chemical smell,' I said firmly.

This was also rehashing an old argument. We all have a dream, as I'd told Daphne. Gan's dream was that he and I could go into business somewhere. The idea of being tied to a shop didn't strike me so much as a dream as an out-and-out nightmare. I understood Hari's neuroses only too well. Put in charge of a business I'd end up just like Hari, swallowing the herbal pills and working myself towards

35

early heart failure. Just thinking about being tied to anything fills me with strong negative emotions, as they say. Scares me witless, in other words.

I'd no present job and I'd no family. But I did, still do, have my independence and it's worth more and more to me as I see the price other people pay for giving theirs up. That's why I was in tune with Daphne. As for not owning anything, that doesn't have to be so bad. Not owning anything means nothing owns you. I have a decent place to live right now, but otherwise I don't have anything (except Gan as a friend but that's worth a lot).

But take Ganesh as an example. He has a close and loving family. But they have expectations of him. That's a terrible burden for anyone to bear. No one has expectations of me, not any longer. Grandma Varady and Dad had hopes of me once but I let them down. I'm sorry about that and always shall be, but there's nothing I can do about that now. There's never anything anyone can do about the past except, possibly, learn from it and that's not easy. 'Learn from your mistakes!' people say with varying degrees of smugness.

'Listen, chums!' I want to cry out. 'We make the sort of mistakes we make because we're the kind of people we are. We're poor judges of character, or easily influenced, too kind-hearted for our own good or just plain lazy. So we go on making the same mistakes over and over again.' I suppose you could say that in the end it gets to be a habit, a way of life.

This is not to say I don't have plans, hopes, expectations, dreams, call it what you will, for myself. I do. But as long as I don't owe anything to anyone but me, Fran Varady, I can't let anyone but myself down. That's the way I like it.

I stood up, collected the dishes and took them to my tiny kitchen. I was feeling rattled because perhaps, despite my earlier claim that no one has expectations of me, I realised it was possible Ganesh did. What's more, I could see now that Alastair did. They both expected me to make good somehow in some acceptable way. Which meant, rejoin the human rat-race. Now there was Daphne as well. If I wasn't careful, the pressure would get to me and if that ever happened I'd have to move on, walk away from them all.

Enough about me. I didn't want to get neurotic.

'How are your people getting on?' I called out as I filled the kettle for tea. 'Any luck with new premises?'

'They've found a couple of possibilities. Jay's sorting out what they can afford.'

Jay's an accountant. An accountant as a son-in-law is useful and the Patels were getting good advice. Ganesh, however, sounded depressed. I guessed that other things weren't going so well in High Wycombe. I went back into the sitting room. Gan had tidied up the table and was now wandering around tidying up the rest of the room.

'Look,' I said. 'They'll sort something out.'

'Yes. They'll either get a place in High Wycombe and expect me to move out there to run it with them. Or they won't get a place and I'll have to stay on here with Hari.'

'Why don't you tell them what *you* want?' I said, exasperated. 'You can't please everyone all the time.'

He grunted.

'In the meantime,' I went on briskly, because there was no point in letting him mope, 'what do we do about Albie?'

He expelled air between his teeth in a hiss and spun round, long black hair flying. 'We don't do anything! We'd have to get him to tell his story again to the police. He probably wouldn't even remember it. We don't even know where he is now.'

'You said yourself, he's always around here. We could find him. He's distinctive.'

'There I agree with you!' He jabbed a finger at me. 'He's also totally unreliable, Fran. When did this—or when was this snatch *supposed* to have taken place?'

'Quite recently.'

'*When*?' he persisted.

'Look, I don't know! We'd have to ask him again!'

So that's why we ended up spending the

afternoon looking for Alkie Albie Smith.

*   *   *

Needless to say, we didn't find him. We went back to the station and asked the railway staff, the taxi-drivers outside, anyone who looked as if he might have been there earlier in the day. Surprisingly, a few people knew who we meant. Albie, it seemed, was quite a local character. But no one had a clue where he went when he wasn't hanging around Marylebone . . . or offering to punch passers-by outside Hari's newsagent's.

'That's it, then,' said Ganesh, sounding relieved. 'We tried. He'll have got hold of some booze and be sleeping it off somewhere. If you see him again, you can ask him again. Otherwise there's absolutely nothing we can do. I still think he dreamed it all up. You'd bought him coffee. You'd demonstrated you were a soft touch. He wanted a quid off you and was spinning an interesting tale. Look, I've got to get back to the shop or Hari will be worrying.'

'When isn't he? We should tell the police.'

'Give over, Fran. They'd chuck you out of the copshop before you finished your story. You didn't see anything. All you know is, Albie reckoned he saw something—and let's face it, the old chap isn't going to impress the police as a reliable witness!'

39

I wasn't going to argue with Ganesh. It's almost impossible at the best of times. Ganesh always makes perfect sense. The more sense he makes, the more I disagree with him. So I let him go. But I wasn't letting the matter go. I don't give up that easily. I could at least try to report it. So that's where I went, the nick.

*   *   *

Contrary to what some people might think of me, I don't have anything against our gallant constabulary. It does sometimes appear as if they've got something against *me*, but that's their problem. It was worse when I hadn't a regular address. But even now I've got a proper address, they treat me like I had a record as long as your arm, which I haven't, I may add. Gan says, what can I expect if I go around with holes in my jeans and a haircut that looks as if someone ran a lawnmower over it. Probably it doesn't help that my temper has rather a short fuse and the plods can be so frustratingly thick. We get into arguments and the Law doesn't like that. Generally, I leave them alone and hope they'll leave me alone.

Walking voluntarily into the local police station that afternoon felt all wrong. I was a fish out of water and probably looked as if I'd come to confess to being the Camden chainsaw killer.

It was a quiet period. A middle-aged desk

sergeant was drinking tea from a mug with 'George' painted on it. A short distance away, down the counter, an intense woman in a red mac and black beret was making a formal complaint about a neighbour to an impatient woman officer who had probably heard it before.

'He exposes himself to me!' said the woman. 'Every evening at the bay window.'

'We made enquiries,' said the WPC. 'No one else has been bothered by him and he denies it.'

'Every evening!' persisted the woman. 'Wearing nothing but one of them baseball caps.'

The desk sergeant, seeing I'd become distracted, put down his mug and enquired, 'Yes?'

I apologised for my inattention and said I'd come to make a report.

'Sergeant Henderson,' he said. 'You wait over there, take a seat. And you're late. Should have been here this morning, ten sharp.'

'Why can't I report it to you?' All he was doing was drinking his tea and—I could now see—doing a crossword.

'If you're on bail and gotta report in daily,' he said, 'you see Sergeant Henderson. He deals with that.'

I explained, very patiently considering the insult, that I hadn't come to report myself but to *make* a report regarding an incident.

41

'An incident?' he asked suspiciously. 'Mugging? Traffic offence?'

'None of those. Much more serious.' He brightened up so I added quickly, 'Well, I didn't actually witness it myself.'

This didn't go down well. He'd picked up a Biro and now he put it down again and a scowl puckered his receding hairline. The suspicion began to grow in my heart that Ganesh had been right.

I started talking quickly before he could interrupt and managed to get out the gist of Albie's tale.

The woman with neighbour problem was interested at least. She'd left off telling her own tale and was watching me closely.

The desk sergeant looked as if pension day couldn't come soon enough as far as he was concerned. 'Now, let's get this straight,' he said. 'You were told by some old fellow who happened to sit down next to you on a public bench that he'd seen a snatch. Why didn't he report it himself?'

'He's living rough,' I said. 'He doesn't want trouble.'

He rolled his eyes upwards theatrically. 'Living rough? Oh well, yes, that makes it a whole lot easier! You wouldn't know his name, I suppose? Because, let's face it, dear, there's not a lot we can do with what you've just told me now. Half those old dossers are doolally. Live in a world of their own, you know. It

42

comes of drinking anything they can find which is alcohol-based. You wouldn't credit what they'll knock back without a blink. Stuff which would poison you and me. They lose all contact with reality. Even if there's a grain of truth in it, the time scale's out. They tell you something like it happened yesterday and it turns out it took place forty years ago. If you knew his name, of course, we could check it out—if we could find him.'

In a general sense he was probably right. But I didn't believe that the drink had scuppered Alkie Albie, despite his nickname. I knew what had done for Albie. He'd dropped out of the regular world the day he'd had to part with Fifi, Mimi and Chou-Chou. The nice kind woman had taken them away to new good homes. But every day of his life since then he'd wondered what had really happened to those poodles (and one of them very likely a canine alcoholic, at that).

'As a matter of fact I can tell you his name,' I said proudly, confident of making an impression. 'It's Albert Antony Smith.'

It made an impression all right. The sergeant dropped his Biro and gave a yell of laughter. 'What? Old Alkie Albie? He's been spinning you one of his tales? Gorblimey, I've been listening to all this and it turns out to be one of Alkie Albie's nightmares?' He leaned on the counter confidentially. 'Listen, we know old Albie here. He's never sober. He's just

43

what you might call one degree more or less drunk. He never saw nothing, darling, believe me.'

'He wasn't on a bender at the time he talked to me,' I said. 'He was drinking coffee.'

'That'd be a bloomin' first! Old Alkie Albie drinking something which wouldn't go up in flames if you put a match near it?'

'I bought the coffee for him,' I insisted. 'I know what he was drinking. I believe he saw it all.'

He smiled at me in a kindly fashion as people do at the innocently deluded. 'Listen, dear. He believes he saw it. You believe he saw it. Perhaps the old git honestly believes he did see it. But then, he sees all sorts, does Albie, when he's had a skinful. Hallucinating, see? He mightn't have been puggled when you spoke to him, but believe me, the night he *saw* this incident, he would've been plastered. Don't you worry about it. Nothing happened.'

'That what they always say!' said the woman to me, in the tones of one who'd suffered long from the incredulity of the police force. 'And I saw him as clear as I see you, and him without a stitch on.'

The WPC said firmly, 'I think you're mistaken, Mrs Parrish, and this is the third time in a week you've been in here. We're very busy, you know! I'll have a word with the social worker.'

'Happens all the time, see?' the sergeant
44

whispered hoarsely. 'In here reporting things every other day, she is. Loneliness is what causes it.'

Perhaps that did it, the notion that they classed me with a nutcase who saw naked men at every bay window. Or perhaps I had a sneaking feeling the sergeant might be right about Albie. I felt foolish and sought to rescue a shred of pride.

'Look,' I snapped. 'I only know what he told me and I'm reporting it. Kidnapping's a serious crime, right? You ought to check it out. At any rate, I've been a responsible citizen and told you and I want it logged into the daybook.'

I knew that much about police stations. They keep a record of reported incidents, day by day in the Occurrence Book.

His kindly smile vanished. 'If you knew the amount of paperwork we have to do, you wouldn't ask me to waste time writing up a report on one of Alkie Albie's meths-visions!'

I just stood there. He sighed. 'All right. Make meself a laughing stock. And your name is?'

I told him and also my address.

'And at least consider it might have happened!' I pleaded.

'Certainly, madam!' he said. 'And I'll ring round the press and tell 'em to hold the front page, and all.'

As I left, the woman was recommencing but about a different man, this time at a bus stop.

45

*   *   *

I was angry and frustrated—more than a little embarrassed, too—but most of all I was determined. I still believed Albie's story and I wanted to prove it true more than anything. I'm ashamed to say, the desire to wipe the superior look off the sergeant's face was a stronger motivation at that moment than rescuing the unfortunate kidnap victim. I'd almost forgotten about her. Not exactly, but she wasn't in the front of my mind, if you understand me.

But as I walked home, I calmed down more and remembered that behind all this was someone in real trouble and it seemed I was the only person who cared enough to try and do something about it. I might like to be free of commitments, but that doesn't mean I don't have a conscience. I had to find Albie and get him to tell his story again. He might dredge up some extra detail from his fuddled memory but the longer I let it go, the more likely it was he'd forget altogether.

After that, I had somehow to help the girl. But at the moment I had no idea how to find my witness, much less how I could secure the victim's freedom. But one problem at a time.

It was late afternoon and the wind had dropped. It was the nicest it had been all day. Perhaps tomorrow would be halfway decent.

46

I'd want good weather if I was to be footslogging round the streets. I let myself into my flat. Good detective work starts with a cup of tea.

CHAPTER THREE

Ganesh came by at eight-thirty that evening, rapping on the basement window in the familiar pattern that was his code.

'Hari was fidgeting about checking the till for ages but that's it, until tomorrow.' He slumped on the blue rep sofa, stretching out his legs towards the flickering little TV screen. He looked tired.

Hari opened up the shop early in the morning because of the newspapers but closed at eight sharp, usually on the dot. There's money to be made by staying open late, but there's always an increased risk of trouble from kids roaming in gangs looking for mischief and, later, from lager louts spilling out of the pubs. A small shopkeeper is a natural target. Hari played it safe.

Either because of the set's age or because of the subterranean location, the screen displayed poor picture reception, each frame showing two newscasters, one a ghostly *doppelganger* hovering at the other's elbow. Ganesh didn't seem to mind. Perhaps he was just watching the moving shapes, not taking in any of it.

'I've just about had Hari,' he said. 'He's driving me barmy. He had me counting rolls of Polo mints today. Not that they don't pinch Polo mints or anything else. Those kids take anything on principle. Just a game to half of 'em. Hauling sacks of spuds around was better.' That Ganesh had reached this conclusion was a measure of how depressed he was. 'No one shoplifts a potato.'

I told him I'd been to the police and the tone of my voice must have revealed with what success.

Ganesh muttered, 'I told you so.'

This didn't help and put me in aggressive mood. 'I'm not giving up. I'm going out again tomorrow looking for Albie. He has to be somewhere.'

Ganesh came awake. 'You can't wander round doorways, talking to winos and psychos, Fran!'

I pointed out to him that not everyone kipping rough was a maniac. There'd been an occasion, when things had been really bad for me, when I'd slept rough.

I'd been lucky because I'd only had to do it for one night. I'd been nothing but a kid at the time, not long after Grandma Varady went into a nursing home. She'd been my only relative since Dad's death and I'd been living with her. But the place we'd lived in had been rented in her name, not mine, and the landlord had

48

wanted me out. So out I went, into the street, with my belongings in a rucksack. Not that the landlord cared about that.

It had been summer and I thought—being innocent or stupid, whichever word you prefer—that sleeping out under the stars might not be so bad if I did it in the local park. Before I left the house, I crept round the back without the landlord seeing me and filched a piece of tarpaulin from the garden shed, with the idea of making a tent. I probably saw myself like a character in a Famous Five story.

I'd forgotten they locked the park gates at night and that was just the first problem. I had to climb over the wall. Then I found I wasn't the only one to do that and every bench had a regular, settling himself down for the night. I hadn't reckoned on company, either.

Some of the company was distinctly unhealthy in more ways than one. Once the danger of it all was brought home to me, I gave up the idea of making a tent. Instead, I wrapped the tarpaulin round me like a sheet of armour, crawled into the centre of a large municipal rosebed, and spent a miserable, sleepless night among the floribundas. I kept telling myself that if anyone tried to come in there after me, he wouldn't be able to approach quietly and I'd know about it.

The next day I was lucky enough to meet up with someone I'd come across before, on the drama course, and he took me along to a squat where he was living and a place was found there for me. It was in a row of condemned terraced houses. The windows were broken and the floorboards rotted, but it was dry and safe. No one who hasn't been out on the streets can appreciate those words 'dry' and 'safe' as an ex-homeless person can, believe me.

That was the first of the many squats I've lived in. Sleeping rough was an experience I'm determined never to repeat. I look upon it as the lowest point of my career and from then on, no matter how bad things could get, they had to be better, and that meant I was on the way up.

Gan and I argued about it and in the end, he said, 'Look, the old fellow told you himself he spends most of the day down the tube if it's cold, and it's been cold. Unless you want to ride round London Underground all day, you're not likely to find him.'

'He might go back to the railway station. Or if not that one, another one. Maybe over at Paddington? That's on the Bakerloo Line. If they throw him off Marylebone, he might just nip down the tube, ride two stops northbound and try again.'

'Check the railway stations, the lot if you like, but if he's not there, leave it until I can get here after work. I'll come round the doorways with you then. That's the best time to look for him. Fair enough?'

We agreed on that one. Ganesh had cheered up by now and suggested we went down the baked potato café for some supper.

*   *   *

The baked potato place was run by an exiled Scot called Reekie Jimmie. (The potatoes were from Cyprus.) If you wanted to know how Jimmie got his nickname you only had to look at his orange fingers and mahogany-coloured nails. But to his credit, Jimmie didn't smoke in the café. He smoked in the corridor accessed from the eating area by a narrow door behind the service counter.

The potatoes came with filling of your choice but the choice wasn't great: usually cheese, chilli or baked beans, and there was a suspicious similarity between the last two. Despite much talk of prime Scottish beef, I guessed that Jimmie created the chilli filling by adding an Oxo cube and a pinch of curry powder to the baked bean one.

This evening, when we got there, there was only one perplexed customer, crouched despondently over a corner table. He was dismembering the contents of his plate with painful intensity, setting it all out in small discoloured lumps of mash and baked beans. It was rather like watching a man who's afraid of swallowing the lucky silver coin with his Christmas pudding. He had probably ordered

51

the chilli and was looking for the meat. I wished him luck.

Jimmie took our order and our money. Jimmie always wisely took your money first before you saw your baked potato. He gave us a numbered card despite the lack of competing custom and told us to sit where we liked.

We made our choice of the greasy tables, I put my numbered card on display, wiped the seat of the chair and sat down. Gan leaned his arms on the table, dislodging the number, and said: 'I've been thinking.'

'Yes?' I said.

'Let's say the old man did see a snatch. Then someone's missing, right? The snatch victim? It's just possible the police might not know about it but someone must know. She's got to have been missed.'

'Go on . . .' I encouraged.

We had time to talk it over. Jimmie had disappeared into the corridor and blue smoke curled through the open door into the area behind the counter. I was pleased Ganesh had changed his tune and was taking Albie seriously at last. It was always worth having Ganesh put his mind to a problem, because what he said generally made sense.

He made sense now. He was right. Someone who normally lived safely in the bosom of her respectable family couldn't disappear without it being noticed. No one would notice if I disappeared except Ganesh, and possibly

Daphne, after a while. Though Daphne might think I'd just wandered off, and if Gan did go and live in High Wycombe, it'd be a long time before he found out. It was an unsettling thought. Fran Varady, the woman no one would miss.

'The kidnappers may have said to the family, don't call the cops or something nasty will happen. The family may be trying to handle this on their own.'

He had a point. It could explain the desk sergeant's indifference. If he knew of a kidnap in the district, Albie's story—no matter who was telling it—would have caused more of a stir.

The microwave pinged. Jimmie reappeared wreathed in swirling smoke like an alien in a low-budget film, extricated the spuds, and approached bearing two plates. He set them down before us with a flourish.

The potatoes were monsters of their species, overcooked to a pale brown all through, their skins dry, wrinkled and dull charcoal coloured, like a rhino's. My cheese had melted to a bright yellow waxy puddle, enveloping the side salad. I should have ordered the beans, like Ganesh.

'There you go, and I've put extra salad.' Jimmie pointed at it.

Yes, he had. There were two slices of unripe tomato and three of dehydrated cucumber nestling in the yellow sea with the crumpled, transparent lettuce leaf.

'And more filling!' he added with the kind of munificence the President of France probably shows when he's handing out the Legion of Honour.

We thanked him nervously. There had to be something behind this and there was.

Jimmie rested his fists and astonishingly hairy arms on the table and addressed me. 'I've been hoping you'd come in, hen. You're an actress, is that right?'

'Ye-es . . .' I said. 'But I haven't got my card yet.'

'You don't need a card for this. I've got a wee job for you.'

Ganesh asked jocularly, 'Has she got to dress up as a potato and run up and down outside advertising this place?'

I wished he hadn't said that because Jimmie obviously hadn't thought of it and began to think of it now. He frowned. 'You know, that's no' a bad idea there. Mebbe another time, eh?'

'Maybe another time, no!' I snapped. Not even for extra salad and cheese.

'But your friend here's not that far off the mark. How do you fancy being a model?'

'Does this involve taking off my clothes?' I asked, because this is what 'being a model' always seems to involve. Not that I'd be prudish in the case of true art. But getting my kit off on a small stage in front of a lunch-time crowd of boozy businessmen was not, to my mind, art. I told Jimmie if this was what he'd got lined up, forget it.

He looked offended. 'No, no, it's a young lad, Angus, an artist. He's a Scot like myself and seeing as he was a bit short of cash, I gave him a job here. He comes in mornings, early, and mops out the place, cleans the tables, that sort of thing. He doesna' make any money out of the art. But he's real serious about it and verra talented.' Jimmie nodded and paused to let all this sink in.

Ganesh twitched an eyebrow in disbelief and turned his attention to his food.

But Jimmie was concentrating on me. 'Now, you see, the thing is this. The lad needs a model. He had one but she let him down. She broke her leg, poor lassie, and is all laid up with a steel pin in her shin. He's got an exhibition all fixed up and he's really in a spot.'

I did see but, still suspicious, pointed out that there were plenty of professional artists' models. Jimmie said there was a little bit more to it than that. It wasn't a question of just sitting there and being painted. Wouldn't I like to come round to the cafe in the morning, around ten? Angus would be there, having finished his stint mopping out, to explain it all to me himself. Jimmie himself could promise me, hand on heart, that it was absolutely legit and a paying proposition.

I needed a job and money so I agreed to come back around ten in the morning, and

55

meet the talented artist. I insisted I was promising nothing. I'd been offered paying propositions before. Besides, if Angus was reduced to cleaning out Jimmie's cafe, it was unlikely he had much dosh to spare and, it followed, not much to pay a model.

'Don't do it!' advised Ganesh when Jimmie had gone back to his counter.

It was good advice but as usual when Ganesh said don't, I did.

*   *   *

We set off slowly homewards—towards my place, that was. It was half-past ten and the pubs were busy with drinkers getting in a last pint before eleven when most of the pubs locally turned out. The Rose at the end of the street had opened all its windows, despite the cool night, to let out the fug and steaming heat of bodies pressed together in its cramped bar.

The Rose is an unreconstructed bit of Old London Town. It has glazed brown tiles cladding the exterior and inside, although it's lost the spit and sawdust of its early days, it's kept the same atmosphere, resolutely downmarket. That's what its patrons like about it. Everywhere else around has been gentrified, yuppified or poncified. The term depends on whether you're an estate agent or one of The Rose's regulars.

There's plenty of life about the old pub.

They had live music in there that night and either something was wrong with the sound equipment or the band was worse than usual. Discordant wails and amateurish guitar-playing escaped in bursts between shouts of laughter, roars of disapproval and the occasional crash of broken glass. All the usual sounds associated with The Rose, in fact. Despite what you might expect, serious trouble there is rare. The landlord pays a couple of bruisers disguised as bar staff to see things stay that way. They don't have women behind the bar at The Rose.

Another thing they don't do at The Rose is sell food, unless you want peanuts or potato crisps. They're a boozer, for Gawd's sake, and not a naffin' restaurant, as the landlord likes to explain if some stranger asks to see the bar menu. Anticipating the nightly exit of unfed but well-watered patrons, a van selling hot dogs had taken up position nearby. Puffs of acrid-smelling smoke wafted towards us. The proprietor was setting up a placard by his mobile eatery. It read: 'Three Hot Dogs for the Price of Two. Unbeatable value.'

I privately thought the mental gymnastics required to work that out were probably beyond the patrons of The Rose by the time they reeled out into what passes for fresh air around there.

'Hi there, Dilip,' Ganesh hailed the cook. 'How's it going?'

He straightened up. He was remarkable for being about as broad as he was tall, solid as a brick wall, with a walrus moustache. 'See that?' He pointed to the placard.

We duly admired it, Ganesh asking tentatively, 'What's with the special offer?'

'You gotta let 'em think they're getting something for nothing,' said Dilip. 'That's the only way you do any business these days.'

They fell to discussing the general slowness of business, whatever its nature. To illustrate the point, a couple of amateur-looking streetwalkers had appeared, both seeming depressed as if business had vanished altogether. One wore tight red leggings, not a good choice on spindly pins that lacked any discernible thighs or calves and were as sexy as two matchsticks. The other wore a short skirt revealing lace tights on legs that contrasted startlingly with her mate's, being bulbous about the calf and tapering to disproportionally narrow ankles. They looked like a couple of upturned beer bottles. She wore a silver blouson jacket. At a guess I put Red Leggings' age at thirteen and her chum in the silver jacket's at fourteen.

They stationed themselves by the wall and Red Leggings took out a pocket mirror and began to examine a zit on her chin.

'Lookit that!' she moaned. 'They bloody know when I'm goin' to work!'

'You want to try that green make-up,'

advised Silver Jacket.

'Who wants a green face?' retorted Red Leggings, offended.

'Honest, it's foundation, but it's green. You put your other make-up on top and it don't look green, not when you've finished.'

'You're havin' me on,' said the spotty one, still disbelieving.

I could've told them both a thing or two about stage make-up, but Silver Jacket was giving me a funny look. She thought I was on the game, too, and had strayed on to their pitch.

I wandered off a little way out of their range and out of earshot of the strangled sounds made by the musical group in the bar. There were cars parked here. Perhaps they belonged to people living in the flats above nearby shops, or perhaps to patrons of The Rose. Among them was a blue Cortina with a long white-ish scratch along one side. I wandered over to it.

There were probably dozens of them. But not all in this one corner of London. I stooped to peer through the window and met Garfield's eyes peering back at me. Avoiding his outstretched paws, I made out what appeared to be a hole where there ought to have been a car radio. That wasn't unusual for city life anywhere. Windscreen wipers, aerials, chrome manufacturers' logos, radios ... the absence, not the presence of these things, counts as standard if you leave your car unattended.

Despite the fact that the vehicle was in the old banger category and appeared to have been done over already, a little sticker in the window announced that it was protected by an alarm system. They didn't depend on Garfield alone.

Not all such stickers were genuine, I knew that. I wondered, if I rattled the door handle . . . I reached out my hand tentatively.

'Fran!' Ganesh called. 'What do you think you're doing hanging round that heap of scrap?'

I beckoned him over. Without speaking I indicated the car. When he'd had time to absorb the make and the scratch, I said, 'And it's the right colour.'

Gan was looking sceptical. 'It could belong to someone who lives up there.' He pointed at the upper windows of nearby buildings. 'And has it occurred to you that if it's parked here regularly, Albie could have seen it? When he needed to describe a car for the story he spun you, this is the one he chose. It doesn't mean it was used in a snatch.'

But I had that certain feeling. Certain, that is, this was the car. 'This is it, Gan. The one we're looking for.'

'No,' Ganesh said firmly. '*We* are *not* looking for it. You, possibly. Myself, absolutely not.'

'Your mate Dilip,' I said, 'does he work this pitch regularly? If so, and the car's a regular, he'll have seen it, too. Go and ask him.'

Ganesh walked back to the van, hands in pockets. Dilip had clambered back inside and was getting his stock ready for the rush. There was an exchange of words and Ganesh came back.

'Dilip doesn't remember it.'

'Then he's in the pub, the driver. That means we can find out who he is.'

The wind was getting stronger. It tugged at Ganesh's long black hair and knocked over Dilip's placard, which landed face down on the pavement.

Gan went back to reposition it, wedging it between van wheel and kerb. He came back. 'So, what's your plan? We hang about here until chucking-out hour? We could be wasting our time and it's getting colder.'

I indicated the warning notice. 'If that's genuine, there's a quicker way of bringing him out here.'

'Are you crazy?' He was horrified. 'What do we say when he charges out with a couple of his mates and accuses us of trying to break into his motor?'

'We say we saw kids running off down the street. We were just standing by the hot dog van, chatting to Dilip. We didn't notice until we heard the noise, then we saw the kids.'

'No!' said Ganesh adamantly.

*   *   *

61

Do you know, that little warning notice wasn't fake? The old heap actually had an alarm and it went off. What I hadn't reckoned on was that with the noise going on in the pub, no one could hear it in there. Result, no one came out to switch the thing off.

What did happen was that lights began to appear in the windows of the flats above the shops. Soon irate tenants were hanging out in varying stages of dress or undress and yelling for someone to do something about that effing noise.

'You started it,' said Gan. 'Now what do we do?'

Dilip, behind his counter, opined, 'Run like hell, I should. I'll tell 'em it was kids.'

But we weren't likely to get another chance. I told Ganesh to wait and pushed open the door into The Rose.

The place was a pall of smoke, totally airless. You couldn't see across the bar. The stench of beer, cigs, cheap aftershave and sweat was awful. I stood there, gasping for breath and eyes smarting as blue clouds enveloped me.

Dimly, through the mist, I made out a raised stage at the far end of the room. The band was up there and had, thank goodness, finished their act. They were starting to dismantle their gear. The walls were yellowed with nicotine deposit and the net curtains (yes, net, no one could say The Rose didn't know what was nice) were greyish-brown. The carpet was so discoloured it was impossible to tell what its original design or shade might have been. Crushed cigarette stubs littered it but with so many holes burned in it already, that hardly mattered.

I edged over to the bar and tried to catch the eye of either of the beefy barmen. Both ignored me. They had a rush of last-minute orders and I was at the end of the queue. Besides, they don't like women going up to the bar at The Rose. They're traditional. There weren't so many women in the place. Those who were there were defiantly raucous, shouting to make themselves heard.

The first thing they teach you at any kind of voice production class is that if you yell, you distort. Voice projection, that's the thing. Breathing. The diaphragm. On the drama course they taught us all about that. Every word to be audible at the back of the gods.

'Who owns a blue Cortina with a scratch along one side?'

I'd given it the finest Shakespearean. Henry Irving would've been proud of me.

It worked. There was a fractional pause. Eyes turned my way. Faces were blank with shock. One of the barmen asked, 'What was that, darlin'?' Not because he hadn't heard, but because he couldn't believe he'd heard it— not from someone my size whose head was not much above the level of his bar.

I repeated my question in my normal voice, adding, 'Some kids are hanging around it.'

To back up my story, in the lull, the repetitive squeal of the car alarm could now be heard.

'Merv!' yelled someone. 'Ain't that your motor?'

The crowd heaved and parted like the Red Sea. Between the ranks, a figure appeared and came towards me. I felt like a very small Christian faced with a very large and hungry lion.

Merv was tall, pale, and rectangular like a slab of lard. He was one of those who think it obligatory to go around in sleeveless T-shirts in all weathers and his muscular arms were tattooed from shoulder to wrist. One displayed a morbid interest in coffins, skulls and daggers. The other showed an old-fashioned cannon and the word 'Gunners' in capital letters, indicating that if he knew what loyalty meant, which I doubted, he'd given his to the Arsenal Football Club. He had pale yellow hair trimmed to a stubble and his round slate-coloured eyes lacked lashes or brows. It wasn't the expression in them that worried me so much as the lack of it. Nothing. A pair of glass peepers would've had more life in them. No doubt about it: I was faced with one of the living dead.

It spoke. 'What about my motor?' it

growled.

'Kids...' I faltered. 'Joyriders looking for a—'

He shoved me aside as he strode out. I staggered back against the bar and bounced off again painfully. The crowd reformed. The barmen went back to pulling pints and the band to unplugging the sound equipment. I trotted outside to see what was happening.

Ganesh had joined Dilip inside the van and was dispensing hot dogs to the tarts. The alarm was silent now but Merv, standing by the car, was exchanging insults with one of the flat dwellers.

'And you!' yelled the householder, slamming his window shut.

Merv, still ignoring me, padded along the pavement to the van, arms dangling, held away from his body and slightly bent, fists clenched.

'You seen 'em?' he croaked.

'No, mate, we've been busy,' said Ganesh. 'You want a hot dog? Buy two, get one free. That makes three,' he added.

He got a glassy stare.

'You see nothin', *no kids*?'

Merv wasn't as thick as he looked. He was suspicious.

Help came unexpectedly. The tart with the silver jacket said, 'I seen a bunch of kids. They was round our way earlier. Joyriders, that's what they are. They're always hot-rodding round there. Residents got a petition up to put them bumps in the road.' She eyed Merv. 'You on your own? Or you with a mate? 'Cos me and my friend, we know a nice little club.'

Merv gave his by now familiar growl and went back into the pub.

'Well, I didn't fancy him, anyway,' said Silver Jacket.

Red Leggings saved dripping mustard from her hot dog by curling her tongue lizard-fashion to catch it. 'He looked like a bloomin' nutter to me,' she said.

Ganesh was climbing down from the rear of the van.

'Are you satisfied?' he asked. 'Now can we go?'

CHAPTER FOUR

Somehow I couldn't get to sleep that night. I kept thinking about Merv, his bashed-up motor and Albie and all the rest of it. I had a bruise just below my left shoulder blade from my encounter with the bar and a personal debt to settle with Merv over that. It spurred my resolve but didn't help me get my ideas in order.

There was another problem. I'd been right to worry about that windowless little bedroom beneath the pavement. Try as I might, I couldn't relax in it. It was unnatural and there was no way I could come to terms with it. The air was stifling even though I'd left the door open. I also kept the door open because otherwise I was sealed in.

I tossed and turned as I stared into the darkness and juggled the oddly assorted scraps of information at my disposal. Like the kaleidoscope I'd had as a kid, each time I tapped my assembled facts, they reformed to make a different picture. The only thing the pictures had in common was that they were all lurid, all tangled and all vulnerable. There was no scenario that was simple, logical and unshakable. Nothing signposted the way to go with my investigations.

From time to time footsteps passed overhead and echoed eerily around my little room. The sense of being buried alive increased. Tomorrow, I decided, I'd make up a bed on the sofa in the living room. This was definitely the last time I'd sleep in a catacomb. Like a mantra, I began to mutter, over and over:

'Now I lay me down to sleep,
I pray Thee, Lord, my soul to keep.
If I should die before I wake,
I pray Thee, Lord, my soul to take.'

That was keeping it simple and dealing with the basics. The words ran round and round inside my throbbing head. The feeling of being

67

trapped and of being in danger increased. My brain was as scrambled as any kaleidoscope. I was afraid to go to sleep in case I dreamed. But despite that, eventually I must have dozed off.

I awoke with a start and a dreadful sense of claustrophobia, even worse than earlier. I didn't know what time it was but I knew it must be after midnight. Despite it being so late, someone was walking up there, above my head.

I'd heard feet earlier but this was different. These feet didn't march assertively or patter briskly past. This was a slow, even footfall and every so often, it paused. I wondered for a moment whether it could possibly be a copper on the beat. But coppers don't pound the beat the way they used to. They drive round, in pairs.

The man above was moving again. I knew it was a man. The footfall was too heavy for a woman and men place their feet differently to the ground. He walked another few steps and stopped again, this time directly overhead, over the thick opaque glass of the sky-light.

I knew he couldn't see me, any more than I could see him. But I knew he was up there and he—I had no doubt of it—knew I was down here, in my cell beneath the ground.

I sat up in bed, swung my feet to the ground and waited. There was a grille set in the door of the room so that I couldn't suffocate in here but there was no draught, just a still, warm smothering air. And quiet. So quiet I might, if I hadn't known better, have thought he'd gone away. But I did know better. I knew, because I could hear him thinking.

I saw a telepathy act once at an amateur variety night. I was also part of the night's programme. I was the drummer in the all-girl band. All right, I don't play the drums very well, but the others didn't play guitar very well. We were terrible. Anyhow, this act was good. We knew it was rigged, it had to be, but we none of us could see how the man rigged it and he wasn't telling. Otherwise, I didn't believe in telepathy. Or I hadn't done until that moment, when sitting on my bed and listening, I seemed to hear a kind of echo inside my brain. The sense of the unknown prowler's presence was overwhelming. I almost thought I could hear him breathing, though that would be impossible. But for a moment there, it was as if his mind and mine had touched.

Cold sweat trickled down my spine. I didn't dare switch on the light because that would've glowed up through the glass disc. I didn't move again. I forced myself to suggest explanations and knew that I was grasping at straws. He'd stopped to light a cigarette, I told myself. Less innocently, he could be a burglar, sizing up the house and contemplating entry. I ought to make a noise, let him know someone was

69

awake and aware of him.

My brain rejected this feeble suggestion at once. 'No, he's not,' a pert little voice argued. 'He's looking for you, Fran. He wants to know where you live. He wants to know about you. He's looking around, compiling a dossier in his mind.'

Above my head, feet scraped and the footsteps began again, moving away, moving more quickly, as if he were satisfied and had found out what he wanted to know. He was gone. I knew he had left completely, and wouldn't be coming back, not that night at least. I was alone again.

I let out my breath with a long sigh, not having been aware I'd been holding it. I got up and padded to my kitchenette to make a cup of tea, switching on every light in the flat as I went.

I turned on my telly as well for a bit of company, longing to hear human voices. It was two in the morning and the reception was perfect, wouldn't you know it? No double-vision. No snow-storm. They were showing an ancient black-and-white film. I settled down to watch, nursing my mug of tea, returning to normal.

The film was about medieval villagers hunting out a witch who was saved in the last reel by the return of her crusader lover. They'd obviously been on a tight budget because they'd employed so few extras. There must have been lots of out-of-work actors like me who'd have given their eye-teeth just to be a bystander in the crowd with a chance to shake their fists at the camera. Yet whether dressed as peasants, or in saggy chainmail and partly disguised by helmets which looked as if they'd been fashioned from tin bowls and probably had, the same familiar few faces kept running past the cameras.

It distracted me for a while. But eventually the film finished and my worries came back. If you're a young woman and live alone, as I did, the risk of a stalker hanging around the place is always there. They see you around the area, follow you home. Sometimes it gets no further than that. They get bored and seek out other prey. Or they get frightened off.

If that was all he'd been, I could deal with it. But another possibility had occurred to me, that the visit had to do with Albie. If so, then logically the visitor had been Merv, yet I didn't believe it. I'd seen Merv walk. I recalled how he'd padded with dull muffled tread in his trainers towards Dilip's hot-dog stall. My man had worn stouter, heavy-heeled footwear. However, it was unlikely that Merv had been drinking alone and Albie himself had seen two men. So, had my visitor been the other man?

Ganesh had warned me about blundering into the pub but the opportunity had been too tempting to pass up. Had my rashness aroused suspicion and had Merv's companion decided to check me out?

It was a thought which sent my already jittery mind spinning off in several directions, conjuring up a variety of alarming possibilities. What if the two men seen by Albie to snatch the girl had realised they'd been observed? Once they'd got the girl away to a hiding place, they might have gone back with the intention of silencing the witness. Not finding him, had they, like Gan and me, gone looking for him? Suppose the other man had been following Albie on that fateful morning of our encounter at Marylebone? The stranger's intention had been to waylay the old fellow, but he'd been thwarted when Albie settled down to talk to me. Subsequently Ganesh had joined us. The follower might have decided at this point that three was a crowd and left, intending to await another occasion when Albie might be found alone. But before he'd left he'd had time to get a good look at me and had recognised me when I'd walked into The Rose the previous evening. If this was what had happened, then I'd really walked into trouble.

I cursed my rashness. It was all very well saying that I couldn't have known, but I ought to have thought more about it. Instead I had sought out Merv, an action too suspicious to overlook. I had truly become a player in the game. Until now, I could have reasoned that by reporting Albie's story to the police, I'd done all I could as a good citizen. But not now. Out there on the streets was an elderly, frail man who carried a dangerous memory in his fuddled brain. It was a memory I shared and someone suspected it.

I was yawning by now and nodding my head. It was beginning to get light outside and with the grey dawn, all my fears began to fade into foolish nightmares, probably induced by the extra cheese on my potato. Perhaps I was wrong about everything.

'Your trouble, Fran,' I told myself, 'is that you've got too much imagination!'

I went back to bed. It really wasn't so bad in the underground room with daylight seeping through the opaque glass overhead. With the new day, last night's walker became a man who'd stopped to light a cigarette. A Cortina parked outside The Rose had been coincidence. Albie's original tale could be dismissed as the rambling of an alcohol-ravaged brain. I could even choose to blame the railway, with everything stemming from a cold wait on Marylebone Station, which had led me to pay altogether too much attention to the incoherent mumblings of an old wino, building a regular house of cards on those poor foundations.

I couldn't allow myself to sleep late because I had to go over to Jimmie's and meet Angus the Artist. I crawled out, heavy-eyed, at around eight and got myself together, washed my hair, which doesn't take long because I keep it very short, and got into my comfy old jeans. If I was going to be an artist's model, I supposed I ought to make a bit of an effort so I dug out my turquoise silk shirt and quilted dark blue Indian waistcoat, both of which I'd found on a nearly new stall at Camden Market just after I'd moved in to the flat. I yawned and hoped Jimmie's coffee would wake me up.

So, there I was, more or less ready for the day, and just about to leave the flat when someone rang the doorbell. One thing I wasn't ready for was visitors. To begin with, normally I didn't get any, other than Ganesh and occasionally Daphne from upstairs. It was too early for Ganesh and a bit on the early side for Daphne. She knew I tended to sleep late. And no one sends me parcels.

I went to the window that gave on to the basement well and peered out. A man was standing before my front door, his back to me. His jacket, which was a sort of sage green overlaid with a grille of white squares, was unknown to me. But the solid build of the wearer and his cropped ginger hair rang a bell—a warning bell. While I was trying to place him, he turned round. Either he had eyes in the back of his head or he'd sensed I was scrutinising him through the window. He came to rest his palms on the outer sill and stared at me through the glass.

Eyeball to eyeball, there was no mistaking him. It was my old adversary, Sergeant Parry.

'Can I come in?' he mouthed, words muffled by the glass and the echo off the basement walls.

My heart sank. I had no idea what he wanted, or why he was even lurking in this neck of the woods. I would find out, no doubt, very soon.

'Surprise!' he said when I opened the door. He grinned at me evilly.

'Hullo,' I said in what I hoped was a deflating tone. 'I'm just going out.'

'Won't take a moment, Fran,' he lied.

'Miss Varady to you,' I told him. 'Come in, then.'

He came marching in and made himself at home, settling down on the sofa. 'Got a cup of tea to spare, then, *Miss Varady*?'

'No. What do you want?' I asked him. 'And what are you doing around here, anyway?'

'I work out of the local nick now,' he informed me. 'And you've been down there, Fran, I hear. Now that interests me. Fran Varady going to the police? Gotta be a story worth hearing.'

He'd read the daybook, that's what he'd done, and seen the entry. It was just my luck that he was now gracing the local CID with his unlovely presence. He was still trying to grow a moustache and still having little luck with it.

'Ask the desk sergeant,' I said. 'He can tell you all about it.'

Parry shook his head. 'You tell me all about

it, eh?'

He didn't sound so much encouraging as minatory. He'd never been my friend and I doubt he was anyone's friend. He had what Grandma Varady would have described as a nasty, suspicious mind, and no social skills. Neither, looking at that jacket, did he have any dress sense. He did have a shaving rash, though, on his throat. Red hair and sensitive skins go together. But if his skin was sensitive to soap, it was as thick as an elephant's in other respects. DS Parry wasn't New Man. He was an old-style bullyboy armed with a police ID, and he was sitting on my sofa, resentful at being refused the tea. But at least he'd arrived in broad daylight and rung the bell. Parry's style was to barge in, not prowl around outside. Nothing subtle about him.

I repeated my tale about Albie and hoped that he'd get up and go away satisfied. I should have known better. Nothing satisfies Parry except getting the better of you, preferably in sadistic fashion.

I told you I don't feel this way about all policemen. Mostly I don't have any opinion about them. It's just that I didn't like Parry and accepted he didn't like me. But at least we understood one another.

He listened in silence, mouth turned down disapprovingly beneath the mangy ginger moustache.

'And you took this load of cobblers

seriously?' he asked at last, when I'd finished.

'Yes, that's why I went and reported it. Not that it did any good. I'm not surprised we've got the crime rate we have. People take the trouble to go and tell you someone's been snatched off the street and no one takes it seriously.'

Even as I spoke the words, I realised I was wrong. Lack of sleep and surprise at seeing Parry had momentarily clouded my thought processes. Now the truth hit me, as they say, in a blinding flash. Parry wouldn't waste time on me if someone wasn't taking something seriously.

It wasn't that they were inclined to pay an awful lot of attention to me. They wouldn't be interested in anything I had to say in the normal run of affairs. The only reason they were conceivably interested enough in what I'd reported to bring Parry over here was because what I'd told them tied in with something they already knew.

I settled back in my chair and smiled at Parry, which gave me the added satisfaction of seeing him look startled. 'There's been a snatch,' I said. 'Albie's right. I'm right. And you lot are keeping it quiet for some reason.'

So under wraps were they keeping it that not even the desk plod knew. This was a CID special.

It was taking him a moment to adjust to the fact that he'd lost the initiative. He played for time. 'Go on, make us that cuppa, love.'

The words were wheedling but the tone wasn't. It was a mix of peremptory and patronising. I stifled my instinctive reaction and got up to make him his tea. I'd won one round and letting him have this little victory was bearable. Besides, it was a sacrifice in a greater cause. I wanted to keep him happy, because I wanted him to relax, and tell me a bit more than he probably intended.

'To begin with,' he said, when we restarted and he'd slurped at his hot tea, 'you've got it wrong. There's been no snatch.'

'No, of course not,' I agreed.

'Don't be clever, Fran.' Parry put down his mug. 'Not with me. You've got a smart mouth and you don't mind using it. It even impresses some people, but it doesn't impress me, right? I'm not going to sit here and tell you there's been a kidnapping on the manor. So I'm telling you there hasn't been one, right?'

'Right, sergeant,' I said meekly.

He gave me a suspicious look. 'But if there had been one, right? Only *if* . . .' he paused but I said nothing, 'then it'd have to be handled very carefully and professionally by the police. There's procedures for handling kidnappings. A technique, if you like. We wouldn't want publicity, Fran. We wouldn't want you wandering around shooting off that mouth of yours about things.'

Making him tea was one thing. Allowing

78

him to sit there and insult me was altogether different and I'd no intention of letting him get away with it.

'I don't shoot my mouth off!' I said coldly. 'Nor do you have any reason to harass me, which is what I reckon you're doing. I'm a member of the public and you're the one with the attitude problem.' He didn't like that and I pressed on with, 'Incidentally, since all this is hypothetical, have you told Albie Smith the same thing? That he isn't to tell people he saw what he saw?'

He relaxed. 'Alkie Albie Smith is an old soak who spends most of his time paralytic and the rest of it hallucinating.' Parry's mouth twisted in the rictus that is what passes for a smile with him. 'No one's going to listen to anything he's got to say.'

'But they might listen to me?' I sighed elaborately. 'Oh, come on, sergeant. Who'm I going to tell? And who'd listen?'

'How do I know?' he retorted sourly. 'You've got a funny way of getting yourself into places where you've no business to be. You get people to listen to you who should know better. Keep out from under our feet, Fran. This is police business and if you go interfering, it could spell disaster. I mean that. A life could be at risk. Leave it alone, right? If you don't, you'll be in trouble.'

Being in trouble was as permanent a state with me as being drunk was with Albie. Parry's threats didn't worry me. But his dismissal of Albie did.

'Albie's your witness,' I said. 'Have you spoken to him? You ought to, urgently.'

Parry hesitated. 'We're looking for him. He's lying low, probably sleeping it off. But we'll find him and find out if he really did see something suspicious—though if you ask me, he dreamed it all up while under the influence.'

'Not everyone might think so!' I snapped. 'Someone might want to make sure, just in case. Someone might want to shut him up.'

'Leave it. No one's going to worry about an old soak.' Parry drained his mug and got up. 'Nice place you've got here, Fran. Better than the dump you were living in last time we met. Fallen on your feet, haven't you?'

'No,' I said. 'A friend helped me out.'

'Yeah, I know,' he sneered. 'Alastair Monkton. That's what I mean with you, see? You sweet-talk people who normally wouldn't dream of mixing with lowlife like you and your mates. You get 'em eating out of your hand and blowed if I can see how or why. Respectable lady like the one who owns this house and lives up there . . .' He pointed at the ceiling. 'Oh yes, I've had a word with her. She thinks you're a nice girl. "Resourceful" was the word she used. I've a better word for it but I didn't like to disillusion her. Even a nice old bloke like Monkton . . . Tsk, tsk!' He shook his

80

head.

I pointed to the door. 'Out!' I said crisply.

'Keep your hair on, Fran. Just remember, I don't want to have to come and see you again about this, *right?*'

'Next time you come, bring a warrant,' I said. 'I've got nothing more to say to you, right?'

'I might just do that, bring a warrant. Just remember, Fran, meddle in this and I'll charge you with obstructing police enquiries.'

He hadn't changed since we last met. He was still a graceless thug. But he wasn't stupid. It was just my luck to have him hovering in the background on this.

*   *   *

I was late setting out for Jimmie's cafe, thanks to my visitor. I hurried there feeling hot and bothered; angry with Parry for upsetting me right at the beginning of my day, and with myself for letting him do it.

There were few people about today, just some women with grizzling toddlers in tow and the usual drifters. I passed Hari's shop and paused to peer inside to see if I could spot Ganesh. He wasn't there but Hari was and saw me, so I had to go inside and ask him how he was and listen to his latest troubles.

'Ganesh has gone to the wholesaler's,' he said. 'I suspect they are cheating me.' His face, small-featured and lined, crumpled up with distress.

I assured him this was highly unlikely, even though I had no way of knowing. But even if they were, Ganesh would deal with it, I added.

'Ganesh,' I said with perfect honesty, 'is very hard to fool.'

It was what Hari wanted to hear and cheered him up. He nodded furiously and said, 'Yes, yes, my dear, you are perfectly right!' and offered me a cup of tea.

'Sorry, I've got a meeting,' I told him, and hurried out.

When I got to Jimmie's it was well after ten and they were open for business. A few people sat around drinking coffee. Generally speaking, it didn't get busy till around lunchtime. Jimmie was leaning on the counter and talking about football with a short, thickset, freckled young man with red hair to vie with Parry's. By his feet rested a large cardboard folder tied with ribbon. This had to be Angus.

Jimmie had spotted me. 'Here she is,' he told his companion. Then he called out to me, 'Go and sit yourself down, hen. I'll bring you and Michelangelo here a couple of coffees!'

Angus came towards me, holding out his hand. He wore ancient jeans and a dark blue Scottish national football squad shirt.

'Hullo.' He appraised me through narrowed eyes, as if literally measuring me up, which was a tad disconcerting. I hoped none of his part-time jobs had been in an undertaker's. 'Thanks for coming,' he said.

His accent was milder than Jimmie's. I guessed that, young though he was, he'd left Scotland some years ago. I shook his hand and apologised for being late. I also noted that he was in exceptionally good physical condition. Perhaps he spent time in the gym or perhaps his line of creative work involved hauling chunks of stone around.

Whereas Parry's red hair and sharp features made him look like a predatory fox, Angus was a friendly lion with round face, blunt features and a mop of copper curls. His eyes were bright blue and, now he'd sized me up, had reverted to a slightly preoccupied expression which I guessed was normal. I'd lived in a creative artists' commune, over at Jubilee Street, before the council razed it all to the ground. I knew that look in the eyes. It meant a mind on higher things, and went with unrecognised talent and, usually, no money. Angus, however, had plans regarding the recognition aspect of his talents, and I was part of them. He didn't waste time getting down to business.

'No sweat,' he said, dismissing my apology. 'Jimmie's explained it all to you, has he?'

Jimmie arrived with the coffees at that point, and answered for himself.

'Only in a general way. I thought you do the explaining better yourself.'

He padded off and disappeared through the door behind the counter into the corridor that was his refuge. Within seconds, a curl of blue cigarette smoke coiled through the crack.

'Right,' said Angus, pushing his coffee cup to one side with a careless gesture, which caused the contents to slop into the saucer. 'It's to do with the Save Our World Resources Arts Festival at the Community Hall on Saturday next.'

I was obliged to admit I hadn't paid much attention to this forthcoming event, although I recalled seeing a few flyposters around.

'That's the one!' he said impatiently. 'Local artists were asked to contribute one work apiece. The theme's the world's vanishing resources. Well, first of all I was going to create a tower of significant objects representing the natural world under threat. Then I thought, no one's going to take any notice of that! It's boring. I want at least to get a picture of my work in the *Camden Journal*.'

He paused to look wistful and I sipped my coffee. 'It'd be nice,' he said, 'if the national press would take an interest but I don't suppose they will. Or local TV . . .' He shook his mop of red curls and sighed. 'But it's not likely. Anyhow, I thought, it's got to be eye-catching. Then I thought, natural world means life, right? So what I'd create would be a living sculpture. It'll just last the one day, and symbolise the ephemeral nature of the world's resources which we're destroying and wasting at a devastating rate. So you see, apart from the chance to get my work on public view, it's all in a good cause, too.'

He stopped on this confident note and looked at me expectantly. Well, I hadn't thought it'd be for the Tate. I realised I was supposed to comment. I assured him I liked the idea. But, I added hesitantly, although living sculptures had worked very well elsewhere, say, the Hayward Gallery, I wasn't sure about trying the same thing in our local Community Hall.

'You're likely to get a load of kids and weirdos in there,' I said, 'making the model's life a misery. I'm not on for that.'

Since I was clearly intended to be the basis of the living sculpture I was going to insist on such practical details being hammered out first. It's not the sort of thing an artist, with his mind on saving the world and creating a masterpiece that would gain him media recognition, would think about. But I had no intention of standing there to be pelted with wads of wet paper propelled by an elastic band. Much less being propositioned with offers that had no place in the natural world at all.

'You'll be absolutely safe!' he promised. 'The organisers have got a couple of doormen lined up to watch out for troublemakers and I'll be there to protect you. After all, you'll be my contribution to the show. I won't want it—I mean, you—damaged.'

It was an unflattering but valid point. Angus himself, moreover, from the look of him, ought to be a competent minder. He saw me weaken.

'Let me show you!' he urged. 'This'll blow your mind!'

He hoisted the cardboard folder and undid the ribbon. Opening it out, he turned it towards me. 'There!' he said proudly, but just a touch anxiously. 'I decided to concentrate on the vanishing rain forests.' His eyes searched my face, waiting for my response.

If I'd have told him the plain truth, I'd have said it looked like nothing so much as an overladen Christmas tree. The human body around which it was built had virtually disappeared beneath festoons of greenery, trailing lianas, and birdlife, which, I trusted, would be made of fabric. I really didn't fancy being turned into a full-length version of an Edwardian lady's Sunday hat. But he was the design expert and I was just the model. I concentrated, instead, on the practical problems.

'How's it all fixed to me?' I'd had a vision of something painful involving pins or, even worse, instant glue.

'You wear a body stocking, dark green. It's very strong and absolutely decent. I sew the other materials to the body suit.'

Sew? A handy chap to have around.

'How do I hold the pose? I mean, I can hold

86

it for so long, but there's a limit before I get cramp.'

'No problem. I've made this.'

He whipped away the picture of the tree and displayed a sketch of what looked remarkably like a medieval torture instrument. It was a big steel coil, rather like a basketball hoop without the net, fixed upright with an opening on one side.

'You stand inside it,' Angus explained. 'On this platform. The ring supports you at waist level, against the small of your back, and you rest your right arm along it. Basically it takes your weight. Once I've arranged all the materials, foliage and so forth, the viewer won't be able to see it—well, hardly.'

So far, so good. One important question remained. 'I'm not a camel.'

'You'll get comfort breaks,' he promised earnestly.

'I see, and do I get to practise beforehand? To get used to the feel and weight of the body suit?'

He folded up the cardboard case and looked a little embarrassed. 'Unfortunately, we can't do that. I've run into one or two hiccups getting hold of all the materials and some of them have to be fresh on the day or they'll wilt. But it'll be all right by Saturday. You turn up early at the hall, put on the leotard and get into the frame. Then I attach all the other bits and pieces to you—I mean, to the body suit.'

87

He leaned across the table and entreated. 'Please say you'll do it. The girl who was lined up has her leg pinned together and had to cry off. I know it'll work perfectly.'

Of course I'd do it. I was a would-be actress being offered a role, albeit static, before a live audience. If we struck really lucky, the local press would print a pic, which meant I'd get my face—and my name—in the paper along with Angus.

'All right,' I said.

Relief glowed in his blue eyes. 'Thirty quid, OK? It's all I can afford and it's a fair rate.'

A *paid* live performance. 'It's a deal,' I told him.

'Fine, then. See you Saturday at the hall, eight thirty, right? Gives us time to get everything fixed up before the public's let in at ten thirty. Exhibition closes four thirty.'

Six hours' legitimate work. It couldn't be bad. At the same time, I privately resolved not to tell Ganesh anything more about it, not unless he actually asked outright. He'd be much happier not knowing.

My mind straying from art, I hoped Ganesh wouldn't drop out of our planned expedition that evening in further search of Albie.

'You look a bit worried,' said Angus solicitously. 'It will be all right.'

That's what they always say.

CHAPTER FIVE

I walked over to the shop that evening to meet Ganesh, as agreed, outside at eight thirty. A light rain spotted my face and I hoped it stayed at that and we weren't in for a downpour. I'd pulled on my black leather jacket as a precaution.

The shop was closed and in darkness. I pressed my nose to the glass all the same, because sometimes someone's in there stacking shelves or doing odd jobs, but it was empty. I moved to the street door alongside, which gives independent access to the upstairs flat and was about to press the bell when without any warning it was jerked open from inside. Ganesh appeared, bolted out, yelling a farewell up the staircase, and slammed the door shut behind him.

I was relieved to see him. After my brief conversation with Hari earlier, I'd more than half expected the problem with the wholesaler to have led to lengthy arguments after work and midnight studying of the accounts. It had happened before that Hari had found some last-minute problem to delay Ganesh and I'd been left hanging about out here in the street, exchanging banter with passing local sex maniacs.

I opened my mouth to ask him how the

visit to the wholesaler had gone, but a glance at his expression told me this wouldn't be a good idea. So I just said. 'Hi. All ready to go?'

'Where first?' he asked, zipping up his jacket to the chin and glancing nervously up at the first-floor bay window in case it was flung open and Hari put his head out to call him back. 'Let's go,' he added before I could answer.

I was happy to move off. A stiff breeze now gusted unimpeded down the street, bowling rubbish and increasingly heavy rain squalls ahead of it and moving had to be better than standing around. It wasn't so late in the year, only September, and it really oughtn't to have turned so cold yet. Another thing affecting our expedition was the shortening of the daylight hours. It was already beginning to get dark. Gan thrust his hands into the pouch pockets of his blouson and we set off in the general direction of The Rose.

'Just to check it out,' I said. 'See if Merv's there. If he is involved then I'd like to know where he is.'

'He's going to get suspicious if we start hanging around, Fran,' Ganesh mumbled, chin down inside his upturned jacket collar.

'It's a pub! People hang round pubs. Anyhow, I don't think he's that observant. He wouldn't remember me. I'm just some woman he shoved back against the bar.'

'You shouldn't have gone in there,' Gan picked up the vengeful note in my voice. 'What did you expect? By the way, did you go round to—'

He was going to ask about Jimmie's artist friend and I didn't want to explain all that, not just now.

I broke in with, 'By the way, I've had a visit from the Monster from the Black Lagoon. Sergeant Parry dropped round to see me.'

Ganesh stopped and turned to me, incredulous. 'What did he want?'

I told him about Parry's visit. Ganesh thought about it, lips pressed tightly together. 'Well, you could be right. Something brought him running over to your place to warn you off.' He paused. 'It *would* be him, wouldn't it?'

'Yes,' I agreed. 'It would.'

We went on our way in a thoughtful silence. I reflected that Parry had, in a way, done me a good turn because Ganesh had temporarily forgotten my modelling job. Only temporarily. He'd remember.

Despite it being a fairly early hour, the homeless had already staked out their pitches if they were begging, or bedded themselves down for the night beneath whatever sleeping equipment they possessed. We stopped and made brief enquiries of anyone we came across on our way to The Rose. We were greeted either with colourful abuse or the request 'Got any change?' Asked about Albie, they replied,

91

'Who's he?' or 'Never heard of 'im.' It wasn't a good start.

We also drew a blank at the pub, much to Gan's obvious relief—no beat-up old wreck parked outside and no Merv inside.

The patrons' musical ears were being given a rest tonight in the absence of a live band. But their tolerance was being tested in another way by a stand-up comedian. He was young, very nervous, and dying on his feet up there on the tiny stage. He'd misjudged his audience and prepared all the wrong material, trying for the witty and satirical when what they wanted was blue jokes, the more politically incorrect the better. At the moment the drinkers were in a fairly good mood and ignoring him. Later, when their tolerance wore thin, they'd start barracking him. The landlord was casting the performer uneasy glances. I could see that at any minute the perspiring jester would be requested to cut short the act, such as it was, and go while the going was good. I wondered if he'd get paid and doubted it. I was sorry for him because he was probably a struggling wannabee, like me, trying to get himself an Equity card.

'Come on,' said Ganesh, rightly judging the mood. 'Before they start throwing things.'

We set off again, seeking information in earnest. I fully realised it wasn't polite, to say the least, to disturb someone who had cocooned himself in a sleeping bag or gone to earth under a pile of old clothes or newspapers, but I quickly discovered it was also hazardous. Shaking a sleeper's shoulder usually resulted in a fist punching out of the huddled shape. We'd also forgotten that the homeless often keep a dog for protection. A close encounter with a large and very unfriendly Dobermann reminded us. The animal chose to go for Gan and not for me, rather to my relief though not to his. Gan escaped with minor damage to his jeans but became especially sensitive to a canine presence after that. He'd exclaim, 'Dog!' as soon as we got anywhere near, long before I spotted the mutt in question.

It was best, in fact, to stand well away from the doorway or alley and call out my request. Sadly, but understandably, street dwellers don't like being asked for information, especially about one another. My polite questions about Albie's whereabouts got me nowhere. 'Never heard of him!' was still the usual reply, followed by, 'Bugger off!' or some variant of same. Frequently we were spat at, and on one occasion the occupant of a doorway shied an empty lager can at us. It missed me by a hair's breadth, hit the pavement with a clang, and rolled noisily away into the gutter.

'Could've been worse,' I said, determined to look on the bright side. Ganesh hadn't been enthusiastic to begin with and noticeably less so since the dog episode. It was up to me to keep the momentum going. 'Could've been a bottle.'

'Could've been a knife,' said Ganesh, who prefers to look on the downside, and had begun to hang back, happy to let me go first as we approached each new doorway. 'Or hadn't you thought of that?'

I hadn't, but I did from now on.

I approached the next likely place with more caution. It was a narrow passage, floored with black and white chequerboard tiles, and running back towards some kind of business entry. It was pitch-dark in there, despite the streetlighting, which had now come on and buzzed fitfully behind me, casting a murky yellow glow on the wet pavement. There was something at the far end of the entry because I could hear movement. Paper rustled.

'Hullo?' I called. 'Is someone there? I'm sorry to disturb you but I'm looking for someone . . .'

There was no reply. The rustling stopped and then recommenced in a flurry. There was a scattering noise across the glazed tiles that made the hair on my neck bristle. A car drove past and its headlights cast a sudden ray of brighter light into the doorway. I had a brief sighting of a shape, raised on hind legs, nose snuffling the air in my direction. Evil little eyes gleamed in the reflected glare of the headlights.

I leaped back with a strangled squeak of horror and cannoned into Ganesh, who yelped and exclaimed. 'What is it?'

'Rat . . .' I whispered, gripping his arm.

I had to admit that was something else I hadn't thought about. There was another reason for sharing your sleeping place with a dog if you were out on the streets. Rats don't like dogs.

I don't like rats. I'd face any street-dweller, with or without dog, bottle or knife, and in any state of mind or out of it, sooner than face a rat.

'We'll give this doorway a miss,' I said.

After that I was more rat-conscious than Ganesh was of slavering hounds. I saw rodents more than once. A pair of them scurried round a plastic rubbish sack in which they'd gnawed a hole. Worst of all, I spotted a real monster crouched on a windowsill, his scaly tail hanging down by the brickwork. That did it. From now on, no matter how hot it got, I'd keep all the windows of my flat closed!

All this time we were getting nearer and nearer to St Agatha's church where I knew, from his own account, Albie was occasionally to be found at night in the porch. So although it had begun to rain steadily and promised to be an unpleasant night, I wasn't yet ready to give up.

Ganesh felt differently. 'I'm getting fed up with this,' he said. 'And I'm hungry.' Rain had

95

plastered his long black hair to his face and he was examining the rip made in the leg of his jeans by the Dobermann.

But I had high hopes of finding Albie at St Agatha's. Enquiries on the way there had only been on the off chance and I hadn't really expected anyone to tell me anything.

'We must check out the porch,' I said. 'This is the last. Then we'll find a place to eat, promise.'

'All right,' he muttered.

I suggested kindly that if he preferred, he could go home. He pointed out that for him this meant returning to Hari's flat above the shop. Seeing as he'd put up with Hari since returning from the wholesalers, he could do with a break, thanks very much. Even if it was only traipsing round the streets with me, risking life and limb disturbing the disturbed.

'You'll see, at the very least we'll pick up fleas!' he concluded.

I'm often grateful to Ganesh for being there, but there are occasions when I wonder if his kind of support is what I really need.

*   *   *

St Agatha's is in a quiet residential area—quiet at night, at least. It wasn't too well lit around there. The mock-Gothic building reared up against the sky like a part of the set in that old film I'd been watching the previous night, all

96

pinnacles and arched tracery, half veiled in shadows. The line of sight was further impeded by trees planted along the frontage. One of the nearby streetlamps had gone out. Iron railings divided the property from the pavement. There was a gate, now secured with chain and padlock.

'That's that, then,' said Ganesh with relief, rattling the gate and turning away.

'Are you kidding?' I asked. 'If you're sleeping rough, you look for somewhere secure. There must be a way in.'

There was, just a short distance down, and disguised by a rampant buddleia bush. The railings had been damaged and two of them removed. We squeezed through and approached the porch, which extended some eight feet out from the building and was doorless. I turned round when we got there to survey the road and work out just what had been in Albie's range of vision when he saw the snatch. Actually, not a great deal, due to the trees. A moment's doubt struck me. Had it all been, after all, an alcoholic nightmare?

Ganesh whispered, 'There's someone in the porch ...'

I'd realised that as soon as I'd poked my head through the arched entry. A sour stew of unwashed human body, filthy rags, booze dregs and nicotine combined in a stench fit to make you gag. Albie hadn't smelled that bad. But I hadn't seen Albie since Marylebone Station and had no idea what he'd been doing meantime. For all I knew, he'd spent the time in a massive drinking session.

I called out tentatively, 'Albie, is that you?'

Whoever it was moved, rustling about like a larger version of the rat we'd discovered earlier, recalling my fears.

'It's Fran,' I called more loudly. 'Fran, the private detective.'

'Who?' asked Ganesh incredulously.

'And actress!' I added, determined to jolt Albie's memory. 'We met at the railway station.'

'Do I know this woman?' Ganesh was asking rhetorically. 'Private eye star of stage and screen? I know a Fran who's usually out of work between spells waitressing or mail-order dispatch packaging.'

'And you might remember my friend,' I explained to the darkness. 'He was at the station, too.' To Ganesh, I added, 'And the word "friend" is variable!'

A wheezing cough came from within the porch. 'Go away . . .' quavered an elderly voice. 'I gotta dog, a big 'un . . . wiv rabies.'

'That doesn't sound like Albie,' I whispered.

'He hasn't got a dog,' said Ganesh, the expert. 'It would've had us by now.'

I ventured into the porch. My eyes were adjusting to the gloom and I could make out the occupant, huddled in the far corner by the church door.

98

'I ain't got nuffin'!' His old voice was tremulous and terror made him smell even worse. 'Why don't you leave me alone? You ain't gonna hurt me?'

'Of course not, I swear. Don't be scared, please. I just want a talk—' I began.

'You ain't goin' to throw me out?' he whined, less afraid and ready to defend his space. 'It's raining. I got me bronchitis again.' He wheezed and spluttered and sounded pretty bronchial to me.

He oughtn't to have been sleeping here. None of the people we'd seen should have been existing like they were. 'If you're ill,' I said, 'perhaps we can get you into a shelter somewhere.'

He spluttered. 'I ain't goin'! You one of them do-gooders, ain'tcha? You Sally Army or what? Well, you can go and shake your bloody tambourine somewhere else . . .' He began to cough, wheeze and hawk in a frenzy. I stepped back sharpish because there was a lot of saliva flying around. Eventually he subsided, like a dying volcano, and mumbled, 'Used to make a living, good living . . .'

'I'm looking,' I said loudly, hoping to penetrate the haze that fogged his brain, 'for Alkie Albie Smith. Do you know him?'

'No . . .' he croaked.

'Oh, come on, he kips here sometimes. If you come here as well you must have run into him. I'm a friend. I've got a message for Albie.

99

It's important.'

Gan, edging into the porch behind me, pressed a couple of coins in my hand. 'How much?' I whispered.

'Coupla quid. Go on, tell him. Then we can get out of here if he doesn't know anything. I'll throw up if we stay any longer and he's probably got half a dozen notifiable diseases!'

'Who's that feller?' quavered the old bloke, taking fright again at the sight of Ganesh. 'Why ain't he got his uniform on if he's Sally Army?'

I pushed Ganesh back outside again. 'I'll pay for information about Albie, right? A quid or two quid if it's special.'

The mound in the corner heaved and another waft of foul air engulfed me. I clapped my hand over my nose and retreated. 'You can stay there and tell me,' I said hurriedly.

From somewhere in the heap of rags and the gloom, a hand emerged, palm uppermost. It looked like something you'd find if you unwrapped a mummy's bandages. 'Give us the two quid!'

I put one pound coin in the withered palm. 'Tell me and you can have the other.'

His claw closed on the coin and was drawn back into the darkness. 'Sometimes,' he grumbled, 'they play jokes. Sometimes they chucks me them tokens what go in the slot machines.'

I waited for him to satisfy himself that the

coin was real. 'I ain't seen him fer a week or more,' he said suddenly. 'I know 'im, yes. Known 'im for years. I come here tonight, thinking 'e'd be 'ere. But he wasn't. So I settled meself down to wait for 'im. Cause he usually comes 'ere sooner or later, see? This is where he kips.'

This much I knew already. A week. I wondered how well the old man was able to keep track of time. 'When you saw Albie last, did he mention anything special? Like he'd seen something unusual happen, outside here, at night?'

'Nothing much round 'ere, ducks. Gotta a hostel fer wimmin down the road. Bit of trouble there sometimes.'

The battered women's refuge. Somehow, it seemed to me, we kept coming back to that.

'Did he tell you he'd seen some sort of dust-up relating to the refuge?'

'No . . . he don't take no notice. None of us does. What you don't see don't get you into no trouble.'

But Albie had seen something and I was afraid it was yet going to get him into trouble. There was no more to be learned from the old bloke. I gave him the remaining pound coin.

'Thanks, ducks,' he said, and wheezed again.

'Satisfied?' asked Ganesh when I rejoined him.

Angry, I snapped, 'That's hardly the word!' Ganesh was silent. I added, 'Sorry, you know

101

what I mean.'

'I know what you mean,' he said. 'But there's nothing you can do about it, Fran.'

We set off back up the street. The air out here was crystal clear and clean compared to the fug in the porch. The remains of it lingered in my nostrils. I wondered why the church hadn't put an outer door on the porch. Perhaps they were sick of it being broken open, and calculated that it was better to let wanderers sleep in the porch than to have them break into the church itself in search of shelter. It was fully night-time now but the rain, which had contributed to the freshness, had eased. The lamplight glittered on puddles and the wet road surfaces. Our feet echoed off the pavement flags. A solitary car splattered past, showering spray from the gutters. As the old chap had said, there was nothing much around there. It was a respectable area and at night people barred their doors and didn't go out. Not on foot, at any rate.

But there was someone about. Ganesh touched my arm and pointed ahead.

A dishevelled figure had turned the corner up ahead and was padding down the pavement towards us, clad in an oversized greatcoat, which flapped like bats' wings as he moved.

I drew in a sharp breath. 'Albie?'

Then it happened.

A car rounded the same corner and screeched to a halt by the lone figure. Two men jumped out, one tall, one shorter, both wearing dark clothing and knitted hats pulled well down over their ears. They grabbed the pedestrian and began to hustle him efficiently into the car. Their victim set up a voluble protest, familiar enough to identify him for sure as Albie to me. He began to thresh about wildly in his captors' grip, kicking out with his feet, but he was already half way through the open car door and in another few seconds would have disappeared inside completely.

Ganesh and I came to life at the same time and yelled out, 'Hey!'

We set off up the pavement, waving our arms and screaming anything we could think of, just to make sufficient noise. Noise is a weapon. If you can't do anything else, yell. It disorientates, frightens and above all, attracts outside attention.

The two thugs by the car paused and looked towards us. Despite the poor light and the little that could be seen of either of their faces, I felt sure the taller one was Merv. In reality, there was no way Gan and I would have been a match for them, whoever they were, but just at that moment, someone pulled back a curtain from an upper window overlooking the road and a beam spotlighted the scene below on the pavement.

The would-be snatchers released Albie, jumped back in their motor and roared off with a squeal of gears and smell of scorched rubber. I did manage to get a better look at the car as it swerved and rounded a corner to the right.

'It's Merv's Cortina,' I gasped.

'I don't know what sort of engine they've got in it,' Ganesh retorted. 'But it's either been souped up out of recognition or replaced. It didn't leave the production line with that one under the hood, that's for sure!'

The beam was abruptly cut off as the person at the window above dragged the curtains together, not wanting to be a witness.

Ganesh and I turned our attention to Albie who was propped against the nearest lamppost, panting and wheezing.

'Are you all right?' Ganesh asked anxiously. An incoherent gurgle responded, followed by a feeble flailing of Albie's hands meant to indicate, I supposed, that he couldn't speak for the moment.

We waited and eventually the poor old devil got his breath back, or most of it. 'You see that?' he croaked indignantly. 'You see what them geezers tried to do?'

'Yes, we did. You remember me, Albie?' I peered into his face, which glowed eerily in the light from the lamp overhead.

Recognition dawned. 'I do, indeed, my dear! You're the actress.'

'And private detective,' said Ganesh, a trifle maliciously, I thought.

'That's it, I remember!' Albie nodded.

'Thanks, dear, for giving a hand and frightening them two off!' He nodded at Ganesh, 'You, too, son.'

I moved away a little and whispered to Gan, 'What are we going to do with him?'

'You're asking me? Nothing.' said Ganesh.

'We can't just leave him out here on the street! You saw what happened. They'll come back, try to snatch him again.'

Albie was searching in one pocket of the greatcoat, his face anxious. 'I bet them buggers have broke it.'

'What's that?' I asked.

'A bottle. I gotta bottle. The good stuff.' He pulled out a half-bottle of Bell's and examined it. 'No, it's all right.' He gave it a tender pat as to a baby.

'You've got more to worry about than a bottle of booze, Albie!' I told him sharply. 'I—we've—been looking everywhere for you. I've just been down to the church. There's a friend of yours down there, dossing. He's been looking for you as well.'

Albie nodded. 'That'll be Jonty. Thought he might turn up tonight. I was just on me way to share this with him. Either of you care for a nip?' he added hospitably.

'No!' we exclaimed in joint frustration.

'Please yourselves, then.' He returned the bottle to his pocket.

'Albie,' I said, 'you remember the story you told me? About seeing the young girl snatched by two fellows, perhaps those two?' I pointed down the road in the direction of the would-be kidnappers' car.

Albie looked shifty. 'I may've said something. Don't recall.'

'Yes, you do!' I wasn't going to let him get away with that, not after all the trouble we'd had finding him. 'Albie, I think you saw a kidnapping. I think the police are looking for the girl. You've got to come with me and tell—'

'I'm not going near no coppers!' interrupted Albie.

'I'll come with you, I promise. You're a very important witness, and after what happened tonight you could be in danger. Those two obviously know about you. The police will put you somewhere safe—'

'Not in the cells.' Albie shook his head. 'These snotty young coppers they got nowadays don't let you sleep it off in the cells the way the old-timers used to. Was a time when the cells were always a good bet on a cold night. All you had to do was shout a bit of colourful language at a few old ladies and chuck a bottle or two in the gutter. After that, you just had to sit on the kerb waiting for 'em to collect you. Then it was off to a nice warm cell and a proper breakfast in the morning. Like a bloomin' taxi service it was. Now they just tells you to bugger off and you're lucky if they don't kick your head in.'

'Not a cell, in a hostel.'

106

'I don't like hostels!' he retorted immediately. 'On account of the baths. They're fixed on baths.' He patted my arm. 'You're a good girl, like I said. Fact is, you're a very nice young woman, and bright. It's a pity I don't still have the act because you'd have fitted in there very well. You ever work with animals? You'd have picked it up in no time. We could've fixed you up with a costume—nothing gaudy, just to catch the eye. Audience would've liked you.' His voice grew sad. 'The dogs would've liked you. They're good judges of character, are poodles.'

He took out the bottle, unscrewed the top and put it to his lips.

'Look, Ganesh,' I hissed, 'he's at risk! We can't just leave him here! Besides, if we let him go, we'll be ages finding him again, if we ever do. I want Parry to hear his story.'

'Take him to your flat then,' Ganesh suggested drily, 'if you're so keen. Then you can go over to see Parry with him in the morning.'

There were limits. I couldn't cope with Albie for twelve hours. Certainly not once he'd drunk the rest of the whisky. Besides, whilst he didn't smell as bad as Jonty, he didn't smell that good either. I'd have to fumigate the flat afterwards.

'I can't do that!' I snapped. 'What'd I do once the whisky got to his brain? Besides, there's my landlady. If she got to know I'd

107

brought him in, she'd throw a fit. I'd be out.'
An idea struck me. 'What about the lock-up garages behind the shop? Hari's got a place there, hasn't he? Couldn't Albie bed down there tonight?'

'Come off it, Fran! You know Hari!'

Albie had been paying closer attention than I'd supposed. 'It's very kind of you to worry about me,' he said grandly. 'But I've got plans for the evening, as they says. I'll be all right. Them fellers won't come back tonight.'

I made a decision. 'Albie, listen to me. I want you to get away from this area round the church. I'm not so sure those two goons won't come back. Go and collect Jonty if you must, but I really believe the pair of you should stay away from St Agatha's, right? I worked out I might find you here and our friends with the Cortina thought the same. I'll meet you in the morning where we first met, on Marylebone Station, understand? Just by the Quick Snack stall. I'll come along early, around eight o'clock. Can you be there? It's very important.' I reached out and took his hand. 'Promise me, Albie.'

'My dear,' he said, 'I'd promise you anything. Putty in a woman's hands, that's me.'

'*Please*, Albie . . .'

'And for a lovely girl like you, what wouldn't I do? All right, dear. I'll be there, early, like you said.' He raised my hand and made a kissing sound, thankfully well clear of contact.

Ganesh and I watched him lurch off down the road on his way to share the whisky with Jonty. I just hoped they could keep from opening it up until they'd left the porch. I had my doubts. Nor could I blame them. At least the whisky dulled the misery for a few hours. In their shoes, I'd probably take to the bottle. I wondered where he'd got the bottle from, if he'd pinched it or paid for it and if the last, what with? But confirmed drinkers always manage to get hold of their favourite tipple somehow.

'He might be at the station tomorrow,' Ganesh said, 'but I wouldn't count on it. It's like I said, Fran. There's no talking sense with him. Still, there's nothing you can do except trust the old soak, I suppose.'

'You saw what happened! You must've recognised that Cortina. You can hardly blame me for worrying!' I said bitterly.

CHAPTER SIX

I was absolutely whacked when I got home that night, but still curiously reluctant to go to bed. The memory of a footstep above my head nagged at me.

I fell on the sofa before the TV set, thinking that a burst of mindless late-night entertainment, or even a serious political discussion, anything, might distract me. It's a funny thing, but you do without something for years and don't miss it. Then you find yourself unexpectedly presented with whatever it is. After that, you wonder how you managed before and can't imagine life again without it. That's how it is with me and the telly.

The last squat I lived in, we didn't have telly, but then we didn't have electricity either. The council had disconnected us, not because we were unwilling to pay the bill, but because they wanted us out of the place.

Then I came here and sitting in the corner was the little television, with its blurred focus and crackling sound, and I was hooked. I know it's a time-waster. But it's also a time-filler and when you're out of a job, it's a sort of cackling companion, rabbiting on about trivia of all sorts and throwing up endless pictures to amuse the eye. I understand only too well why so many old people, especially those living alone, switch on first thing in the morning and don't switch off until they go to bed.

But tonight I only stared at the blank screen, lacking the will or the strength to turn the thing on, even for my regular old film fix.

It wasn't surprising I was dog-tired. It'd been a long day, what with not having slept very well the night before, getting up early and finding myself involved in an unexpected skirmish with DS Parry. Then there was arranging with Angus about the forthcoming

Saturday, and traipsing around looking for Albie, plus rescuing him from Merv and his pal.

I was worried about Albie, where he'd gone after I'd left him and whether he'd turn up on time in the morning. I was also having serious second thoughts about having committed myself to Angus's loony art project. I was only thankful I hadn't told Ganesh any more about it. To top it all off, I kept thinking about rats. My brain churned. I was developing a full-scale panic attack. 'Stop it, Fran!' I ordered myself aloud.

Ganesh and I had found a pizza place after leaving Albie, so I wasn't hungry. I *was* thirsty but making tea was beyond me. I hauled myself upright, staggered to the kitchen and drank two glasses of water. Then I went to the subterranean bedroom, removed the duvet and pillow from the bed and brought them back to the living room and the sofa. A brief expedition to clean my teeth and I fell on the sofa, tugging the duvet around my ears.

Tired as I was, I lay awake for quite some time, wondering whether my visitor of the previous night would return. At first I quivered with tension at the sound of every passer-by and that night, just for the purpose, everyone seemed to be taking a short cut home down our street. As time wore on, the pedestrians were fewer. That was worse. Now each one was a possibility. Anyone walking slowly set my nerves jangling and had me sitting up on the sofa, alert to jump up and be ready, though for what I didn't know.

But no one stopped or even paused by the house. Last of all, the next-door neighbours arrived home by car, headlights sweeping the front of our house like air-raid search beams. They—a carload of them by the sound of it, perhaps they had houseguests—staggered out on to the pavement, the women's voices shrill and excited with drink, the men hoarse, incoherent with that drunken bonhomie that can so quickly turn sour. They giggled, guffawed and swore as someone, stumbling up the steps, had trouble with the key. Eventually, they too had gone indoors with a final echoing slam of the front door. I was left to myself, my imagination, and the ever-present distant rumble of London traffic.

I began to be angry with the absentee. How dare he keep me from my well-earned sleep like this? *If you're going to come, come*! I addressed him silently. But he didn't oblige and eventually I ordered myself to put him on one side, like a half-read book, and go to sleep. At least, I told myself, I wasn't in that tomblike bedroom. Out here, in my living room, I felt safer. I wasn't, but I felt it.

*   *   *

When I eventually passed out, it was

completely. I didn't dream, not even in the circumstances. I was too far gone for that. It was a wonder my old-fashioned wind-up alarm clock woke me at seven. Thinking I must have been barmy to have arranged such an early rendezvous with Albie, I staggered around the flat getting myself dressed, and set off for Marylebone.

I hopped on a bus that took me there by a more direct route and made it to the Quick Snack stall by about ten past eight. If Albie had been prompter, he wasn't to be seen. But I didn't think he'd have given me up already.

Looking around, I realised I'd forgotten how busy railway stations are at that hour of the morning. Commuters poured off every train and swept by me, a solid sea of determined faces. The concourse had the appearance of a disturbed ants' nest as people scurried towards the main exit or the Underground entry within the station precincts. To spot even Albie's distinctive figure in the throng would be difficult. I got myself a coffee and sat down, as I had before, on the metal seat, with a definite sense of *déjà vu* or at least *déjà* been there.

From here I could watch the entry to the Underground, over to my left as I faced the coffee stall. It was clogged with office workers pushing through the barriers. There was a notice informing them the down escalator was out of action and that there were 121 steps to negotiate. That would add to the poor souls' enjoyment. When I worry, as I occasionally do, that I haven't a regular job, sights like that cheer me up no end.

Fewer people were coming up from the tube and through the barrier into the station, and none of them looked remotely like Albie. I began to wonder if he'd taken my advice and moved away from the streets around St Agatha's. I knew that, on the whole, it was unlikely. He and Jonty would have started on the whisky, and after that they wouldn't have bothered to move on.

The seat seemed to get harder and harder as if there were no flesh padding my bum at all and my joints rested directly on the metal. I'd drunk the first coffee and another one. The commuting crowd had thinned out. Eventually the last of them vanished. A different sort of passenger was arriving off the trains now. Not workers, but shoppers and people coming up for the day for one reason or another, who had no reason to fight for the early train, or could take advantage of cheaper tickets by travelling later. It was well after ten. I'd been here two and a half hours and I knew Albie wasn't coming. Perhaps I'd always known it. I stood up and eased my cramped legs.

Damn it! I thought. He probably hadn't even remembered. He was sleeping it off somewhere. I quelled the fear that some other reason detained him. I simply should have

114

known better than to attempt to make any kind of firm arrangement with someone like Alkie Albie Smith. Ganesh and I would have to go out tonight and try to find him again. Ganesh would love that.

I went home. I'd had nothing to eat with my coffee and it was getting on for lunch time. I set about making toast in my kitchen and was debating whether to scramble a couple of eggs, *haute cuisine* as far as I was concerned, when I was interrupted by the ring of the doorbell followed by the noise of someone hammering on the front door.

Footsteps scuffed outside in the basement and as I walked out of the kitchenette into the main room, a face appeared at the window and a hand tapped urgently on the glass. Faintly I could hear my name being called. It was Parry.

'Go away!' I shouted.

'Let—me—in!' he mouthed back.

'Get a warrant!'

'I—need—to—talk—to—you!'

I unlocked the front door and he stepped in, uninvited.

'I'm just getting my lunch,' I groused. To back me up, a strong smell of burning toast wafted into the room. I belted back to the kitchen and whipped two charred squares from beneath the grill. Cursing, I hurled them into the bin.

Parry appeared behind me. 'Here,' he said, 'I'll do that. You make us a cup of coffee or

115

something.'

His offer of help convinced me more than anything else could have done that he was the bearer of bad news. There were only two people he could have come about. Ganesh or Albie.

I asked, 'Is it Gan?' because when all was said and done, Ganesh mattered more. I felt cold and my heart gave a little hop of fear.

'No,' he said, his back to me. 'As far as I know, your Indian mate is still selling bars of chocolate and girlie mags in that shop. You putting anything on this toast?'

He obviously wasn't going to blurt it out. But so long as it wasn't Ganesh, it could wait five minutes and I wanted that five minutes. Whatever Parry had come about, I wanted to be ready to deal with it.

'Eggs,' I said. If the man liked to cook, I'd let him.

*   *   *

Well, he wasn't a great cook but who am I to criticise? I sat at my table and ate my lunch and he lounged on the sofa, drinking his coffee and smoking. He didn't ask, as he took out the ciggies, whether I minded. When I'd finished, I picked up my coffee mug and swivelled round on my chair to face him.

'All right,' I said. 'Let's hear it.'

He squashed out the cigarette stub in a

116

saucer he'd found in the kitchen to serve as an ashtray. The man was certainly making himself at home but I was too worried to care.

'I'm really sorry, Fran,' he said. 'It's your mate Albie Smith. We fished the old bloke out of the canal this morning, half seven. Early morning jogger along the towpath spotted him.'

It's possible to be shocked without being surprised. The niggling fear I'd first felt at Marylebone when Albie'd failed to appear had remained with me and now it was proven well-founded. But being to some extent prepared was no protection against the feeling of horror and dismay. I stared at Parry in silence, unable to find words. All I could think was that, all the time I'd been waiting on the station bench, down by the canal Albie's waterlogged corpse had been laid out on the towpath, surrounded by the coppers he'd mistrusted so much.

I knew if Parry wasn't sure he wouldn't have told me, yet I still played for a few moments to come to terms with the news. I managed to ask, 'You've identified him, definitely?' My voice sounded unnatural, hardly mine at all.

'Yes.' Parry waved vaguely at the table. 'I thought you ought to get some food inside you before I told you. I know you took a liking to the old devil. But let's face it, he had no kind of life. Maybe he's better off wherever he is now, eh?'

I could have argued but lacked the will to do

so for the moment. Parry, with a rare lapse into niceness, was attempting to console. But he was making the mistake generally made by people whose lives fall into the category of mortgage, car and two point four children.

They see life as being one of those questionnaires with little boxes that you tick or cross according to your circumstances. Tick enough of them and you are Doing All Right. Too many crosses and you're seriously disadvantaged. They assume we all want the things our consumer society reckons essential to health and happiness. But what about the ability to find hope and happiness in little things? Some people would look at me and say my life wasn't worth much. They say it about the severely disabled, the mentally ill and drink-sodden old dossers like Albie. I'm not saying Albie's life-style couldn't have been improved. But the last I'd seen of him, he'd been making for the porch with a half-bottle of Bell's and the prospect of finding his mate Jonty. He'd been quite happy. True, he'd just had a nasty experience from which Gan and I had saved him, but he'd forgotten it already. It was a pity he'd done that. He might be alive now if he'd scared more easily or if the prospect of a drink hadn't numbed his brain to more important things.

Unwarily, I said, 'He must've stayed around the church.'

'Whazzat?' I swear Parry's nose and ears

quivered.

So I had to tell him all about the previous evening's adventures. 'I wanted to persuade him to come with me to see you,' I concluded. 'I wasn't interfering. I was trying to help.'

I suppose I sounded defiant. He grunted and said, 'We were looking for the stupid old git as well. I sent a man I could ill-afford to spare to check out Marylebone and Paddington railway stations and every tube station between there and Oxford Circus. I even went myself to that old church, the one he reckoned saw the snatch from. He wasn't there. There was another bloke hanging around, stank to high heaven. It wasn't Albie and he scurried off when he saw me. They're never so far gone they don't recognise the police!'

'Probably,' I muttered, 'because you're so obvious! You were there too early. He came later and so did the two men looking for him. Albie saw the snatch from the porch of St Agatha's, just the way he said. But the kidnappers realised he'd seen them, so they came back last night to silence him. I'm pretty sure I recognised one of them. He's called Merv, a big bloke with an Arsenal supporters' tattoo and nearly white hair. He drinks at the Rose and drives a scratched blue Cortina. The Cortina Albie saw the girl bundled into—and I saw last night when they tried to grab Albie!'

'A burned-out Cortina was reported last

119

night,' Parry said, a tad thoughtfully. 'Alongside the park. Fire engines called out to it at four in the morning. No sign of anyone in it. Firecrew reckoned it might've been joyriders who torched the motor when they'd finished with it.'

'Merv and his chum knew Ganesh and I saw the car,' I explained as patiently as I could. 'So they got rid of it.'

Parry was still in an argumentative mood. 'If you're right, and they came back to take out a witness, why didn't they leave his body in the car before they torched it? That way they'd have got rid of him altogether, give or take a few charred bones.'

No wonder our crime rate is what it is.

'If the firecrew discovered a charred body in the car, the police would set about identifying it,' I pointed out. 'If, in some way, it was found to be Albie's—and Merv couldn't be sure it wouldn't be—then you'd want to know what the hell Albie was doing in a car. They wanted Albie dead, but it had to be in some way that'd look like an accident. Unfortunately for them, Gan and I saw them earlier, trying to grab Albie off the street!'

Parry fixed me with his bloodshot gaze. 'That's right,' he said. 'They know *you* saw them—and *they* saw you.'

That shut me up. They had seen me. They might even come looking for both Ganesh and me. I remembered the incident two nights before. That had been bad enough. Just a solitary stroller had got my imagination working overtime with creating scary scenarios. Now there was a real possibility of flesh and blood thugs on my trail. I wondered briefly if it were worth telling Parry about the man out there on the pavement, above my head as I lay in my dungeon bedroom. But there was nothing to tell. No facts. The police like facts although when presented with them they seemed, in Albie's case, to have made precious little effort to follow them up.

I glowered at Parry and saw that he'd lit another cigarette. I was badly upset by what I'd learned and the sight of him sitting there quite at home was the last straw.

I lost my temper with the frustration of it all and yelled, 'If you'd tried harder, you'd have found Albie and he'd be alive now! I spent all morning sitting on Marylebone Station hoping he'd turn up! And all on your behalf! So that he could tell his story to you! What's up? Don't you want to find the snatched person, whoever it is?'

'Come on, Fran, be reasonable!' he wheedled. 'We don't pass up any lead. You were quite right to report what he'd told you. But even if we'd found him, we'd always have had to take any testimony he gave with a big pinch of salt. Even you can't say he'd strike a jury as reliable. We always knew we couldn't ever have put him on the witness stand and no identification he made would've stood up for two minutes if challenged! The most we could've hoped for was that he'd have given us a further lead and that was doubtful, too. Look, his brains were as scrambled as those eggs I made you.'

It was not a nice simile and made me distinctly queasy. 'He was still your witness! You didn't worry about him, but they did, Merv and his mate! They kept looking until they found him and they killed him!'

He leaned forward, foxy features sharp. 'So you keep telling me, Fran. But just hold on a minute. You're talking murder, here, and the fact remains that you don't know what happened after you left Albie. He had a bottle, for crying out loud! He was all set to drink himself senseless. You've got at least to consider that he reeled off and fell in the canal, full of whisky. He drowned, Fran, and despite what you tell me you saw earlier, he didn't need any help in doing it. He fell in, poor old sod. Couldn't get out—finish. There's no *evidence*, Fran, to show otherwise. Evidence points to accidental death.'

'What was he doing down there by the canal?' I snapped. 'I left him heading for the porch.' With a stab of guilt, I remembered I'd urged him to move elsewhere. Perhaps he had, perhaps the canal path had seemed safer. 'Did anyone see him go in?' I asked.

'No one's come forward to report hearing a

splash or a cry,' Parry said unwillingly. 'But that's not surprising, is it, at that hour of the morning? Give it time. We're asking around.'

'Did *you* see his body? Did you see Albie in the water?' I couldn't believe he was taking it so calmly. They'd lost their only witness, and now had a murder on their hands. All Parry could say was that Albie was better off where he was now.

'No. I got down there after they'd dragged him out. I understand he was found floating face down with an empty whisky bottle in his pocket.' He made sure I took that point in.

I sat back and asked, 'So where's Jonty?'

'Jonty?' His nose quivered again.

'The old man he was going to share the booze with. The old man you saw scurrying away! Look, there were two of them going to drink a half-bottle of Scotch. That makes a quarter-bottle each and that wouldn't be enough to send Albie tumbling into the canal!'

Parry was shaking his head. 'Naw, he had a whole bottle. He was wearing that big old coat he always had on. When he fell in, that coat would've made it impossible for him to clamber out. The bottle was still in his pocket, Fran, just like I said. It was empty and I saw it with my own eyes.'

'No, *I* saw it,' I told him triumphantly. 'I saw it last night. He offered me a nip from it. A half-bottle of Bell's whisky. A half-bottle, sergeant! You can check that out with Ganesh

123

Patel. If there was a full-size bottle in his pocket this morning, someone put it there. And hey, why on earth should he return an empty bottle to his pocket, anyway? Once it was empty he'd have chucked it away. It was a plant!' Sarcastically, I added, 'I'd have thought you'd know enough to recognise a plant when you saw it!'

Parry didn't like that. His mouth pursed up tight and his little eyes glared at me, but he didn't say anything. I'd got him. He couldn't ignore a significant discrepancy.

'No signs of violence on the body,' he said at last, sulkily, I fancied.

'What do you expect?' I asked. 'Albie said they weren't amateurs. I saw them hustling him into their motor. They nearly got him inside for all his kicking and yelling. They're a couple of professional heavies. They waited around until the coast was clear and went looking for him again. They found him.'

My voice quavered unexpectedly on the last word and I was horrified to realise I was near to breaking down. Only determination not to give way in front of Parry stopped me.

'They found him in the porch,' I went on, 'and gave him another bottle of whisky. Maybe they took him elsewhere first. They made him drink it, which wouldn't've been difficult. *Stopping* him might have been. When he'd passed out drunk, they put him in the car, drove over to the canal and heaved him in. The car had become a liability, too recognisable, so they drove it to the park and torched it.'

Parry's cigarette had smouldered to a spray of ash, which suddenly collapsed and dropped on to the sofa. He started, swore and brushed the ash quickly to the floor. 'You say Albie was on his way to meet up with the old geezer I spotted, the one who smelled like he'd been dead himself a month?'

'His name's Jonty and I'm not surprised he ran away from you. He's terrified of everyone. He could never have fended off an attack. I hope they didn't get him too!'

Parry chewed his thumbnail for a moment before taking his hand from his mouth and heaving a sigh. 'So what you're telling me is, I've got to go out looking for yet another deadbeat? All right, you got a closer look at him than I did. Can you give me a more detailed description? To me he just looked a moving pile of rags. Got any idea of his surname or where he hangs out during the day?'

'No idea,' I confessed. 'I reckon he must be as thin as a skeleton to go by his hand which was the only bit of him I really saw.' Something occurred to me. 'He mumbled about making a good living once,' I said. 'I thought he was rambling but—'

'Probably made a good living begging,' Parry interrupted, 'until the smell put people off!'

'I was going to say, perhaps he was on the

125

halls, like Albie. Perhaps that's why they were friendly.'

He thought that over and shrugged. 'We'll never find him,' he said, and something about the way he said it made me shiver.

Jonty had either run away in terror and wouldn't come back to this part of London, or Merv and his pals had got rid of Jonty too, somewhere else. Just one more old man dead in a doorway. What's new?

Parry got to his feet. 'Merv, you say, and drinks at The Rose?'

'That's right. People there knew him. They called out his name when I asked about the car.'

Parry was staring down at me thoughtfully. 'You and your pal, what's his name, Patel? You both stay away from that pub, you hear me? In fact, from now on, you stay right out of this altogether, Fran. Remember, the two blokes saw you and there's something about you, Miss Varady, that people remember!'

I watched his legs and feet disappear up the basement steps and after a moment or two, I went upstairs too, to call on Daphne.

*   *   *

'I just wanted to talk to someone,' I explained.

She peered into my face. 'My dear,' she said. 'You've clearly had a terrible shock. You need a drop of brandy.'

126

I hadn't realised my face betrayed so much or just how shocked I was. The brandy was welcome, though it's not something I drink much of. I spluttered over it a bit and said I was sorry to have disturbed her. The large, old-fashioned sit-up-and-beg manual typewriter still stood on the table with what appeared to be a fresh pile of paper beside it.

She shook her head vigorously. 'No, not at all! What's happened?'

I couldn't tell her everything, so I just said, 'An old man I knew died. His name was Albie Smith. He was just an old tramp, but he used to have a variety act, years ago. He had a troupe of performing poodles. He—' I hesitated. 'A jogger spotted him in the canal and called the police.'

'Oh dear.' Daphne leaned forward, her hands clasped and resting on her bony knees, which were outlined through her jogging pants. She had a different pair of hand-knitted sock-slippers on today. 'Years ago,' she said, 'I remember seeing some performing dogs at, let me see, oh, at the Theatre Royal in Portsmouth. They were very clever. One of them pushed another one along in a little pram.'

'That might have been Albie's act,' I said. But she couldn't remember the name of the turn and anyway, he'd probably had a stage name.

'Why did he fall in the canal?' she asked.

127

'The police think he was drunk. That's to say, he probably was drunk.'

How he got drunk was another matter, but it didn't concern Daphne.

It concerned me. I should have made sure Albie spent the previous night in a place of safety. At the very least I could have gone with him to collect Jonty and chivvied them both elsewhere, somewhere they could have drunk themselves into a stupor hidden from Merv.

'What are you thinking?' Daphne asked.

'I saw him last night. I wanted to take him to a hostel, but he didn't want to go.'

'There might not have been a place free for him,' she said. 'And if he didn't want to go, you couldn't make him.'

I was grateful to her for that. 'Do you think,' I asked, 'that poodles have souls?'

I'd have felt foolish asking anyone else but Daphne. She didn't bat an eyelid. She thought about it and then said, 'I don't know. Nobody knows, do they?'

'Sergeant Parry, who came to tell me about Albie, said that wherever Albie is now, he's probably better off.'

'Ah,' said Daphne, 'we don't know that, either. Because he was a tramp, doesn't mean he wouldn't rather be here than there, wherever there is. On the other hand, there's no reason to suppose he isn't perfectly all right there now. Why shouldn't he be? Personally I believe in reincarnation. If I'm right, then

128

Albie's got the chance to start all over again. On the other hand, if the heaven theory is right, then it seems logical to me that if there's a heaven, it's a sight better organised than we've made our world down here. There might not have been a place for him here, but there should be there, wherever heaven is. I imagine heaven is what we want it to be. In your friend's case, a sort of ever-open hostel, perhaps, with unlimited beds.'

'Hope they don't make him take a bath,' I said wryly.

'Because our bodies may be dirty doesn't mean our souls aren't clean.' Daphne gave a deprecating cough. 'I don't lay any claim to that burst of wisdom. It was something I was taught in Sunday school, aeons ago. The children used to sing, "And your souls shall be whiter than the whitewash on the wall!" I've no idea if those are the correct words. It's what we sang, anyway.'

'I like to think,' I said, 'that we've all got souls, the animals, too. Wherever Albie is now, I hope that Chou-Chou, Mimi and Fifi are all there with him, that they're together again.'

'Why not?' asked Daphne. 'Because we can't be sure of anything, doesn't mean it isn't so. We just haven't got any proof.'

Bingo! I thought. I couldn't be sure what happened to Albie, but that didn't mean my suspicions weren't correct. I just needed proof. Parry was wrong, quite wrong, if he thought I was going to give up as easily as that. Just because he'd warned me off? Never. And because of Merv and his mate? Even less. Now I really had matters to settle with Merv.

I thanked Daphne for the talk and the brandy and told her I felt better now.

'Any time,' she said. Then as I was leaving she added, 'You won't do anything hasty, will you, Fran?'

She understood me a lot better than I'd imagined. It gave me something to think about.

*   *   *

I went down to the canal. It was a visit I had to make.

Albie's body had long been removed, of course. All that remained to mark his demise at that spot was a fluttering blue and white tape that had cordoned off the area. And even that was broken down.

The strip of mud and straggly grass beside the concrete towpath was strewn with cigarette stubs and sweet wrappers and trampled by police-issue boots. But the visitors, both official and simply ghoulish, had all gone for the moment and I was alone. I was glad of it, because I had a little ceremony to perform and I didn't want an audience. I placed the spray of carnations I'd brought with me neatly in the middle of the wet, flattened grass. The next

130

person to come that way would probably pinch my floral tribute, but I wanted to do the right thing and mark the spot of Albie's passing in a decent manner, if only for minutes. I stood back, like they do at the Cenotaph, and remained with bowed head as I said a brief prayer for Albie.

As I came to the end of my short act of memorial, it seemed to me I wasn't alone after all. I looked up quickly, thinking someone might be watching me from the railings atop the steep bank, or had come along the towpath unheard, or was even in one of the quiet houseboats.

But there was no one. The canal itself was covered with a scum of debris, everything from waste paper to discarded condoms. Water slapped against the houseboats as they groaned and creaked. Yet I still felt that tingling between the shoulder blades that you get when someone is watching. I wondered for a moment whether it was Albie's ghost. Except that Albie's spirit would have been well disposed towards me and what I felt was alarm, some age-old instinct, as if an unfriendly presence had manifested itself and prowled about me.

The mood was broken as, with a whirr of wheels, a cyclist appeared at the far end of the towpath and pedalled determinedly towards me. He was all kitted out in a special helmet, goggles, thigh-hugging black cycling shorts and a tight jersey. I had to clamber up on the bank, almost trampling my flowers, to let him past. The ignorant oaf just cycled on without so much as a nod of thanks, not even slowing down. Yet I was pleased to see him because just then any sign of another human life was welcome.

I didn't agree with Parry that there would have been absolutely no one around down here in the early hours of the morning. There's a whole world out there that seeks the darkness and the lonely places. But if there'd been anyone and if they had seen anything, they would be keeping quiet. It was as Albie'd said. Those who move about the city streets by night see and hear a lot, but they say very little about any of it. It's one of the laws of survival out there.

But Albie had seen something and, against all the rules, had told me. He'd put confidence in me because we both hankered after the theatre: he, because he'd lost the life, and I, because it shimmered before me like a mirage, vanishing whenever I tried to grab at it.

He'd trusted me and I wasn't about to let him down.

CHAPTER SEVEN

It was after four when I left the canal and started to walk home. My mind was busy planning how to go about my enquiries. There were two lines of approach, as I saw it. One was Jonty, assuming I could find him again, and the other was the women's refuge run by St Agatha's.

The refuge had cropped up a couple of times and the more I thought about it, the more I felt it tied in somehow. In fact, St Agatha's church seemed to feature large in all of this, one way and another. It would only be a slight detour to call in there on my way home. I turned my steps in that direction.

In daylight St Agatha's mock-Gothic looked less like a backdrop for a *Hammer House of Horror* special. The gate in the fencing around the place was unlocked and pushed open wide. The porch was empty and clean and reeked of extra-strength commercial disinfectant. The church door also stood open and from within came the whine of a vacuum cleaner. I put my head through the gap.

I'd never been inside but I could have made an educated guess and been more or less right. It was a fairly typical late-Victorian church, with oak pews and pillars bearing wooden boards for hymn numbers, and brass memorials to local worthies. There were a lot of flowers around, either in free-standing arrangements or attached as posies to bits of the architecture or fittings. It suggested that recently the church had seen either a wedding or a funeral. A woman was standing on one of the pews, tin of metal polish in hand, rubbing energetically at one of the brass plaques with a rag. Further away, up in the chancel, another woman pushed an ancient upright Hoover back and forth. Both were intent on their tasks. I walked in, up to the brass polisher and cleared my throat loudly.

She turned and looked down at me from her vantage point on the pew. 'Oh, hullo,' she said. 'Can I help?'

I apologized for disturbing her and indicated I just had a couple of questions, which wouldn't take a moment.

She seemed glad of the chance to stop work and chat, and clambered down from her pew, puffing. She was a little on the heavy side to be climbing up and down furniture. Her companion in the chancel had switched off the machine and was struggling to extricate the full inner paper sack from the outer bag.

'It's our turn on the cleaning rota, Muriel's and mine,' my new friend explained. 'I'm Valia Prescott. My husband is captain of the bell-ringers. If you want the vicar, I'm afraid it's his afternoon off. There's an emergency number on the notice board. If it's a baptism or a

134

wedding, that's not emergency, I'm afraid, and you'll have to get in touch with him tomorrow.' She paused for breath.

It can't be helped, but some given names don't age with their owners. I suppose it will be odd being called Francesca when I'm eighty. Perhaps one ought to be able to change one's name as one goes along, to suit one's years—turn into a Maud, Doris, or a Muriel like the wielder of the vacuum cleaner. The name Valia, to me, suggested some sort of wood nymph cavorting about veiled in nothing but her long hair. But this Valia was sixty something, grey hair set rigidly in a tight perm, and she wore a hand-knitted tangerine-coloured pullover, which clashed nicely with her flushed rosy complexion. None of the information she'd so kindly reeled off for me was of any use. I nodded brightly to show I'd taken it all in and then explained my business.

'My name's Fran Varady. I'm trying to find an elderly homeless man who might have been sleeping in the porch out there last night. His name is Jonty.'

She first looked a little startled, this being an out-of-the-ordinary request, then her good-natured expression became grimmer. 'Someone was there last night, all right! The smell out there was still dreadful when I got here with Muriel around two. It's difficult to get cleaners for a place this size and paying someone's out of the question, so the Mothers' Union got up a rota. I don't mind doing it—I quite like cleaning brass.'

She paused to glance up complacently at her work. The memorial was to a 'physician in this parish', paying tribute to his observance of his 'duty as a Christian and as a man of healing'. His patients had lost his services in 1894. His testimonial gleamed like gold, testifying to Valia's efforts. I complimented her and she beamed at me as brightly as the brass plaque.

'I don't mind doing anything, really, but anyone would draw the line at having to clean out the porch. Not that I had to clear away the worst of the mess. Ben, our caretaker, had done that this morning. But the smell was such that we just had to throw a bucket of Jeyes down there and brush it well out. It's the vicar, you see.'

Fortunately I was able to decipher her meaning. 'You mean the vicar lets the homeless sleep out there?'

'Not exactly *allows* it, but doesn't stop them. We used to have a wire mesh outer door but vandals broke it down. Then this vicar got the idea that we ought not to refuse shelter to a homeless person, even if it meant letting him sleep in our porch. Of course, one wants to be charitable . . .' she drew a deep breath, her ample bosom filling like a pair of water wings, 'but there are limits! As I say, the vicar doesn't have to clear up after those people.

Sometimes—well, I won't tell you what kind of disgusting mess they make out there.'

'This Ben, the caretaker,' I asked. 'Would he still be around the place?'

She looked vague. 'He might,' she said. 'If so, he'd be seeing to the furnace. We've had a lot of problems with it. It's very old. It's in the basement, entry outside the church. If you go out of the door there where you came in, turn right and make your way along, you'll see the door, down a couple of steps.'

I thanked her and went to find Ben the furnaceman. If he had been the one to clear up the porch first thing, it was just possible he'd seen or found something that might give a clue to what happened here last night.

I made my way along the outside wall of the church. The area between building and street was untidily planted with shrubs and might once have been a garden. Someone, perhaps Ben, had cut the grass, but otherwise the shrubs had been left to grow straggly and misshapen. As I approached one clump, from behind it came a metallic clang and rather to my surprise, Muriel, the wizard with the vacuum, appeared. She was holding the crumpled emptied paper liner. St Agatha's cleaning rota, economical souls, reused them. She started on seeing me and stopped, clasping the bag to her flat chest.

'Sorry,' I said. 'I'm looking for the furnace room. Valia said it was along here.'

'Oh,' she looked relieved. 'Yes, just behind there.' She hurried past me, back to the safety of the church.

I saw now that the bushes served both to hide a row of refuse bins and the steps down to a low door in the side of the church. I wondered whether St Agatha's had a proper crypt. Probably not, but possibly some cellars, one of which now housed the furnace.

I paused by the refuse bins and eyed them. If Ben, or anyone else, had found anything, it might have been tossed into one of these. Gingerly, I took off the nearest lid. A layer of grey dust, fluff and unidentifiable scraps covered the top. The contents of Muriel's dust bag, no doubt. I peered at them.

'What're you looking for, then?'

The voice came from behind me, male, hoarse and suspicious. I jumped round.

He was elderly, red-faced beneath a greasy cap, and stout. He wore dark blue overalls and carried a folded tabloid newspaper.

'Ben?' I asked.

'That's me. Who're you, then?' He wheezed as he spoke and I saw the redness of his skin was accentuated by purple threads.

I explained who I was, what I wanted, and that Valia had directed me to him.

He snorted and went past me down the steps to unlock the door. He disappeared inside, but left it open, and I assumed I was meant to follow.

Once inside, I saw I was in Ben's personal sanctum. Most of it was taken up with the furnace, an ancient and alarmingly rusty-looking monster. Just enough room was left for a small table, a wooden kitchen chair, a small paraffin heater and a billycan. Ben had placed his newspaper on the table and added to it a packet of cigarettes and a box of matches. He indicated I should take the chair.

'You belong to one of them charities, then?' he rasped.

'No, it's—it's personal. Ben, do you ever see any of the men who sleep in the porch or have they always gone by the time you get here in the morning?'

He prised a cigarette from the packet and lit it. Shaking both the match to extinguish the flame, and his head at the same time, he said, 'No—not hardly ever. They clear out before they see me because they know I'd help 'em on their way with me boot.'

So much for the vicar's charity. It wasn't shared by his staff.

'So you wouldn't know an old man, rather smelly, called Jonty? Or another, a bit cleaner, called Albie Smith? I think Albie slept here regularly.'

'Journalist?' Ben asked, ignoring my question.

'No, not a journalist. I told you, it's private.'

He looked disappointed. It occurred to me that journalists have been known to pay. But I didn't have any money. All I could do was stand my ground and wait.

'It smelled bloody awful this morning,' Ben observed. He didn't seem to hold it against me that I'd not offered any money. It'd been worth a try. 'I wish I did know who done it because if I'd got hold of the bugger I'd have made him clean it up! Gawd knows what they were doing in there last night.'

God probably did know. I was trying to find out. 'Was there anything left behind like clothing or blankets?'

'Just a few rags. I slung 'em in the furnace there.' He pointed. 'Not that it's lit. But if I find anything what burns, I sling it in the furnace. It's all fuel.'

Hesitantly I asked, 'Is it possible to get them out again?'

He looked at me in amazement. 'Think I got nothing better to do than to spend my time raking rubbish out of the furnace just to amuse you, whoever you are?'

I glanced down at the table, the newspaper and the cigarettes. He scowled but took the point.

'It's my tea-break,' he said sulkily.

'What time do you go home, Ben? I mean, what time do you lock up?'

He pointed to the ceiling. 'When them women finish their polishing. They generally goes off around five. I lock up at six and that's it. Can't leave the place open. Sometimes the vicar wants it of an evening and then he lets me know. He's got his own keys, of course.' He shuffled about and curiosity got the better of him. 'These rags, what do you want 'em for?'

'Just to see them, in case I recognise any of them.'

Ben expelled his breath in a hiss between his yellowish stubs of teeth. Then he picked up a long metal rod fashioned into a hook at one end. Alarmed, I wondered if he meant to drive me off, but he inserted the hook into the handle of the furnace door and tugged it. The round metal door swung open. Ben reached in with the useful hook and poked around, eventually emerging and turning toward me. A grimy and tattered piece of gabardine, once the skirts of a raincoat, hung from the rod.

'This 'ere's part of it. Make you happy?' He raised his eyebrows. 'There was a bit of blanket as well. I can try and find it.'

It meant nothing to me. I shook my head. Ben pushed the rag back into the furnace. He swung the door shut and tapped the metal behemoth with the rod. It replied with a cavernous echoing groan. 'Pipes is buggered,' he said. 'Whole lot wants replacing.'

'And that's it?' I asked. 'You found nothing else?'

'Only what you'd expect,' he said. 'Whisky bottle. Live on alcohol, them old blokes. No matter how badly off they are, they always

141

manage to get themselves a drink. A bottle and a fag packet. I put the packet in the furnace and the bottle in the dustbin, one of the bins outside there.'

Crossing my fingers, I asked, 'Would it still be there? Could I look?'

'Course it's still there. Haven't been emptied, have they? Take a look if you want. Leave it all tidy, that's all I ask. Don't go chucking stuff around.'

'Which dustbin?' I'd remembered there were three of them.

He frowned. 'End one, as I recall. Where you was looking just now.'

I thanked him again and left him settling down to read his paper as I climbed up the short flight of steps to the outer air and the lines of refuse bins behind the bushes.

I took the lid off the bin in question and stared down at the grey mix of dirt. I didn't fancy putting my hands in that. What I needed was something like Ben's furnace hook. I retraced my steps. He was reading the football page and looked up crossly.

'What d'you want now? No, you can't borrow it. I needs it.'

'You're not using it now,' I pointed out.

'Ah, and if you go running off with it, I won't never be using it again, will I?'

I promised faithfully I wouldn't leave the premises with the poker. He picked it up and gazed at it as if it were made of precious metal,

142

before handing it over to me, laid ceremonially across his two hands, like a symbol of office. Perhaps, to him, it was.

I lugged it back up the steps and began to scrape little trial trenches in the dirt. At first I turned up only crumpled sweet wrappers and other assorted scrap paper. But eventually, after much diligent probing, the metal poker chinked against the glass and the round neck of a bottle appeared. I picked it out carefully— an empty Bell's whisky half-bottle.

I replaced the lid of the bin and made my way down to the furnace room. Ben, who evidently read his newspaper from back to front, had progressed from the sports news to the indiscretions of a politician on page two. I propped the poker against the furnace and thanked him for the loan of it.

He glanced down at it sternly, checking it was undamaged. I held out the Bell's bottle.

'Is this the bottle you found?'

'That's it.' He nodded and lost interest. He turned over the last sheet of newsprint so that now he'd reached the front page. It was nearly filled with a photograph of the erring politician arm in arm with a leggy bimbo. Ben, sucking his teeth, studied the picture carefully and gave his verdict.

'Oh well, good luck to 'im, anyway. I didn't vote for 'im.'

'You don't mind,' I asked, 'if I take it away?'

'What? That empty old bottle? Blimey, you

got some funny ideas, ain't you?'

'Yes,' I said simply. 'Have you got a bit of paper I can wrap the bottle in?' I didn't want to walk along the street holding an empty bottle. I had my standards.

Ben had decided I was a joke. He got up chuckling and began to rummage in a black plastic bin-liner in the corner. He emerged with a crumpled and grubby plastic carrier bag. 'Here, take this. I find 'em floating around the place and I keep 'em because they come in handy.'

'Thanks,' I told him.

'Just don't come back again,' he bade me kindly as we parted.

*   *   *

I set off with my plastic carrier containing the Bell's bottle. Much as I disliked the idea of dealing with Parry again, he'd have to know about it. It supported what I'd told him, that Albie had had a half-bottle of whisky last night in the porch and not a large bottle.

Of course it wasn't proof unless they could get Albie's fingerprints off it. I wondered, uncomfortably, where Albie's body was. Lying in a morgue? Would they carry out a post-mortem? I thought they probably would. Stray deaths have to be accounted for. They'd confirm he'd died by drowning and we'd be no further forward. I glanced down at the plastic bag with the bottle. Jonty would've handled it and after that Ben handled it and lastly I picked it up, though I'd been careful. Other rubbish had rubbed against it in the bin, unfortunately, and Ben's hands had been like shovels. If there had been prints, they would've been smudged or obliterated by now.

I realised at this point that I wasn't walking towards my flat. I was walking the other way, towards St Agatha's refuge. It seemed I was meant to go there.

* * *

The refuge looked like a quiet, respectable house not unlike Daphne's and in a similar street. The only real sign that anything unusual ever happened there was a wooden board temporarily nailed over the lower half of the window to the left of the door, signifying a breakage. That, and the tiniest, most discreet of notices beside the bell push, reading 'Women's Refuge'. I stood on the step and wondered what I could say that would sound convincing. No story came to mind so I rang the bell anyway and trusted to luck and inspiration.

The door was opened by a thin-faced woman with a wary expression. Her hair, cut in an old-fashioned, dead straight page-boy bob and dyed an unlikely reddish colour without variation in texture or shade, had to be a budget wig.

'Come in,' she said, without preamble, and I found myself standing in a narrow hallway that smelled of cooked vegetables. From the rear of the hall, through a half-open door, came the rattle of crockery as if someone were laying the table for the evening meal. Upstairs a baby wailed, and a sudden burst of shrill voices was cut short by the slam of a door. The air of tension about the place was palpable. I'd been surprised by the way the woman had hurried me inside without question and then I realised that possibly they didn't like leaving the front door open. I remembered the boarded window panes. They had a bit of trouble here sometimes, so Jonty had said.

'You want a bed, I suppose?' The woman sounded partly resentful and partly resigned. Her gaze took in the plastic carrier. 'Is that all the stuff you've brought with you? Just as well, we've got very little room to store personal effects.'

Embarrassed I explained that actually I didn't want a bed, I'd only come to ask a couple of questions.

Her thin features reddened. 'Oh for goodness' sake!' she snapped. 'If you want to do a story, you might at least phone first! And in any case, we don't want too much publicity. We get more people coming here than we can cope with as it is.'

It was the second time that day I'd been

mistaken for a journalist. I explained to her that I wasn't from the media.

'So what do you want?' Her temper was getting shorter by the second.

I told her my story. 'The old man said he saw a girl running away from somewhere around here. So I wondered whether you'd missed any of your—' I wasn't sure what to call the women who came here, so ended up, 'clients.'

She pressed her lips together. 'We don't discuss anything which happens here with anyone outside. We don't discuss the circumstances of any of the women here nor do we give out any names or details which might allow them to be identified. They come here knowing that all their problems will be heard with sympathy and the information received in complete confidence. I don't know who you are, but it's clear you have no valid reason for being here at all. Please leave.'

She moved past me and opened the front door.

'Look,' I pleaded, 'perhaps this girl meant to come here but never reached you? She may have been snatched on the way. You might not know about her but she knew about you! Wherever she is, she still needs your help!'

'If you refuse to leave,' she said, 'I shall fetch help to put you out.'

She meant it. I left.

I walked home thinking that I'd handled that particularly badly. It would be difficult for me now to go back there again. But the woman I'd seen couldn't be on duty all the time. If I returned tomorrow at a different time, say in the morning, there was a chance someone else might answer the door. Provided the first woman hadn't passed on a warning message about me, another refuge worker might be more helpful.

I turned into my street. I didn't know what time it was but the meal-time activity at the refuge had reminded my stomach I hadn't eaten since Parry cooked scrambled eggs for me at lunchtime.

I hurried towards my flat. Daylight was failing and it was that peculiar hour of the day when objects begin to blend into their surrounds. What with the poor light and my mind being occupied with food, I failed at first to realise that a large car was parked opposite the house, shielded by a gnarled, unhealthy city tree and the gathering dusk.

My attention was called to it by a slam of the driver's door. He'd got out, a big solid bloke in a pale grey uniform-type suit and a dark tie, and was walking towards me.

I cast a despairing glance at my basement steps. No way could I get down them and indoors before the hulk reached me.

'Miss Varady?' he asked in a flat, unemotional voice.

I had a choice of answers. 'No' would be pointless because he'd already identified me. I said, 'Yes?' and looked up at Daphne's windows, hoping against hope she was looking out. But there was no sign of her.

'Mr Szabo would like to talk to you,' the hulk said. He nodded towards the parked car.

I took a look at it. It had tinted windows.

'I don't know him,' I quavered.

'He's waiting in the car.' The hulk's voice grew slightly reproachful. 'He's had a long wait. You're late coming home tonight, Miss Varady.'

'Look, this has to be a mistake . . .' I began. But I got no further. He took hold of my arm, not roughly, just firmly, and guided me across the road with gentle persuasion.

The rear passenger door swung open and with it the interior light came on. But I still couldn't quite make out who sat in the back seat because he was leaning away from me into his corner. But I heard his voice.

'Miss Varady? Please don't be alarmed. My name is Vincent Szabo. I believe I knew your father.'

The tone was precise, a touch old-maidish. As a chat-up line, it was different.

CHAPTER EIGHT

When I was a kid I was told, as kids are, never to get into a car with a strange man. I've hitchhiked a few times and broken the rule, but the choice had always been mine. Get into the car or not. This time, given any kind of choice, I'd have decided not. This wasn't the sort of lift I'd have accepted. Nevertheless, before I knew it, there I was sitting in the back of Szabo's plush motor. I was torn between wondering whether I was ever going to be allowed to get out of it again and a curiosity to see the owner of the voice.

The chauffeur hadn't joined us. He was hanging about outside somewhere, making sure we weren't disturbed. Szabo had asked the man to set the interior light to 'on', so that we shouldn't be left in the gloom when the door was shut again. Now we eyed each other in the resultant cosy intimacy.

I'd had no time to imagine what he'd be like but even if I had done, I wouldn't have been anywhere near the mark. He was a small man with a round head and a halo of grey curls. His face was pale, lined with worry, and his eyes—blue or grey, I couldn't be sure which—anxious. He was about as frightening as your average lollipop lady. I began to understand the chauffeur. If you haven't got muscles of your own, you have to hire 'em.

Szabo's appearance was further undermined by his clothes, which were expensive and stylish but looked too big for him. He seemed to be sitting inside his overcoat as in a tent, and his shirt collar stood away from his neck. Something about it all niggled briefly at my memory, but I couldn't put a finger on what he reminded me of, other than a white mouse. The coat rustled as he leaned forward and his hand, small as a woman's, emerged from a sleeve to reach over and pat mine.

'Don't be alarmed, my dear,' he said again, reassuringly. They really were more suited to be a woman's hands, tiny, and the fingertips very soft with nails professionally manicured. He took his hand away, not letting his fingers linger, but I still didn't like the gesture or the velvety feel of his skin. The guy was a toucher. There's the paternal kind and the groping kind, but it adds up to the same thing in my book. They want to get their grubby mitts on you.

Perhaps he sensed he'd made a wrong move. He made a vague, deprecating movement of the hand in question and withdrew it into the baggy sleeve of the overcoat. Then he folded both hands tightly, after the fashion of an imperial Chinese mandarin, to show he had them under control. I wondered what else he had up his sleeve, in both senses.

Urgently he repeated, 'I really do mean I knew your dad.'

151

'My dad's dead.' I managed to make icicles form on the words, and squeezed up in the corner as far away from him as I could, just to let him know the touching hadn't gone unremarked and sitting there with his hands clasped like a mother superior didn't fool me.

I supposed him to be about fifty, which is what my dad would have been if he were still alive, or forty-seven, to be exact. Though Szabo in no way resembled my father, who'd been stockily built, there was something in his cast of features that was identifiably Central European. Szabo was a Hungarian name as common as Smith, and I supposed it was just possible he was telling the truth.

'I was very sorry when I heard Bondi had died,' he went on.

My father's first name had been Stephen but Grandma Varady had always called him Bondi. No one else to my knowledge had even done so until this man. I knew then that somehow, though I'd no idea how, he might well have known Dad. Nevertheless, I said, 'He never mentioned you.'

'Why should he?' Szabo unfolded his fingers and pressed the well-manicured tips together. The sleeves of his coat still came halfway up his palms. 'We were boys at the time. Let's see, we'd have been ten, eleven years old? We played in the local Catholic boys' football team. How time flies. My parents moved to Manchester and took me with them. I lost

152

touch with Bondi. I've always regretted it. We were good friends for several years. Happy days . . .' He sighed.

I wondered what line of business he was in. Whatever else had happened after their lives diverged, Szabo would appear to have made money. Dad hadn't. Or rather, Dad had made fair amounts from time to time, but always had trouble keeping it.

Hungarians have a name for being good at business, highly entrepreneurial, hard workers, quick to learn, and are usually welcome as immigrants anywhere. 'A Hungarian,' so the saying goes, 'is a man who goes into a revolving door behind you, and comes out of it ahead of you.' Szabo was probably a perfect living example of this.

My dad had been the exception that proves the rule. The one who'd somehow got stuck in the door's workings and gone round and round, always heading somewhere and never arriving anywhere.

'You're wondering about me,' Szabo was saying, 'wondering how I got to you, what I'm doing here. What I want, I dare say.'

'Yes, I am.' The only thing I was fairly sure of was that Vinnie here wasn't just kerb-crawling. I might still be wrong about that, of course. On the other hand he was being so damn polite, looking so worried, was so anxious not to offend. What did he need from me?

'Of course you are!' Szabo nodded. 'I'm

sorry there wasn't a—a less alarming way of introducing myself. But now I have, I'd better explain myself.'

I settled back. I could have scrambled out of the car, I suppose, and set up a yell if the chauffeur had tried to grab me. But I wanted to hear what Vincent Szabo, self-styled friend of my father's youth, had to say. After all, the man would have appeared to have gone to a lot of trouble to meet me.

'You don't mind if we talk in the car?' he asked. I didn't point out I'd not been given any choice in the matter. He was watching me anxiously, as if my agreement mattered.

'Go ahead,' I said.

After all, I might learn something. There had to be a reason for all this. Besides which, what can't be cured must be endured, as Mrs Worran, who'd lived next door to us when Dad had been alive, had been fond of saying. I'd heard her say it to Grandma after my mother walked out. Later, when Dad died, she'd said it to me. There was something in her grim acceptance of Fate that had struck me then as worse than despair. I still found it irksome as a philosophy, but sometimes, like now, it described the situation perfectly.

'You see,' Szabo was saying, 'I like my privacy. I'm essentially a private man, a family man, you'd say. I don't care to discuss my affairs in a public place or to think that others might be discussing me in that way, for all and

154

sundry to hear. I find it distressing. That's why I find this meeting distressing and I've chosen to conduct it in this way. I hope you'll understand.'

I waited. He had paused as if he expected me to speak and when I didn't, he rubbed his small neat hands together and began again, his voice staccato, the words chopped into broken phrases.

'What I have to say is particularly sensitive. Oh dear, this is quite—You see, I hardly know how to begin. To have to talk of it at all. And of course, I shouldn't, shouldn't be talking to you or to anyone. But then, when I realised you were Bondi's girl . . . I thought, that would be different. Almost as if I were talking to him. He was a dear friend.'

'Excuse me,' I said, irked by this continual dropping of Dad's name, 'but I honestly don't remember my father mentioning your name.'

'Why should he?' For a moment Szabo seemed even more downcast, if that were possible. 'Life took us in different directions.' Suddenly his manner changed, becoming all at once confident and almost cheerful. 'Oh, those were the days! He was a real scrapper of a kid, your dad. Always getting into fights with bigger kids and coming off worst. Never learned.' He gave a rusty chuckle as if he'd got out of the habit of laughing of late. Then amusement faded. 'He should have learned, but he never did. It doesn't always pay to go straight in there

155

with fists flailing.' He tapped his forehead with a manicured nail. 'Use this.'

Well, I already knew *that*. If I hadn't got in the way of using my brains before this, I wouldn't have survived as long as I had. Before now I'd have been one of those bodies they find in the canal, like Albie's, all shot up with booze and drugs. I knew enough to keep clear of trouble. I can't help it if sometimes trouble seeks me out.

I glanced at the little man in the opposite corner and wondered if Vinnie had early learned to use his brains because he wasn't built for the rough stuff. Undersized children sometimes tag along with a tough kid for protection, like a moon orbiting a powerful planet. Had that been the nature of the link between Dad and this man? Had Dad protected him from the playground bullies? The football team story could still be right. A small kid like Szabo could still have been nippy about the football field and a nifty player, despite his present unathletic appearance.

'I'm here because of something so—appalling, something which has quite, I don't exaggerate, turned my world upside down,' Szabo said earnestly. 'My dear, you're confused. I'm confusing you. It'd be best, perhaps, if I explained events in the order in which they happened. You'll soon see why I want—why I need—to talk to you.'

His manner had changed. Now he'd made

up his mind to tell me his story, he began speaking briskly and in a coherent way. I was relieved because his manner had been making me jumpy. I'd even begun to wonder if he wasn't on something.

'As I was saying, my parents took me away from London to Manchester.' He sounded brighter, as if the change had been a turn of luck for the better. 'I went into the soft furnishing business, wholesale, not retail, supplying upholstery fabrics to the trade. It's a good business—or it was before the recession set in. The housing boom did me a power of good. Everyone buying a new home and each new home filled with nice new furniture and curtains.'

He sounded cheerful again, remembering his successes. 'Oh, I didn't forget your dad,' he said. 'Even if, as you suggest, he might've forgotten me! No, I remembered him and when I started to do well, I wrote suggesting he come up North and join me in business. He wrote back refusing. Felt it wasn't his style. That was the last time we communicated. I'd no idea what he did after that.' He raised his eyebrows questioningly and paused for me to fill in the detail.

'Not very well,' I admitted. 'Although sometimes better than others.'

He shrugged. 'I was afraid of that. If he'd joined forces with me, I'd have guided him. On his own, Bondi was always—erratic. However,

I did well for a long time and then we had a few setbacks. The bottom fell out of the housing market and it hit me as it hit a lot of suppliers to the trade. Carpets, housepaints, bathroom fittings, you name it. The whole shebang took a hell of a knock. Saddled with negative equity, who buys a new three-piece suite? But I'd made my money by then and besides, I'd got a good export business going. Speciality fabrics to the Middle East.'

He gave a coy, old lady's giggle, indicating he was about to make a joke. 'Many a harem's fitted out using my fabrics. They're mad about velvets.'

'Great,' I said vaguely.

'I've also diversified into other interests,' he went on. 'It doesn't do to keep all the eggs in one basket, as they say.'

He didn't explain what these other interests were and I didn't ask.

His manner, which had continued to veer between the depressed and the almost hilarious, changed again. His state of mind was beginning to worry me. He was either under intolerable stress and barely coping, or seriously nuts. I wasn't sure which.

'I was married for twelve years and I count myself blessed to have had an extraordinarily happy marriage. My wife was a widow at the time we met. She had a little girl, Lauren, aged just six. It's difficult for a woman on her own, bringing up a child, especially with the world

158

being like it is today,' he concluded earnestly, leaning forward slightly to impart this wisdom.

Within a stone's throw of where we sat we could've found half a dozen single mums who could tell him a thing or two about how tough it was. But this prissy little fellow, with his success hanging smugly about him, seemed to think he'd made the discovery.

'I adopted Lauren and brought her up as my own,' he said, emphasising the last word just a little. 'I'm as proud of her as *any* father. I've done my best for her. Good school, dancing lessons, elocution classes, cordon bleu cookery course . . .' He rattled off the list with simple pride.

I nearly told him *I'd* been to a good school and had acting lessons, and look at me! But I didn't.

'My responsibilities towards Lauren increased after my wife died.' His blue eyes rested on my face, watching for my reaction. 'She had cancer.' His gaze moistened and I felt an awful lurch in the diaphragm and hoped he wasn't going to snivel. Poor little guy. Perhaps he'd lost weight when his wife fell ill and died. That could be why the wretched overcoat was too large.

'After that I had a double duty towards Lauren. I had to play the role of both father and mother. I owed it to my late wife to take every possible care of her and see she wanted for nothing. I did make sure she lacked nothing. Like I said, she's had everything, the best money could buy. I made sure of it. Anything she wanted, she only had to ask.' He leaned towards me again and I guessed it was a substitute for touching. He'd realised I didn't like the hand-patting, but he couldn't help himself. He had at least to imitate a physical contact.

Well, all right, all right, I believed him. But I'd got control of my emotions, and was thinking straighter. If he'd done his homework on my background, as he surely had, he'd know that my father had been left with the care of me after my mum cleared out. Szabo was making a bid for sympathy, assuming I'd appreciate his problems and the effort he'd made to tackle them.

He'd probably done his best, just like he'd said. But I don't know whether spoiling a kid rotten is the kindest thing to do in the long run. I also wondered if he'd been there to listen when Lauren burbled about her dreams, as my dad had been for me. But perhaps I was misjudging him. Maybe he idolised Lauren.

As if he sensed my thoughts, he burst out emotionally, 'She's a lovely girl, a beautiful girl, with a sweet nature!'

Well, there have to be a few examples of pure young womanhood around like that, even in this wicked world. Perhaps he'd kept Lauren locked up in a tower, like Rapunzel. Lauren, he said, had been aged six at the time of her mother's marriage to Szabo and the marriage had lasted twelve years. I didn't know how long his wife had been dead. 'How old is Lauren now?'

'Nineteen,' he said. 'So a little younger than you.'

He obviously knew I was twenty-one. The man probably had the equivalent of a *Who's Who?* entry on me.

He drew a deep breath, as if he'd surprised himself by the outburst, and resettled himself in his corner of the back seat. 'I'm successful. It's attracted jealousy and resentment in some quarters,' he went on. 'It's inevitable. I can live with that. Unfortunately money also attracts another kind of attention.' Emotion entered his voice again. 'What I'm about to tell you isn't to be repeated to anyone, you understand? No gossiping among your friends.'

'You're sure you want to tell me?' I asked, since he was getting het up again and the muscles around his mouth were wobbling.

'Not particularly, to be truthful. But I'm in an unusual and unexpected difficulty. My daughter has been kidnapped.'

He broke off and seemed to be waiting for my reaction.

It was blunt enough as a statement and was meant to shock. But I couldn't sound surprised. I knew that a snatch had taken place. That an identity had at last been given to the snatch victim came almost as a relief. I said I was sorry.

'Sorry?' He picked up my word and shook his head. 'You can have no idea what it means. Oh, kidnap—everyone thinks he knows! But when it happens to you, when someone you love, someone you've cared for, watched grow from a young child to a lovely woman, is taken from you . . .' He twitched. 'Not to know where she is, if she's well or hurt, who has her prisoner, in what circumstances they're keeping her, what kind of people—' He broke off and twitched again. I hoped he wasn't going to break down. Instead, he rushed on, 'I say, what kind of people? But I know what kind. Only depravity of the worst sort could do this, only a mind dulled to any human emotion could even contemplate it!'

I felt I ought to say something so I said, 'They have no reason to harm her.'

'They don't reason like you or me. What's happened is worse than death,' he said quietly. 'You can mourn a death and bury a body. I don't know whether I'll ever see Lauren alive again, or whether it's a body they'll bring back to me. Or neither. It could be that I'll never know. At least they are still sending their messages and while there's contact, I have hope.'

'They've named a ransom?'

He nodded. 'I've received a ransom note for a quite exorbitant sum. I'm a wealthy man but

I'm not a millionaire. Perhaps, given time, I might raise the money but even if I did, there is no guarantee Lauren would be returned. I am not a fool. Until I pay, they need Lauren. She is their security as well as their hostage. We're hampered in everything we do, knowing she's in their hands. But once they have the money, they don't need her any longer. She's an embarrassment and worse, a weak link in their armour. They will be taking precautions so that she can't identify them. They probably have her blindfolded, or keep her in a dark room. She'll be distraught, terrified. But she may still have heard a voice, smelled some distinctive odour, caught the sound of something unusual out in the street, recognised some peculiar feature of the house ... any of these things could lead to their capture and conviction. So why shouldn't they kill her, once they have the money? After that, all that will matter to them will be their safety.'

I was following this as best I could and trying to deduce what I could from it. Some of what he was saying sounded semi-official. Before, he'd said 'I', but now he was saying 'we'.

'You've been to the police,' I said, not a question.

'I knew I had no choice but to go to the police!' he retorted vehemently. 'They have their procedures. The first thing they organised was a blanket ban on news

163

reporting. Despite the fact that I'm not accustomed to following orders, I've been following their instructions in negotiations with the kidnappers to the letter. Meantime, the police have been trying to locate my girl. They've not done so and I'm beginning to become impatient, not to say out of my mind with worry. One can't know what those creatures who hold my daughter will do. My confidence in the police is dwindling. In fact, it seems to me they're floundering, with no more idea what to do than you would have, if I gave the job of finding Lauren to you.'

I thought that he underestimated my ingenuity, but it wasn't the time to argue. I nodded.

It seemed to encourage him. He began to sound more determined. 'I think it's time I took a more active hand. Now, I understand from Sergeant Parry that you had some conversation with an elderly vagrant who claimed to have seen a girl, answering Lauren's description, snatched from the street?'

So that was it. That's how Szabo knew about me and I came to be sitting here, listening to all this. Parry had grassed.

'That's right,' I said. 'I did. And if you've seen Parry today, you'll know the old man's body was found floating in the canal this morning. Parry declares there is no evidence to suggest it was anything other than an accident but I don't think so.'

'I've spoken with Sergeant Parry and with his superiors. Like you, I feel it's unlikely the death was accidental. And if those men killed the old man, why shouldn't they kill my girl? I can no longer afford to sit back and leave it to the authorities! Tell me what the vagrant told you, all of it, exactly as he said it.'

I told him, but only that, not what I had seen. Szabo listened intently, looked dissatisfied and tapped his pale fingers on the knees of his quality worsted pants.

'And the two men?' he asked. 'Did the tramp describe them?'

I was being manoeuvred rapidly into a no-win corner here. If I answered all these questions, I was likely to end up on the receiving end of aggro from Parry. If I didn't, Szabo could turn awkward. He might look harmless but I'd an idea he was used to getting his own way and I hadn't forgotten the beefy chauffeur. 'Look,' I said, 'do the police know you're talking to me?'

'Naturally,' he said, sounding rather starchy. 'Recognising a Hungarian name, I asked the police what they knew about you and Sergeant Parry appeared to know your background quite well. I informed him that you were almost certainly the daughter of my boyhood friend Stephen Varady and that I'd seek you out as a matter of courtesy, if nothing else.' He sniffed vengefully. 'The police didn't like it, perhaps. But since they've come up with absolutely nothing so far, they were hardly in a position to argue with me. I've put through some tough business deals in my time. I know when to call someone's bluff!'

So take that, he might have added.

'All right,' I said. 'He didn't describe the men. He described their car.' I gave him the description and told him a car like that had been torched during the previous night.

'And the men?' Szabo practically bounced in his seat with excitement. 'Perhaps the old man didn't describe them, but I understand you can give a description of at least one of them?'

I cursed Parry and wondered what on earth he was playing at, putting Szabo on to me. I wasn't sure how much I was supposed to tell him. But if the police had wanted to keep Vinnie from questioning me, Parry should have kept his mouth shut. I wondered why Parry had given out the information. It could be that Szabo was a difficult man to refuse, or that the sergeant thought I was holding out and might tell Vinnie here more than I'd told the plods.

'I saw one of them, I think,' I said. 'Very tall, possibly a body builder, all muscles and tattoos. Ugly mug. Not nice.'

He leaned forward intently. 'Tattoos? What kind of tattoos? Any special marks?'

'Gunners' supporter,' I said. 'Arsenal Football Team, that is. Got it tattooed on one arm.'

'You've told the police?'

'Of course I have,' I said sharply. 'I don't keep things like that from the coppers!'

I might do if I thought it advisable, but I wanted Szabo to think I was a law-abiding type. I didn't want him to get the idea he could use me in some way with Parry none the wiser.

My companion was searching in his inner breast pocket and took out a little silver case and a silver pen. From the case he took a business card and with the pen wrote a phone number on the back. He handed it to me.

'I can always be reached on this number,' he said. 'If you see this man again, I want you to get in touch with me immediately, do you understand? Whether or not you tell the police, I want you to tell me directly. Or if you come across anything else, or remember anything, however insignificant it might be, which the old man said, you understand? Get in touch with me!'

'I understand,' I said, pocketing the card. I hadn't said I'd do it, but he took that as read. His mistake.

He'd put away the card case and pen and brought out his wallet. 'Look, my dear, I hope you won't take this wrongly. Obviously things have been difficult for you since your father died. I know if the situations had been reversed, Bondi would have tried to look after any daughter of mine who was in need. I'd like to help. If I'd known about you, I'd have offered my help before this.'

'It's not necessary,' I said sharply. 'I can manage.'

'Please!' he urged. 'I'm not offering charity! I understand you're proud, like your dad, but look at it this way. Let me pay you for your time this evening. You've been more than patient and I do appreciate it. I apologise again for any alarm you may have felt. Matson, my driver, lacks, er, tact. Call it compensation?'

He took out several twenty-pound notes and fanned them out like a magician, inviting me to pick a card, any one. The notes were all crisp and new. I nearly asked him, jokingly, if he'd printed them himself, but he was probably deficient in a sense of humour right now, and if they were duds, he wouldn't be passing them himself.

There were five of them. 'One hundred pounds,' he emphasised, peering at me in the poor light. 'Do you feel that's adequate?'

There are moralists among you reading this who would feel I should have refused the money. But I took it because, fair's fair, he *had* taken up my time and originally given me a heck of a fright. Nor would he have liked being refused. Besides, I was broke, and it wasn't like he hadn't known Dad.

'And you won't forget what we agreed?' he asked.

As I recalled it, we hadn't actually agreed

168

anything, but there was only one answer. 'No, Mr Szabo,' I said meekly, pocketing the readies.

He smiled and nodded and almost patted my hand again, but remembered just in time. 'You know, I feel as though I've managed to do something to help Lauren at last. It's been so frustrating with the police, they always reckon to know best—though I've begun to doubt it. Just talking to you, telling you, it's been such a help. I want to thank you. You're a good girl. You're like your father. I knew I couldn't go wrong seeking out Bondi's daughter.'

I'd been going to give him a nice bright smile back, but it faded. The last person to call me a good girl had been poor old Albie.

'Can I go now?' I asked.

'Of course!' He looked stricken and tapped on the smoky window. 'I've held you up, such a long time, I'm so sorry . . .'

The door beside me opened and the chauffeur waited outside on the pavement, hand outstretched to help the little lady out.

Halfway out, I made a mistake. Curiosity got the better of me. I turned back and asked, 'Why was Lauren walking around at night on her own, near St Agatha's church?'

I don't know if Szabo heard the question or not. The chauffeur's deferential touch turned to an ungentle grip. I was hoicked smartly out of the motor and deposited on the pavement. The car sped away, leaving me rubbing my upper arm.

Bruise on my shoulder from Merv and bruises on my arm from Szabo's minder. I was keeping the wrong sort of company.

CHAPTER NINE

Ganesh came over in the evening with a bag of takeaway food and a bottle of wine. I was glad we hadn't to go out to eat, not least because I wanted to avoid Jimmie's until the art show was over. It was already Thursday, which meant I'd only one clear day left before my debut as a living work of art. I still hadn't told Gan about it and wasn't keen to.

So when he asked, 'What's been happening?' I concentrated on telling him about Albie, St Agatha's and an edited account of my meeting with Szabo.

'I'm sorry about the old fellow,' Ganesh said, 'even if he was a disgusting old drunk. I'd like for the two thugs to get caught. But it's a job for the police, Fran. You should hand that whisky bottle over to Parry at once. I remember it. I mean, I remember that Albie definitely had a half-bottle of Bell's.'

'That's handy,' I said. 'You can tell Parry, back my story.'

But Ganesh was frowning, his mind running on something else. 'This Szabo, you reckon he really knew your family?'

'Yes, I do. I don't think he'd claim he had if he didn't and he seemed to know all about them. I know my dad never mentioned him, but why should he? Vinnie was sitting up there in Manchester turning out the quality loose covers and making a fortune out of the chintz and cretonne business generally. Dad was down here making one bad business decision after the other, probably regretting he hadn't joined Vinnie when he had the chance. But then, I don't know what capacity Szabo had in mind when he asked Dad up to Manchester to join the business. I don't somehow think he was intending to make him a partner. Dad might've ended up driving his old footballing pal around town, wearing a chauffeur's suit like Matson. Perhaps that's why he declined the offer!'

'He sounds a bit dodgy,' said Ganesh, who said that about pretty well everybody.

'Szabo? He's a funny little guy. Lots of brains and a dab hand at business, that's for sure. Thought the world of his wife and of course, the kid, Lauren. I don't know, but it's occurred to me . . .'

'Go on,' Ganesh urged when I stopped, embarrassed.

I put into words something I'd been mulling over. 'All right. It's occurred to me that perhaps Vinnie married a widow with a child because it seemed a good deal businesswise. I

171

don't mean he wasn't nuts about them both—
but it took some of the uncertainty out of
getting married. She'd been married before.
She already had a kid. He didn't mention any
other children so I don't think they had any
together. It was like, well, buying a package
holiday. You know exactly what you're getting.'

'Hah!' said Ganesh with feeling. 'Usha and
Jay bought a package holiday and got food
poisoning.'

'So there's always a risk in any business! I'm
just saying, Vinnie took the best option. I don't
imagine he's ever been the type to sweep
women off their feet! There was this young
woman with a child, looking for a nice home
and there was Vinnie, looking for a family. It
worked out well. Everyone got what they
wanted.'

Ganesh was looking dissatisfied. Chewing
and waving a piece of naan bread at me to
emphasise his words, he said indistinctly, 'I still
don't see why he had to turn up like that and
nab you. I understand the man's desperate,
but—don't get me wrong—talking to you was
really grabbing at straws.'

'I think he only came to find me when he
realised whose daughter I was. Szabo's getting
tired of waiting about for the police to pull the
chestnuts out of the fire. He wants Lauren
found, fair enough, and found quickly. And
he's used to doing things himself, his way,
calling all the shots. More than that, he's

172

isolated. He's come down from Manchester. London's a place he left as a kid. He doesn't know people here. This isn't a situation where he can call in business favours and get things done. Suddenly, there I am, Bondi's daughter. I'm almost family!'

'I understand how he feels, but he could screw up the whole investigation,' Ganesh said, still disapproving and scraping the rest of the chicken korma out of the foil tray on to my plate. It was kind of him to think of bringing meat for me. He's vegetarian himself. 'And *how* did he learn that you were a friend's daughter? I mean, what made Parry send Szabo to you?'

'Hah!' I said darkly. 'Wouldn't we all like to know what Sergeant Parry's up to? He's got a nerve, setting Szabo on me! What did Parry expect me to tell Vinnie I haven't already told the police? Does Parry think I'm holding out on him? I've already told them all I know and a fat lot they've done with the information.'

We sat in silence eating. Ganesh was deep in thought and I didn't disturb the process because generally he's good at figuring things out and exceptionally good at finding weak links in arguments, especially my arguments.

'It seems to me,' he said at last, 'that you're looking at this from the wrong point of view. That's to say, from your point of view when you ought to be looking at it from Parry's. What I mean is, I don't think Parry thinks

173

you're not telling all you know. I think he thinks *Szabo* isn't telling all he knows. I'm not saying Szabo is a crook. He probably just sails a little close to the wind sometimes and it's not in his interest to tell the coppers all his business, right? At the very least, he's probably got money offshore and the tax people are sniffing round.'

'He likes privacy, he told me so,' I informed him.

'Exactly. Normally he'd probably go a hundred miles out of his way to keep the police or any other official authority out of his hair. Who's to blame him? Look what happened to Hari. But now this girl, Lauren, has been kidnapped. Szabo's had to open up and let the cops put their big feet over his threshold. But no more than he's got to. He's not letting them into the front room and offering them cups of tea. The police would like to know more about Szabo and just how it's come about that his daughter's locked in a cupboard somewhere while a couple of thugs put the squeeze on her family. Perhaps there's a lead or a connection which is slipping by Parry because Szabo's trying to be clever. The man wants his daughter found, but he's a businessman, and he's trying to cut a sort of deal with the police. He wants Lauren back but to give away as little as possible in return. Parry's not using Szabo to shake you loose. He's using *you* to shake up Szabo.'

'Poor kid,' I said. 'As if she's not in enough trouble, Szabo and Parry are playing silly games instead of getting together. I hope she's not having too rough a time. She must be scared out of her wits.'

We sat in silence for a while, both of us aware of the brutal reality of Lauren's situation. Some kidnappers, according to press reports of past cases I'd read, kept their victims prisoner in Dark Age squalor, locked in airless cupboards as Ganesh had just suggested, or even worse, boxed in coffin-like horror, possibly underground. No wonder Szabo was half out of his mind with worry. Even if they got her back in one piece, what sort of mental state would she be in?

I pushed all this gruesome speculation from my mind. It didn't help Lauren and rescuing her was what we all ought to be concentrating on, that and nothing else.

What Gan had said made sense to me. I ought to know enough about Parry to realise he hadn't sent Vinnie along to me without some dastardly plan behind it all. Never mind if I get the fright of my life, abducted by a goon into a motor with tinted windows, to be faced with someone I never saw before but who knows all about me.

Just you wait, Sergeant Parry, I promised myself. I can be very awkward about this. You weren't told to do things this way at Hendon Police College. Or perhaps you were. Come to think of it, Parry had been rather clever for once. He couldn't bully Szabo in the way he liked to bully people, so he had to manipulate the situation. Neat, Sergeant P., but, from my point of view, nasty. The boys in blue are a devious bunch.

'God, Parry's a creep,' I said fervently.

'Sure he is,' said Ganesh. 'But he fancies you something rotten.'

That startled me so much I dropped my plastic fork. 'You're barmy!' I yelped.

'No, I'm a bloke and I can read the signs. He gets that gleam in his eye when he sees you. Now he knows where you are, he'll be back.'

'Thanks for nothing,' I said.

'Let me know if you want me to rush round and defend your honour.' He started chortling away happily to himself.

'I'll have you know I can look after myself!' I snapped. 'Parry? *Parry*? Parry waltzing round my bedroom reeking of aftershave and lust? I'd sooner face a firing squad!'

'Well, they used to call it a fate worse than death!' said Ganesh. He laughed so much he choked on a cashew. I had to thump his back until he yelled out for me to stop before I fractured his spine.

*   *   *

My unknown visitor came back that night.

Before going to bed, I had managed to

176

convince myself that I'd imagined it all two nights ago. It was that sealed little bedroom, I'd told myself. Now I was sleeping out here in the living room, my mind wouldn't be tempted to create wandering ghouls. Anyone lying in the subterranean room, listening to footsteps overhead, would be bound to start making up scary tales. In this way, a late-night, homeward-bound stroller had stopped for a quiet ciggie and in my imagination I'd built it up into a Gothic novel.

Whereupon he proved me wrong. He came back. He even ventured a little closer. He came down the basement steps into the well and stood by the window. He couldn't see in because I'd drawn the curtains and all the lights were out.

I woke up with a start and a sick feeling in my stomach that was fear, not indigestion. Even in my sleep I must have been aware of his approach. Now, as I sat up on the sofa hugging the duvet around me, I saw him.

To be exact, I saw his silhouette on the curtain, slightly distorted by a fold in the curtain. The lamplight outside the house shone down into the basement well and there he was. Not a tall man, not Merv certainly. A squat figure, burly, and somehow familiar. He stood still and silent for a moment or two and then he moved away. I heard his heavy footstep, wearing strong boots of some kind I guessed, as he reclimbed the steps. Then he must have walked off in the other direction, and not back past the basement well, because I heard only the faintest footfall and then, very distantly, a revving motorbike engine. But traffic noise out on the main road travelled at night and the two last things needn't have been connected.

I went into the kitchen, got the bottle from the fridge and drank what remained of the wine Ganesh had brought. With the Dutch courage it provided, I wished I'd had the presence of mind to jump out of bed, snatch back the curtains and glare at him, eyeball to eyeball. Ten to one, it'd have scared him off. He was a prowler, a creeper in the shadows. He played out his fantasies in secret. He didn't like to face his victim.

Victim? I tipped up the bottle but it was empty. Was I indeed to be a victim? If so, what sort? He could just be a nutter. There were people like that who went out at night and roamed about. They had given rise to tales of werewolves and vampires in ages past. Now we just knew them for psychos. But what could he want?

I ran through the possible variations on this theme. He might be a rapist. Basement flats were notoriously vulnerable to break-in. But I had a chain on the door and bolts on the windows.

Or he might be a burglar. But surely he didn't think my place worth robbing? I ought to tell Daphne, though. He might think she had valuables around the place, or money. But I didn't want to frighten her, that was the thing. If he were interested in the rest of the house, why hang about in the basement? If I were the sole object of his attentions, why trouble poor Daphne?

Did he know, I wondered, that I was aware of him? Tonight had he known that I'd woken and seen his shadow on my curtain? He hadn't rattled at the window, trying it. So what the hell was he playing at? To frighten me? Was that his aim?

I raised the empty bottle to him in salute. 'You're doing a good job, friend,' I said. 'I'm frightened.'

I could tell Ganesh. But Ganesh would go berserk. I could tell Parry. No, things weren't that bad.

I crawled back beneath the duvet, but I didn't sleep much.

*　　　*　　　*

Dawn came at last and I fell asleep for a restless hour. I reawoke around six thirty and jumped off the sofa. I couldn't afford to waste daylight. Not now. One thing not on my side was time—amongst all the other things which weren't on my side, of course. Come to think of it, *nothing* was on my side.

If you added to that The Shadow hanging round the place at night, I didn't lack good reason to get moving. But at least I now knew where to start looking. I showered, dragged on jeans and a sweater, and trotted off to St Agatha's women's refuge.

I can't say I was feeling very chipper. But once away from the flat, the sheer normality of daily life all around encouraged me to believe I'd sort it all out somehow. Besides which, I had Szabo's hundred quid in my pocket and being in funds is guaranteed to brighten the outlook. I hadn't told Ganesh about the money. I knew he'd say I shouldn't have taken it. He'd probably argue that I'd implicitly put myself under some sort of obligation to Szabo and that's certainly what Vinnie intended. But I make my own rules.

There was some activity at the refuge this morning. They'd had a visitor of their own since I'd been there. Not content with just heavy breathing like my nocturnal caller, this one had kicked in the front door, which was off its hinges and leaning against the wall. A couple of carpenters were replacing the wooden panel. A skin-headed glazier, half his shaven skull tattooed with a spider's web, was fixing the broken window, getting everything shipshape till the next time. Fixing up St Agatha's must be like painting that Scottish bridge.

There was a transistor radio on the pavement blaring out pop music, and what with that and the sawing and hammering and the workmen all shouting at each other about football, it was bedlam.

I couldn't get past the carpenters so I had to stand next to them and shout. 'Excuse me!'

'My pleasure, darlin'!' said the younger one, all purple singlet, muscles, body odour and dirty blond locks tied back with a bit of ribbon.

'He lives in 'opes, he does,' said his mate to me, winking. 'You want to go in there, do you?'

Oh yes, we'd got a quick thinker here! I was only standing on the step, trying to get past.

'What's up?' enquired Purple Singlet. 'Your old man give you a thick ear?'

'I've just come to see a friend,' I explained, hoping to shut him up. I edged past them both.

The radio had stopped blasting out pop and a presenter was waffling on about something. The shaven glazier burst out unmelodiously into song, informing the world he was forever blowing bubbles.

'You don't want to go in there,' said the second carpenter. 'Right funny lot in there.'

'I wouldn't mind getting in there,' said Purple Singlet.

''E's sex-obsessed!' shouted the West Ham supporter from the windowsill.

'Well, 'oo in't?' Purple Singlet justified his interests.

I left them arguing it out and managed to get past the damaged door into the hall.

The door to the dining room was shut, as

was a door to my left. But the door to the right marked 'Office' was ajar and the rattle of a keyboard could be heard. I knocked.

As I'd been hoping, the dragon with the fright wig wasn't on duty this morning. She'd been replaced by a motherly but competent-looking woman wearing a silk shirt, a drooping skirt and, yes, an Alice band securing faded fair hair. I knew where I was with this one. It was time to polish up the legacy of a good education (in my case, gone wrong, but that didn't matter).

'I'm terribly sorry to bother you,' I said with a diffident smile.

'Not at all,' she said cheerfully. 'Come in and do sit down. Just a moment, I'll make a space.' She swept a pile of papers from a chair. 'We're all at sixes and sevens this morning, I'm afraid.'

'Gosh, yes,' I burbled. 'I saw the damage. Frightful.'

'Nothing to worry about,' she reassured me. 'Just a bit of a nuisance.' She lowered her voice. 'They *will* play that music.'

I sat on the chair, keeping my knees together as taught. 'The reason I've come is that I've been terribly worried about a friend, well, an old schoolfriend, actually. I hadn't seen much of her since I left school but I bumped into her a little while ago and we had a coffee and a sort of catch-up talk, you know?'

She was smiling and nodding, but her eyes were watchful.

I plunged on. 'She didn't seem to be awfully happy. She had some sort of man problem which she wouldn't talk about. The thing is, she's rather disappeared. I've asked for her all over the place and no one's seen her. So I've started looking anywhere the least bit likely. That's why I came here. Her name's Lauren Szabo. She's got longish hair and the last time I saw her she was wearing jeans and a sloppy sweater and had a hairband like yours.'

'Oh dear,' said the woman. 'You understand we don't give out names or personal details. We just can't. We operate here on a principle of trust.'

'Oh yes!' I breathed earnestly. 'I mean, I wouldn't expect you to! I just would be happy if I knew she'd been here and was safe.'

'Well, yes . . . I do see your problem. The trouble is—'

There was a rap at the door and Purple Singlet put his head round. 'You know your frame isn't square?' he demanded.

I cursed him silently and tried telepathy to get him to clear off and sort out the crooked frame for himself. After all, he was the carpenter. But telepathy didn't work.

'We'll have to plane the door down or it's gonna stick, otherwise. All right?'

She looked flustered. 'I'll come and see.' She turned to me. 'Could you just wait a

183

moment? Oh, um, not in here. Just come this way, would you?'

She led me past the carpenter, who winked at me and asked, 'All right, then darlin'?'

'Thank you!' retorted my guide for me before I could answer. She scurried down the hall and opened the door to the dining room. 'Please, if you don't mind?' She gestured at me to enter. 'Back in two ticks!' she promised, and shut me in.

The room smelled of stale vegetable water and old grease mixed with the vinegary aroma that scouring powder manufacturers call 'lemon-scented'. I sat down at the table wondering what they were all going to have for dinner that evening and glad I wasn't going to be eating it myself.

The door creaked and I turned my head. It opened slowly. I waited. There was a scuffle on the other side and a child put her head round.

'Hullo,' I said.

'What are you doing?' asked the child suspiciously.

'I was told to wait in here,' I said truthfully.

It seemed a satisfactory explanation. She came in and closed the door. She appeared to be about nine, with a round, wary, tough little face and straggling brown hair. She wore a sleeveless denim pinafore dress, which was too big, crumpled off-white socks and black PE plimsolls. She climbed up on the dining chair at the head of the table, leaned her elbows on the scarred table-top and surveyed me closely.

'You've got no bruises,' she said reproachfully, as if I'd failed some test.

'Yes, I have,' I said, 'I've got a bruise on my back and on my arm, as it happens.' I pushed up my sleeve to display the imprint of Szabo's chauffeur's fingers.

But it wasn't judged good enough. She sniffed scornfully. 'That's nuffin'. My mum's got a broken arm. Gary, her boyfriend, he bust it.'

'I'm sorry,' I said. 'What's your name? I'm Fran.'

'My name's Samantha,' she said with dignity. 'I was named after a Page Three girl.'

'It's a pretty name. So you and your mum, you're here because of your mum's friend.'

'I never liked him, I never liked Gary,' she confided. 'I liked the boyfriend she had before. He was called Gus. He could make all his fingers crack, like this . . .' She tugged fiercely at her small fingers but, disappointingly, they refused to crack. 'She should've stayed with Gus. He had a job and everythin'.'

Clearly we had here a budding Agony Aunt. And perhaps she was right, at that. Being able to crack your fingers is an achievement of sorts. Not everyone can do it, after all. Throw in a steady job and I was inclined to agree that Samantha's mum had been unwise to leave Gus for violent, workshy Gary.

Then I remembered the brief discussion between the workmen. Gary probably had the charisma of a pop star and, when he wasn't belting the living daylights out of a girlfriend, was the life and soul of the party. While poor old Gus had sat there evening after evening, cracking his fingers, before turning in early because he had to get up to go to work in the morning.

I just hoped Samantha here remembered all this when she grew up. It might be better to phrase that 'when she grew older' since she appeared to have grown up already.

'Whatya doing here?' she asked shrewdly. I wasn't battered enough to be a genuine refuge-seeker. I had to be after something else.

I glanced at the door. It was taking the woman a long time to sort out the carpentry problem, but this might be to my advantage.

'I'm looking for a friend,' I said. 'Have you been living here long, Samantha?'

'For a bit.' She looked vague. 'We bin here before, lots of times. I don't know how long we're staying this time.'

'My friend's name,' I prompted, 'is Lauren.'

'Oh, she's not here no more,' Samantha said immediately.

I fairly jumped off the chair in triumph. So Lauren had been here! But there might be more than one Lauren.

I said tentatively, 'My friend's got long hair and an Alice—hairband—like that woman in

186

the office wears on her hair.'

'That's Miriam in the office,' said my informant. 'Lauren had one of them on her hair. I'd like one too,' she added, her gaze growing thoughtful. 'Do you think my hair's long enough?'

'Yes, I should think so,' I assured her. 'When did Lauren leave?'

'Dunno,' she said vaguely.

'Did she stay long?'

Samantha frowned. 'She didn't stay. She didn't live here. She used to come in and help out—'

The door opened and Miriam reappeared. Seeing Samantha she halted and exclaimed, 'Oh!' Then she rallied. 'What are you doing in here, Sam? Your mum's looking for you. Go on, run along, dear!'

Samantha slid off her chair. 'Goodbye,' she said to me politely. She trotted past Miriam into the hall and could be heard there, equally politely greeting someone else. 'Hullo. What you doing here? They don't let no men in here! You a boyfriend?'

'No,' said a familiar voice. 'I'm a policeman.'

'Oh, one of *them*,' chirped my small pal dismissively.

I couldn't have put it better myself.

CHAPTER TEN

They taught us all about entrances and exits when I was a student of the dramatic arts. A good entrance is important, but a good exit is *really* something. Shakespeare's *'Exit, pursued by a bear'* is a good one. But on balance, and without boasting, I'd say not as good as the exit made by Sergeant Parry and me from St Agatha's refuge. That was exceptionally dramatic. That would've had 'em on the edge of their seats and without a pantomime animal in sight.

Once he'd caught sight of me chatting peaceably to my little friend Samantha, Parry had stormed into the dining room in fouler than usual mood.

'Get the kid out of here!' he'd snapped. Unnecessarily, as it happened. Poor little Samantha had already learned when it was time to disappear and had nipped down the hall and scuttled away upstairs out of reach of his anger.

'All right, Fran!' he'd continued. 'I might've guessed it'd be you. You're leaving now, right?'

'I've not concluded my business here,' I said with dignity because one shouldn't lower one's standards to match this sort of thing. They taught us that at school. A lady acts with calm and poise no matter what the circumstances. She doesn't descend to exchanging vulgar abuse, not even with the police.

The woman with the drooping skirt, who'd been through the same kind of social schooling only in her case with better result, was looking equally askance at his manners. She stood ramrod straight by the door, her bosom quivering while she made little disapproving clucking noises, just as if she hadn't phoned him to come over, which she clearly had.

'Oh yes, you have!' Parry snarled to me.

'Oh no, I haven't!' I couldn't resist.

But Parry has no sense of humour. He grabbed my elbow in the manner recommended for arresting officers. He then frogmarched me past the snitch in the doorway, down the hall and through the gap where the front door had been removed. Out into the street we shot, linked like Siamese twins, and there the fun really started.

The workmen, all three of them, must have marked Parry down as a copper when he arrived. I think it's the purposeful way they walk that betrays plainclothes officers. Either that or the fact that no one but a plod in mufti would emerge in daylight wearing a sports jacket like the one Parry had. So they were curious, and ready for us, when we emerged.

'Oy! Whatcha doin' with the little lady?' demanded Purple Singlet aggressively, barring our way.

The older carpenter asked sternly, 'You got a warrant, mate, or what?'

The skinhead glazier hopped from his ladder in happy anticipation of a chance to put the boot in. I noticed he'd also slipped a chisel in his back pocket and this worried me. I foresaw having to throw myself across the wretched Parry to save him. The picture didn't appeal.

Parry turned a clashing red to his moustache and yapped, 'Out of the way, please!'

All three stayed put. 'What's she done?' asked Purple Singlet. 'You taking her down the nick, or what? Here, let go of the poor little mare's arm before you dislocate her perishing shoulder. Pick on someone your own size.'

The glazier didn't quite jump up and down and shout 'Me, me!' but his expression grew more eager.

'The lady's not under arrest!' growled Parry. 'But you all will be if you persist in causing an obstruction and hindering a law officer in the performance of his duty.'

'Ooh!' cried the glazier in a shrill falsetto and stamping one of his Doc Martens. 'He's getting angry!'

'Watch it!' ordered Parry, nearly as purple as the carpenter's singlet.

'Isn't he masterful?' admired the glazier. He'd obviously got tormenting the constabulary down to a fine art.

The older carpenter was proving himself a

saloon bar lawyer. 'If she's not committed an offence, she don't have to go with you.'

He then turned to me. 'You don't have to say nothing, ducks, right? You tell 'em you want a lawyer. And mind they get you a proper one and not some pensioned-off old geezer they got in their pocket. If you don't know a lawyer, Mr Eftimakis in Dollis Hill's very good. You give him a ring and tell him Harry Porter recommended him.'

'You're going to need him yourself,' squawked Parry, 'if you don't get out of my way! She's not under arrest. I'm escorting her home!' He immediately lived to regret this indiscretion.

'Aha!' chorused all three of my knights champion with varying degrees of ribaldry.

The glazier leered and enquired, 'Goin' to show her your handcuffs, are you?'

'One more word,' panted Parry, 'and you're nicked!'

'Goin' to arrest us all?' asked Purple Singlet with interest, eyeing the car parked at the kerb. 'Goin' to squeeze all five of us in that motor? Cosy.'

'If necessary,' said Parry, clearly meaning it. 'I'll call backup and we'll get you all to the nick in style!'

It was time for me to cool things down. 'Thanks for the support, fellers,' I said. 'But the sergeant and I are old acquaintances. I can manage. No grief, OK?'

191

They parted reluctantly to let us through, the older carpenter calling out final advice to ring Mr Eftimakis in Dollis Hill.

'Nice to think chivalry's not dead in England!' I piped as Parry gunned the accelerator and we roared away from the refuge.

'Bloody yobbos!' he muttered, crouched white-knuckled over the wheel.

'No, they're not, they're British craftsmen!' I defended my new friends. It seemed only fair to return the favour.

'British ruddy football hooligans more like. I don't care what they do on a weekday. Come Saturday afternoon that lot'll be rampaging round the terraces, when they're not kicking in shop windows or chucking one another off trains! I know your common or garden yob when I see him!'

'They were only trying to look after me,' I said placatingly because I was afraid Parry might collapse at the wheel with an aneurysm. His neck had swollen up and bulged over his collar and his eyes popped out of his head.

He rolled a red-veined eyeball at me. 'Strange as it may seem, Miss Varady, I am also trying to look after you!'

It was a pity he said that because up to that moment I hadn't been too worried by his appearing. I'd been confident of dealing with the situation and secretly pleased he'd not wanted to talk in the dining room, because it gave me more time to think up a reasonable excuse for my being there. But now I remembered Ganesh's loony notion that Parry fancied me. My presence of mind completely deserted me.

'Where are we going?' I quavered.

'Where I said, I'm taking you home. Then we're going to have a little chat.'

'I don't mind going to the station. I'll come and talk about it at the station, if you like.'

He glanced at me in puzzled annoyance. 'What's the matter with you all of a sudden?'

'Nothing!' I cried unconvincingly.

He was normally of a suspicious disposition and now he demanded, 'What's back at your place you don't want me to see?'

'Nothing! I've already told you.'

'We'll go there then, right?'

We went there.

*　　　*　　　*

When we got out of the car I made a last-ditch stand to prevent him following me down the basement steps. Custer had better luck.

'We can talk here!' I began on the pavement, lolling nonchalantly on the gate like a cut-price tart.

'Whaffor? We can talk in your flat, private.'

That's what I didn't want, privacy with Parry. I changed tactics.

'Whatever you've got to say, say it here!' I

now declared in ringing tones, barring access to the basement steps by gripping the iron railings with one hand and bracing myself against the house wall with the other.

'You're hiding something, you are!' He stood over me, glowering.

A window above our heads was pushed up and Daphne's head appeared. 'All right below there? Fran? Is that man harassing you?'

'It's fine, thanks, Daphne!' I called back. 'I can manage.'

'I can easily fetch help!' cried my landlady. 'Who is that strange man?'

'He's a police officer, Daphne. Sorry and all that.'

'Are you sure, Fran dear? Ask to see his identification. There are a lot of confidence tricksters about, always pretending to be policemen or that they've come to read the electricity meter. Why isn't he in uniform? Why's he dressed like that?'

'It's plainclothes, madam!' howled Parry. He waved his identity card up at her. 'I called to see you the other day, if you remember? Sergeant Parry?'

'Oh yes, so you did. I haven't got my glasses on. But now I recall the jacket. Is there something wrong?'

'No, madam, just checking out something.'

'Well, please do it quietly!' she ordered him, and slammed down the window.

'That's right,' I grumbled. 'Get me thrown

out of my flat. Come down if you must.'

I led him down to the flat and let us both in. He pushed past me and marched into the living room, eyeballs swivelling all over the place like bagatelle balls.

Not seeing anything likely to cause a breach of the peace, he whirled round. 'All right, what are you playing at now? What's your little game, eh? Why were you at the refuge asking about Lauren Szabo? What d'you know about her?'

'Only what Vincent Szabo told me, after you'd so kindly told him all about me, including where I lived,' I informed him crisply.

It threw him off balance slightly, but not for long. 'Well, he's a respectable businessman, isn't he? Drivin' round in a Roller with a chauffeur and all. Thought you might like to move up a class for company. Anyway, he reckons he knew your dad.'

'He probably did. Not that my father ever mentioned him.'

Parry sat down uninvited on the sofa. 'So he did turn up, did he? I wondered if he would. He didn't lose time. What did he say to you?'

'Private conversation,' I told him. 'None of your business. But if you want to put something in your report, put down that I don't like being used.'

'Don't come the injured party with me. You're always keen to stick your nose in. What

195

did Szabo have to say?'

I sat down too. It was, after all, my flat. 'He told me his stepdaughter has been snatched. He's not happy with the lack of progress being made by the police. If I heard anything, I was to tell him. So I told him more or less everything I told you.'

He chewed at the end of the mangy moustache. 'Why did you go to the refuge?'

'I'm not sure,' I confessed. 'Probably because when I asked Vinnie if she was likely to have been walking back from there when she was picked up, his tame gorilla tossed me out of the car.'

'She helped out there,' said Parry. 'She's one of them wealthy girls with nothing else to do, so they go round doing good works. No need to earn any money. Daddy makes 'em an allowance.'

'Why shouldn't he want me to know that?' I asked, puzzled.

'He disapproved. She was doing it behind his back, the voluntary work there. The impression I got of him, he's on the overprotective side. On the other hand, he might've feared something would happen to her, mixing with the wrong sort. Perhaps he was afraid she'd fall for some sandal-wearing social worker with long hair and granny glasses. You know, fortune-hunter. How do I know? He's rich, for Gawd's sake. Rich people have to worry about things like that. The kid's the apple of his eye. His wife's dead. She's all he's got left. He's a worried man.'

I reflected that we'd come a long way since Parry had sat on that sofa, pretending there was no snatch and poor old Albie hadn't seen anything. I said as much.

Parry had the grace to look sheepish. 'Yes, well, that was when I still hoped you'd keep your nose outa things. I should've known better. Stay quiet about all this, right?'

'You told them at the refuge to call you if anyone came asking about Lauren Szabo. Were you thinking of me?'

'Routine,' said Parry, which is what they always say when they don't want to answer.

'Or were you expecting someone else to be asking after her? Has she got a boyfriend?' That was a new idea to strike me. 'You said Vinnie was afraid she'd meet someone unsuitable. Did she?'

'We've followed that line up and got nowhere,' Parry said, tugging at the sleeve of his jacket with a frown. 'She's been dating some Hooray Henry what works in his own family's firm. Suppose they had to give him a job. Strictly between you and me, he hasn't got the brains to organise a teddy bears' tea-party. Anyway, he's got an alibi for the night she was snatched.'

'Of course he has,' I said patiently. 'He would, wouldn't he? He wouldn't do it himself. What's his name and where can I find him?'

197

'Forget it!' Parry snapped.

'All right,' I said, to keep him happy. 'Have you tried looking for Merv? He can't be that difficult to find.'

'We've got your description of him,' he said. 'Give us time. We'll pick him up. But we won't necessarily be able to link him with the old man.'

'Of course you can! Ganesh and I saw Merv and his mate try to snatch Albie!'

'So you say, but that's not good enough,' Parry retorted aggravatingly. 'It was late at night. Poor streetlighting. All over in a few seconds. Can you describe the second man?'

Unfortunately I couldn't. Merv I'd recognised, but in the circumstances all I'd noticed about his pal was that he was shorter, broader and either dark-haired or wearing a dark woolly hat. I told Parry this.

'There you are then,' he said. 'I can't haul anyone in on the basis of a description like that. Adds up to mistaken identity, doesn't it?' He shrugged. 'Your word and Patel's against his. Not good enough, like I said.' He crouched aggressively on the edge of the sofa, flexing his mitts, which were sprinkled with long red hair like an orangutan's.

A thought had occurred to me. 'If you want to know what Szabo and I talked about, ask Szabo himself. Or doesn't he talk to you? What *was* the big idea sending him along to me?'

Parry scratched his chin. The shaving rash was clearing up, but if he carried on rubbing it like that, it'd come back. Serve him right. I hoped he came out in boils like those people in the Bible.

'You're near enough his daughter's age. He knew your dad. He might've said something to you he—he overlooked when talking to us.'

'I'm two years older than his daughter and I don't think Szabo would draw any comparison between me and his Lauren. Szabo's gone out of his way to protect her from life's nastiness until now, whereas he sees me as someone who can be bundled into a strange car by a minder and asked a lot of nosy questions.' A new idea leapt into my head. 'Have you got a picture of her, of Lauren?'

'The girl? Sure.' He fumbled in a wallet and produced a couple of snapshots. One showed a young girl with long fair hair, apparently sitting at a pavement cafe table. The background looked continental and big city, probably Paris. The labels on the bottles of soft drink were French. The girl in the photo leaned on her elbows and stared at the camera with a cool challenge in her eyes. She was a good-looker.

The other picture was a studio portrait, one of those little polyphotos, all varying poses, which the photographer gives the client for him to make his choice. Her hair was tidier and she wore a lot more make-up for this one but I was more taken by the difference in her expression. In the cafe picture she looked as if she were in charge. In the polyphoto she looked trapped and angry. She hadn't wanted that picture taken. I wondered who had taken the informal snap. Looking at Lauren's picture made me uneasy. Before, she'd been a name, and a vague description by Albie. Now she was a real person, a prisoner somewhere, frightened and in danger. I handed them both back to Parry who put them away.

'So,' he said, 'what else you got to tell me, Fran? Now's your chance. Withholding evidence is a criminal offence.'

I got up and fetched the empty Bell's bottle and put it down on the coffee table in front of him.

'What's all this?' His eyes began to turn pink again.

I told him. 'I was going to bring it to you, right? You know as well as I do that Albie saw Lauren snatched and this—' I pointed at the bottle—'this shows he didn't just fall in the canal unaided.'

'It doesn't show anything of the sort,' he retorted.

I hadn't expected thanks, but this annoyed me. 'No wonder Szabo's fed up with the slow progress you're making!' I snapped. 'You lose your one witness and now you've got tangible evidence you don't know what to do with it. Can't you fingerprint it or something?'

'I told you before,' he said, 'that you're a

200

mouthy little madam. I remember when you lived in that squat with all those other dropouts. You were a right bossy little piece then, issuing orders right, left and centre. Don't try it with me. You're sailing close to the wind, Miss Varady. You say you were going to hand over the bottle to us, but you did your damnedest to stop me coming down here.'

'That wasn't because of the bottle,' I began. 'It was because—'

But I couldn't tell him it was because Ganesh reckoned Parry lusted after me. I didn't know where Gan had got that idea from. If the sergeant here fancied me, he'd got a funny way of showing it. I finished lamely, quoting Szabo, 'I like my privacy. This is my home. I don't want you marching in and out just as you like.'

'Actually,' he said. 'I don't like it. Think I've got nothing better to do? I'm a busy man investigating a serious crime. Don't mess me about, Fran. If you do, I'll get you on a charge, right?'

'Oh, will you?' I challenged. 'I could make a formal complaint against you for sending Szabo to me.'

He treated me to a wintry smile. 'You overlook that, Fran, and I'll overlook the fact that you didn't hand the bottle over at once, also that you went to the refuge, causing trouble—'

201

I opened my mouth to protest because he'd caused the trouble there, not me.

He overrode my objection. 'So keep out from under my feet, right? That way we can stay friends.'

'We are not friends,' I told him coldly.

I was treated to another of those gargoyle grimaces. 'Oh, come on, Fran. I think you and I could get along rather well!'

'In your dreams!' I corrected him icily.

'Please yourself. I'm taking the whisky bottle, right? Got a paper bag?'

I gave him Ben's plastic bag. He stood up. 'So find yourself something else to do, leave the sleuthing to the professionals. Weekend coming up. Go away somewhere nice. Go to Margate and get some sea air.'

'As it happens,' I informed him, 'I have a job this weekend as an artist's model.'

His ginger eyebrows shot up to meet his hairline. 'What? In the buff?'

Simple soul that he was, I hastened to disappoint him.

'No! In costume.'

'What sort of costume?' he asked with interest, his limited mind running on bare-breasted bimbos hiding the essentials behind a pair of unzipped jeans lodged at crotch level.

'A tree,' I told him. 'I shall be dressed to symbolise the threatened Amazonian rainforest.'

He burst out laughing and made a pretty

good exit of his own, warbling about talking to the trees in a surprisingly good baritone.

I was fed up so I ran myself a bath to wash away all contact with the law. The hot water steamed up the bathroom mirror. I wrote I HATE PARRY on it so that I could meditate on it as I lay in the bath. But the moisture on the mirror began to trickle and changed my slogan to I HAVE HAPPY. Sometimes nothing works.

CHAPTER ELEVEN

The long soak in the tub, a grilled cheese sandwich and three cups of coffee succeeded in erasing the tainted air of Parry's presence from the flat. A single ray of sun, angled down through the basement window, told me it was after two o'clock and encouraged me to go out and try something else. My brain was working again. If at first you don't succeed and all the rest of it. Thanks to Parry, I now knew Lauren had a steady boyfriend. The first thing to do was to find out if Szabo had known about this and what he'd felt about it.

Dressed in clean jeans and my best silk shirt and quilted waistcoat, I ran up the steps to Daphne's front door and rang the bell.

She must have seen me coming and the door was opened almost at once. 'You are all right, aren't you, dear? What *is* going on?' she demanded breathlessly.

'Sorry about the bit of bother earlier,' I said.

'There was no need to come up and apologise for that!' she returned, and fixed me with a reproachful gaze. 'If that was the same police officer who came to see me the other day, I thought him uncouth.'

'He is uncouth,' I said. 'But he can't help it. May I use the phone?'

'Help yourself!' She waved at the instrument and trotted back to her ever-growing pile of manuscript. I was momentarily distracted enough to wonder again what it represented, but it seemed rude to ask.

I punched the number Szabo had given me and after a moment, his high-pitched, nervy voice asked, 'Hullo? Yes?'

'Mr Szabo?' I said. 'It's Francesca Varady.'

'You've seen the tattooed man again?' He quavered with eagerness and I imagined him standing there, the mobile phone pressed to his ear.

There was a sound of movement in the background and Szabo, his voice fading slightly as he turned his head, snapped, 'Yes, yes, just leave it there!'

I deduced he was sitting in a probably expensive hotel room and the room service had just delivered something. I had felt sorry for the man, because after all, there was nothing he could do but sit there all a-jitter and wait. But my sympathy was tempered by the thought that at least he was doing it in comfort.

I had to disappoint him. 'Sorry, no, I haven't seen the man again. But I've been thinking and I wondered whether anyone has talked to Lauren's friends.'

'Why?' He sounded edgy and a little annoyed that I'd falsely raised his hopes for a moment.

Trying not to antagonise him further, I began, 'Suppose she'd noticed that someone appeared to be watching or following her—'

He broke in with a terse, 'She'd have reported a stalker.'

'I wasn't thinking of anyone so obvious as a stalker. Just a face which seemed to be turning up more often than coincidentally, but not often enough or aggressively enough to make her report it to the police. If no one made an actual approach or spoke to her, what could she have reported? She might not have told you either, not wanting to worry you, or thinking she might sound neurotic. But she might have mentioned it to a friend.'

A pause. 'The police have already followed up this line of enquiry,' he said discouragingly. 'Naturally they've spoken to all her close friends.'

'Oh, the police . . .' I let my voice tail away.

He thawed. 'Well, yes, I do see that a casual approach might turn up some little, overlooked fact, something which appeared too trivial to be mentioned to the police.'

'Or too embarrassing,' I pursued. 'A situation like that can be awkward for a woman.'

'I take your word for that,' he said, terse again. Perhaps he'd made the connection between this and his own cautious fencing with the police. I had to be careful not to tip Parry's hand.

Silently cursing the sergeant, I asked, 'I wondered whether your daughter had a particular boyfriend, someone in London?'

'I fail to see the relevance,' Szabo's voice had grown icy. 'You mean, I take it, that she might have confided her fears to Jeremy. But Jeremy would have reported anything like that to me at once. He'd know I'd want to be informed of anyone annoying my daughter!'

'She might have asked him not to.'

'Jeremy is a thoroughly reliable young man,' he replied, apparently unaware that the word might mean something different to him than it did to Lauren. 'I've no reason to doubt his judgement. He's extremely fond of Lauren and would have insisted she went to the police immediately if there were the hint of any threat.'

I said nothing, letting him think it over.

'Very well,' he said at last. 'I'll call him and tell him to expect you. I'm willing to try any avenue which might get my daughter back safely and soon.' His voice broke and trembled. 'You can't imagine what the uncertainty is doing to us, to me and to Jeremy, what it's like . . . I'll ring him at once.'

The last thing I wanted was to appear to Jeremy as Szabo's stooge. 'No!' I said hastily. 'Don't do that. Far better if I drop by and tell him I've been trying to get in touch with Lauren. That we had a lunch date or something and she didn't show. As you said, we want to keep it casual.'

It was important to make him think this was basically his idea. It worked. Though I still expected him to put up more argument, he folded almost at once, went along with the plan without any fuss, and told me Jeremy's full name and where to find his business. Really, handling him was a doddle.

I replaced the receiver, put a fifty-pence piece by the phone, called my thanks to Daphne, and set out.

*   *   *

Thais Fine Arts was located in a narrow blind alley in the New Bond Street area. The alley looked as if its original purpose had been to provide a back entrance to the block, for removal of garbage, that sort of thing. It had been spruced up since those days and the dustbins taken away. But it wasn't the sort of place you'd ever find if you didn't know it was there, which meant the business wouldn't attract the casual passer-by. Perhaps it dealt with recommended customers only. There were places like that. Or perhaps it dealt in export and import.

Further investigation confirmed my suspicions. This was by no stretch of imagination a shop, gallery, showroom, call it what you like. The premises consisted of offices at the top of a narrow flight of stairs. The name appeared on a discreet but well-polished plate on the outer door by a bell. I pressed. It buzzed and the door uttered a disgruntled click as the locking mechanism was released. I pushed it open, thinking that the person within hadn't bothered to check who rang.

Then, as I went through, my eye caught the tiny camera up in the corner of the stairwell, trained on the door. The person inside knew exactly who was out here and had watched me climb the last stairs, peer at the doorplate and fidget about making up my mind to ring. I didn't like that and marched in belligerently.

I found myself in a reception area, a large square room decorated predominantly white like a hospital ward. White walls, white leather chairs, oatmeal carpet. The only splashes of colour were provided by a tall green plant in a white pot and the dark blue of the business suit worn by the receptionist. Above her head flickered the screen on which she'd seen me arrive and on her stainless-steel and glass desk stood a dinky little wooden nameplate with the gold-painted legend 'Jane Stratton'. This was a nice place to work, all right. It must be really neat to have your name in gold, stuck there in front of you for all to see. Ms Stratton rose to intercept me. Greet was not the word.

'Yes?' she asked.

She was a human version of an Afghan hound, long, lean, thoroughbred. Her narrow face was perfectly made up and her long blonde hair sculpted and lacquered into rigid waves and curls. The overall effect was intended to be glamorous but failed for lack of warmth or personality. She had eyes like twin lasers.

I ignored the permafrost welcome and asked cheerfully if I might see Mr Copperfield.

'You have an appointment?' she enquired, faintly incredulous.

'No, it's personal. I'm a friend of Lauren Szabo.'

She hesitated then pressed a switch on the intercom and relayed the information. It squawked a distorted reply.

'Do take a seat,' she said to me, marginally more gracious. 'Mr Copperfield will be out to see you shortly.'

I sat on one of the white leather chairs and studied my surrounds, wondering what constituted fine art. I also wondered whether I was to be interviewed by Copperfield out here, or whether I'd be admitted to some inner sanctum. It depended how much he wanted the chilly receptionist to overhear, although she could overhear whatever she wanted through the intercom system.

There were two doors in the walls facing the reception desk but neither carried a nameplate. The only example of a fine art object stood near me atop a plinth perched on a glass-topped table. It was a marble bust of a cherub and would, to my mind, have been more suited to a monumental mason's showroom than an art dealer's. It was an extraordinary ugly thing. Its fat cheeks bulged and rosebud lips were pursed as if it ought to be blowing a trumpet, but someone had taken away the musical instrument. This meant the overall effect was that it blew a raucous raspberry towards the entrance door.

I wouldn't have fancied it around the home, but then it was unlikely I could ever have afforded it so the problem didn't arise. It didn't carry anything so vulgar as a price tag.

I caught the Ice Queen's eye, nodded towards the cherub and asked, 'How much?'

'Fifteen hundred,' she said, and allowed herself a smirk of satisfaction when she saw my mouth fall open.

She returned to her work, rattling a keyboard with scarlet talons. At her elbow, a red light suddenly glowed on the telephone.

She ignored it. After a few moments, the light went out. I wondered if it signified an outside line was in use.

Without warning, one of the twin inner doors opened and a bulky figure filled the aperture.

'Miss Varady?' He moved solidly towards me, spectacle lenses glinting, hand outstretched. 'Jeremy Copperfield. I'm sorry to have kept you waiting. Do come through. Would you like some tea or coffee?'

The receptionist paused in her work and raised a forbidding eye.

'No thank you,' I said. 'I won't take up much of your time.'

I followed Copperfield to his office, which closely resembled the outer room in colour scheme and general furnishings. He invited me to sit on one of the ubiquitous white leather chairs, and eased himself into a beige leather executive chair with stainless-steel arms. He placed his fingertips together and swivelled gently to and fro before me, all the while watching my face over the top of his specs.

Fighting the impression that I'd strayed into some private sanatorium and was facing an expensive medical consultant, I forced myself to relax on my chair, and studied him back. There was silence while we eyed one another in polite antagonism.

Lauren's boyfriend was about twenty-eight and had a weight problem which, if he hadn't got to grips with it by now, he never would. His belly bulged over his waistband. His jawline was lost in the cushion of double chins, which in turn made his mouth, with its pink pouty lips like those of the cherub, look too small. It struck me that he showed little sign of the distress he ought to be suffering. But perhaps he was good at hiding his feelings.

'I don't recall,' he broke our silence to say, 'that Lauren ever mentioned your name to me.' He stopped swivelling the chair and rested his hand on the steel arms, raising his head so that his eyes were still fixed on me but this time through, not over, his glasses. The lenses were thick and made his eyes appear piggy. He wasn't my cup of tea, but then I wasn't Lauren, and the choice was hers.

I'd already decided to use the story that had worked well at the refuge until I'd mentioned Lauren's name.

'We hadn't seen each other for a while when we bumped into one another. We fixed up a reunion lunch but she didn't show. I did think she seemed worried about something, so that made me concerned. I've been trying to get in touch with her.'

Behind the jam-jar-bottom lenses, his eyes blinked at me. As if I hadn't spoken, his voice flowed on, 'So I took the precaution of phoning her father. He says it's in order to talk to you. You know there is a possibility she's being held somewhere against her will and the police are involved. You understand all this is highly sensitive and mustn't become public knowledge.'

So it *had* been an outside line. So much for the approach I thought I'd agreed with Szabo. Now I was left looking foolish. But I had to admit that without Szabo's go-ahead, Copperfield wouldn't be talking to me.

'That's fine,' I said, abandoning that line. 'I understand the circumstances and believe me, I'm very sorry. You're all under a terrible strain.'

'Yes,' he said, 'we are.'

But he still didn't look it, not to me. Curiously, I asked, 'Have you been dating Lauren very long?'

Blink. 'We've known each other several years,' he said, pursing his fat little lips and suddenly looking so like the marble head out there in reception that I had a job not to grin.

'Is Mr Szabo also involved in the art market?' I asked, 'I thought he was in loose covers.'

Copperfield ignored the question and his stare informed me that he considered it improper. Worse, he suspected me of mockery. His opinion of me wasn't high. But there again, neither was my opinion of him. It was clear to me already that far from being the love of Lauren's life, this man was her Malcolm Tring.

I should explain. Obviously, Jeremy here was Szabo's choice for Lauren, a man who saw

213

things his way and could be relied upon to report back to her stepfather at the first sign of trouble. Szabo himself would deny this was the reason for his selecting Copperfield. He'd roll out a whole list of Jeremy's virtues. Personal charisma wouldn't figure among them, but neither would Szabo see it as a disadvantage. If anything, he'd see it as an irrelevance.

That's the way it goes. Families judge by a whole different set of criteria to that favoured by their offspring. Which is where Malcolm Tring comes in.

Malcolm figured briefly in my life when I'd just turned fourteen, and all because Grandma Varady liked a game of cards. She belonged to a whist club and there she met a fellow fanatic called Mrs Emma Tring, a well-to-do widow. Mrs Tring, it soon turned out, had a grandson, one Malcolm.

'A really nice boy,' enthused Grandma V. to me, as she ladled out the goulash soup one evening. 'Just a year older than you, fifteen, and doing very well at school. He escorts his grandmother to the whist club regularly, such a kind boy. Not many his age would give up the time! He's always polite and so well spoken, and the family has a pine furniture business in the High Street. I understand from Emma it's doing very well, and my goodness, she has some beautiful pearls.'

Grandma paused for dramatic effect and chinked the ladle on the soup tureen. 'And he's an only child!' she whispered.

'I want to be an actress,' I said, correctly divining the drift of all this. 'I don't want to spend my life selling pine furniture.'

'Actors starve,' she said, correctly as it happens. 'A business is handy to fall back on.'

'Especially if it's furniture!' I quipped, and was rapped on the knuckles with the ladle for not taking the matter seriously. But how could I take seriously anyone connected with a business that advertised itself as selling 'FURNITURE TO MAKE YOUR HEART TRING'?

Grandma did take it seriously and needless to say, I was eventually dragooned into accompanying her to the whist club, there to meet Malcolm Tring. Also needless to say, he was awful, and I'd have had to be out of my skull to want to fall back on him. Nor did I think his grandmother's pearls all that great. They looked fake to me. I was already something of an expert on stage props by then.

Malcolm reciprocated my feelings. It was mutual dislike on sight. Grandmothers Tring and Varady engineered one more meeting and then, a stroke of luck, Malcolm had to go into hospital for his adenoids, and that was that.

I don't think Grandma V. ever quite forgave me. Not even when the furniture business burned down eighteen months later. It was in the *Standard*, and arson was suspected. So perhaps it hadn't been doing all that well. I always knew those pearls were false.

Jeremy offered the kind of reassurance to concerned families that Malcolm had appeared to offer. No doubt the marble cherub business was doing well. Every home should have one. Szabo probably saw in this young entrepreneur something of himself when younger. Jeremy would guarantee Lauren a nice big house and a generous personal spending allowance. Jeremy wouldn't stray and he wouldn't ask where Lauren spent her money or her afternoons. Business would always come first with him, women a long way back second. I was even prepared to bet Jeremy Copperfield was an only child.

The scepticism in my face succeeded in rattling Copperfield. He flushed and said loudly, 'We were about to announce our engagement!'

By 'we' he meant himself and his prospective father-in-law. I doubt Lauren was in full agreement.

'Then you'll want to find her,' I said.

The flush turned to beetroot. 'I would feel any other suggestion to be insulting, Miss Varady!'

'I want to find her too.' I ignored the huffing and puffing. I wasn't here to listen to Copperfield's bluster. I was here on business.

My voice must have told him so and it was an attitude he respected. His own manner changed. The flush faded, he sat up straighter

216

in the executive chair, folded his plump hands and asked crisply, 'And what would be your interest? You don't know Lauren personally. Is Szabo paying you?'

It was possible Szabo thought he was. I didn't. 'My interest,' I said, 'is in what happened to an elderly man whose body was taken from the canal yesterday morning early.'

Copperfield's small sharp eyes gleamed behind the lenses. 'Has this any bearing on what's happened to Lauren?'

'I think so.'

'I'd appreciate your reasons,' Copperfield said.

'Fair enough. I believe he saw Lauren snatched off the street. The men involved knew he'd been a witness. They arranged his death.'

There was a silence. Then Copperfield said carefully, as if picking his way through a verbal minefield, 'You are suggesting murder. That's a very serious matter. Where do the police stand in all this?'

'You'd better ask them,' I retorted.

'I shall, believe me.' He unfolded his podgy paws and tapped the armrests of his chair. 'And what do you think I can tell you, Miss Varady, that the police or, indeed, Vincent Szabo can't?'

'I had wondered,' I confessed, 'whether Lauren had told you of anything unusual that had happened to her lately, during the time

217

leading up to her disappearance. Had either of you made any new acquaintances? Started going to new places? Had anyone been asking about her, making some excuse or other?'

'Much as you are doing?' His cheeks shuddered as a sarcastic smile rippled away from the edges of his mouth.

'OK then, much as I'm doing. Was there anyone?'

'If she'd told me any such thing,' he said, 'I'd have insisted she report it to the police.'

Time to shake him up a little. 'Did you know,' I asked innocently, 'that she was a regular volunteer helper at a refuge for battered women in the area where she was snatched?'

I was wrong in fancying that would bother him. He looked annoyed, but not surprised. 'The police have already investigated that angle, as I understand it. I'll be frank with you, Miss Varady. I didn't approve of such good works, laudable though they might have been. The simple fact is that when a young woman stands to be heiress one day to, well, not exactly a fortune perhaps, but certainly a comfortable amount, she has to accept the risks that go with having money. She becomes a prey for spongers, spinners of hard-luck tales, penniless young men and unsavoury elements in society of all kinds. Her family and friends will try to protect her but she must also protect herself.

'I knew she gave her time to the refuge, amongst other similar hostels. I tried to dissuade her. The very nature of such a place is that she must meet all kinds of riffraff there and that sooner or later, one of them may try to gain advantage from the situation.'

I couldn't let that pass. I nearly jumped out of my chair to remind this well-heeled slob that the women at the refuge had received horrendous treatment. They weren't there by choice. They were there often because their very lives were in danger. To describe them as 'riffraff' was unacceptable and I'd be glad to hear him withdraw it.

'On the contrary,' he said. 'What you've just said confirms my view. The women in those places are there because of violence. They are associated with violent men. So it follows that anyone associated with those women is also likely to become the target of violent men.'

I remembered the broken window and damaged door at the refuge and reluctantly conceded he had a point. 'So you're saying,' I said, 'that it's through her voluntary work that Lauren became known to her eventual snatchers?'

'I think it's highly likely, don't you? I fancy the police think so too. Look, Miss Varady . . .' he consulted an expensive-looking wristwatch, 'I've given you quite a lot of my time this afternoon and frankly, I can't see to what purpose. There is nothing I can tell you that isn't more properly learned from the police. In fact, I suspect the police would be strongly opposed to my talking to you at all.'

He wasn't going to talk to me any further, he was saying. So I could just get out. I got up and prepared to go, but I had one last query.

'Tell me,' I said, 'that cherub thing out there,' I pointed at the door and the reception area beyond. 'Is it really worth fifteen hundred smackers?'

'Cherub?' He looked puzzled. 'Oh, you mean the zephyr! Yes, a lovely piece. Exquisite. Italian Renaissance and established provenance. It was salvaged from the ruins of a pleasure villa on Lake Garda at the close of the Second World War.'

'Salvaged', I suspected, might be a euphemism. 'Trophy of war?' I asked.

'Certainly not!' His full lips pressed together and disappeared into a thin line. The flesh around them had turned white with anger. 'Good day, Miss Varady,' he said, opening the door.

There was a motorcycle courier in the outer office. It was a tribute to the soundproof quality of the office doors here that I hadn't heard him arrive. Leather-jacketed, metal-helmeted and high-booted, he was a space-age vision, even more out of place in these surroundings than I was, even though he was here on proper business, not part-time detecting.

The Ice Queen handed him a package. He growled, 'Right!' and clumped away, casting me no more than a dismissive glance. If he wondered about my presence, he didn't show it. Perhaps I hadn't even registered with him. A man who spent his days weaving in and out of London's packed traffic probably didn't worry much about anything except staying upright.

The receptionist gave me a glance that was only marginally more aware than the courier's. 'Mr Szabo is waiting for you downstairs,' she said, and returned to her work, wiping my presence from her mental screen.

*　　　*　　　*

Vinnie Szabo was standing in the doorway, sheltering from the draught that cut through the alley. Perhaps he also wanted to avoid the scrutiny of any passer-by who might glance down the narrow way and wonder what he was doing lurking there.

'Hi,' I said dourly, because I was cross with him.

We left the alley awkwardly, obliged to walk in single file. I went first. The courier had made it out into the main road, mounted his machine and was already zigzagging away. There was no sign of Szabo's car or the muscular driver. He wouldn't have found it easy to park around here. Perhaps Szabo had wisely taken a cab. He edged out of the narrow

221

entry behind me, and stood unhappily on the pavement. He was wearing his overcoat and it looked even more oversize than it had in the car. His small hands barely poked out of the sleeves and the skirts nearly reached to the pavement.

He peered up at me, Mole from *The Wind in the Willows*. 'You've seen Jeremy? Did he—Was there anything?'

'No,' I said. 'But then he knew exactly who I was and why I was there. I thought we'd agreed I'd say I was a friend of Lauren's?'

'But he phoned me,' he protested in dismay. 'I had to tell him.'

'I might have got more out of him if you hadn't,' I said, still feeling sour about it.

'He wouldn't have spoken to you at all,' Szabo defended himself. 'When he phoned me, he was worried you might be an emissary of the kidnappers.'

That certainly hadn't occurred to me!

'Never mind,' I said, conceding the point. 'He wouldn't have believed the other story anyway. He doesn't know anything. I don't think Lauren would've told him if she'd had anything on her mind.'

'She certainly wouldn't have wished to worry poor Jeremy. He is devoted to her.' We'd fallen into step and he spoke these words confidently as he scurried beside me.

I wasn't getting into an argument over that one. I'd have been surprised if Lauren spoke much to Jeremy about anything.

We'd reached the corner of the street and parted with a minimum exchanged of farewell words. I promised to ring Vinnie if I learned anything but it was clear from his expression he no longer held out any hopes of my turning up any information of value. He'd been desperate when he'd contacted me. That I'd failed him hardly made any difference. He hadn't really expected much.

He headed off in the direction of Mayfair, a small dejected figure in a too large coat, padding along the centre of the pavement. An air of loneliness and loss hovered around him and I knew what it was that niggled at me whenever I looked at Szabo. In his own way, he reminded me of Albie, a lost soul, someone out of whose life the heart has been wrenched.

I set off in the opposite direction, making for the Underground and home.

* * *

Back on home turf, there didn't seem to be anything else I could do. But I hadn't forgotten Jonty and, wanting to do something, even if I knew I was wasting my time, I went looking for him again.

Unsurprisingly, I didn't see any sign of him. I hoped the poor old fellow was all right and polluting the environment somewhere safer for him than around here. I was in two minds whether to go to the shop and talk to Gan, but I remembered that tomorrow was the day of the art exhibition in which I was to figure, literally. It would be best to avoid Ganesh until it was all over.

Suffering from severe doubts about the whole project myself, I went to Reekie Jimmie's instead. I was hoping unrealistically that I'd be told Angus had unexpectedly been called back to Scotland and the proposed display was off. Suddenly even the prospect of thirty quid didn't compensate for looking an idiot all day.

CHAPTER TWELVE

As a hope, it'd only been an outsider and not surprisingly, it never got out of the starting traps. Angus, apparently, had been in that morning doing his mopping out stint, and was all keyed up and worrying about keeping the vegetables fresh.

'Can't talk about anything else but tomorrow, the lad is that excited,' said Jimmie. 'He reckons it's his big chance. He's counting on you, hen. We all are, eh? Ah, we'll show the auld enemy where he gets off!'

He beamed at me fondly. Somehow or other I'd become the focus of Scottish aspirations, in this part of London, anyway. But something he'd said sounded an ominous note.

'Veg?' I asked hollowly.

'Aye, to pin on your wee costume. Would you like a cup of tea or coffee, on the house? It's bottomless cup tonight, you'll have seen the notice.'

He pointed to the wall behind him where, above the microwave, was a poster showing a steaming coffee cup and emblazoned 'Special Promotion. One night only. Pay for first cup! Refills on us!'

I accepted a bottomless cup of tea and began to wonder how Angus was proposing to fix a couple of pounds of mixed veg to a body stocking without making it sag disastrously. I hoped Jimmie had got it wrong. I didn't think we got our vegetables from the rain forests.

Jimmie had left me to take some orders. The café was filling up and trade threatened to become a rush. This couldn't be, surely, because of the special promotion?

'Friday night,' he told me when he rejoined me. 'Lot of 'em got paid and the weekend starts here!'

He began slicing a cucumber at a furious rate, the knife flashing wickedly near his fingers, missing by a miracle. 'Would you happen to be free for the rest of the evening?' He swept the cucumber slices into a bowl and reached for some greeny-orange tomatoes. 'I know you've a busy day tomorrow, but as you can see, I'm fair rushed off my feet here. The

225

cashier's not turned up. You wouldn't fancy lending me a hand? I can manage the till and taking the orders if you keep the spuds coming. It's not difficult. There's plenty of salad done ready, see?' He waved the knife under my nose. 'Just put a bit out on the plates beforehand. Then all you need to do is pop the spuds in the microwave. When they're ready, add a filling. We've got another one now, tuna and sweetcorn, going very well. It's all mixed up in a bowl over there.'

I followed the line indicated by the point of his knife and saw a huge plastic bowl of unappetising beige and yellow gunge.

'That's all there is to it. Put a few quid in your pocket,' he concluded artfully.

Why not? I couldn't do anything about Lauren tonight and though it mightn't be *haute cuisine*, it would stop me brooding on the next day. 'Sure,' I said.

'You'll find the uniform on the coat rack in the corridor,' he told me. 'And go easy with the cheese.'

*　　*　　*

By the time I left Jimmie's at ten, I was whacked. Business had been nonstop all evening, to Jimmie's joy and my despair. I burned my fingers trying to keep the spuds coming along. As for the 'bottomless cup', that had proved a nightmare. The patrons, unused to being offered anything free here, had seen it as a challenge. They'd kept coming back and holding out empty cups, determined to take full advantage. The coffee percolator hissed, gurgled and spat dementedly and the tea urn ran dry. But at the end of it all, I had a tenner in my pocket and half a pound of left-over grated cheese in a washed margarine tub.

'Make yourself Welsh rarebit for your supper,' suggested Jimmie. 'Save a few pennies.'

'Tomorrow, perhaps,' I said. Food had temporarily lost its appeal. I never wanted to see another potato in my life. The smell of melted cheese, singed potato skins and baked beans clung to me even after I'd peeled off the rayon overall that Jimmie called staff uniform. My hair must stink of it. But provided Angus paid up the next day as promised, I was doing all right this weekend on the financial front.

It had rained while I'd been juggling hot spuds and ladling out the beans. Surfaces gleamed in the lamplight. There were comparatively few people about and not much traffic, but as I walked away I heard a motorcycle engine cough and splutter into life a short distance behind me. Enjoying the cool damp air on my perspiring face, I took little notice.

With a low growl the machine caught up and passed me. It wasn't travelling fast and that did strike me as odd. Most bikers like to take advantage of an empty road. I remembered then that I'd heard a bike before, revving up in the distance on the occasion of my night visitor's second call.

I didn't want to end up seeing and hearing things every time I stuck my head out of doors. But I decided to take a different route home, just in case. I turned the corner and left behind the lighted main road with its pubs, cafes, and security-lit store windows.

I was walking through deserted residential roads now. Curtains were drawn and doors locked against the night and its dangers. The only sign of life within was the flickering phosphorescent glow of television screens, playing on the blinds. My footsteps echoed on the pavement. I'd ceased to enjoy the coolness, and shivered as a cold draught whistled uncomfortably round my neck. Greasy paper wrappings from fried food and empty foil trays, discarded back there in the main shopping area, had been scooped up by the wind and diverted into this side street. They bowled past me, rattling and fluttering along the uneven flags. Occasionally one wrapped itself unpleasantly round the back of my legs. I pulled up my collar, shoved my hands into my pockets, in one of which I'd wedged the tub of cheese, and head down, hurried on.

The motorcycle roar, coming from directly behind me, broke into the quiet solitude like a wild animal let loose. Had I stopped and turned to face it, I'd have been a goner. As it was, instinct made me leap first without waiting to see. I scrambled up someone's front steps as the machine raced past along the pavement. The tug of air as it swept by almost knocked me off my feet. The rider was crouched low over the handlebars, a dark helmeted faceless shape.

'Maniac!' I yelled after him. 'What're you trying to do?'

The margarine box of cheese fell out of my pocket and bounced away down the pavement.

My question had been both stupid and unnecessary. What he was trying to do was run me down. His speed carried him on to the end of the street. I hammered frantically on the door behind me, knowing it was useless. No one, hearing any kind of fracas outside, would open up at this time of night.

I jumped down the steps and began to run back towards the main road. Behind me, the biker had skidded round in a U-turn and the engine snarled as he began the run back. I couldn't make it to the lights and safety ahead. There was a side turning and I dived into it. The machine swept past. He was faster than me but less mobile. He had to slow and turn again before making his third and possibly successful attempt.

I had no option but to run and no time to think where I might be running to. All I knew was that I had to find a hiding place. I pounded round the next corner and found myself in a broader street but even more poorly lit and not residential like the one I'd left. One side of it was entirely taken up with a large building, which, judging from the general architecture, had probably once been a warehouse. Despite that, a peeling sign advertised it for rent and specified a large amount of office space. The sign looked to have been there a long time. The building was in complete darkness and its windows stared down at me like so many blind eyes. Nothing suggested a security patrol or even a caretaker was there to look out and see my predicament.

The other side of the road was bordered by iron railings and bushes. It was eerily empty of all life. I couldn't have chosen worse.

Since the commercial building offered nothing but a solid wall and ground-floor windows barred with iron grilles, I crossed to the fenced side of the street. I raced down the line of metal posts, hoping for a gap or at least a place where the spikes were broken and I might climb over. And there was a gap! I leaped into it just as the motorcycle's headlight swept around the corner of the street.

I'd hoped to be able to scramble away among the bushes, but in my haste I'd miscalculated. The gap was the entry to a flight of steps leading downwards. I lost my footing and rolled and bounced to the bottom, where I landed face down in the dirt. I was bruised and my hands scraped but I had no time to worry about injuries. I crawled into the nearest bushes and crouched there. My heart was thudding and my breathing sounded so loud I thought my hunter must hear it. The machine was put-putting slowing along the street above. He was looking for me. He'd see the gap in the railings and he'd guess I'd gone down here.

The machine moved on. Had he missed the gap? Cautiously I put my head out and, for the first time, took note of where I was. A fresh breeze rippled past my face. Water lapped and nearby somewhere there was a creak of some wooden object. A pungent, tarry, muddy, faintly stagnant smell pervaded the air. It was familiar. I was on the canal towpath, not far from where poor Albie's body had been taken from the water. I edged out and stood up. There was a bridge some way down and about fifteen feet from me, the same two houseboats were moored. I began to move towards them and then let out a yell as I stubbed my toe painfully against some hard projecting object.

It was a metal ring set in a lump of concrete. Attached to it was a length of coiled rope. The houseboat it was presumably meant to secure was missing from its mooring.

I cursed myself for having given away my position by the shout, and stood, straining my ears for my pursuer. Faintly, some distance ahead of me, I heard the splutter of an engine. Then almost at the furthest point of visibility along the towpath from where I stood, a sudden bright beam flashed and swept across the bank, path and water like a searchlight. A menacing engine cough told me it was the headlamp of the motorbike.

Dear Lord! I thought, my heart leaping sickeningly into my throat. He did see the gap and realise where I am. Now he's found a way down on to the path! He's coming down here!

I had to get rid of him. I could only elude him so long before our cat-and-mouse game finished suddenly, messily and horrifically. I looked down by my bruised foot and saw the coil of rope. I snatched it up and leaped into the tangle of shrubbery and nettles on the bank, hauling the rope behind me. As fast as I could I pulled it taut and secured it to a stump of tree-trunk. Then I poked out my head.

The biker was waiting at the far end of the towpath. Cunningly he'd switched off the headlight. But I knew he was there, watching for a movement in the shadows or an outlined figure in the pale towpath lights. I remembered the cyclist who'd sped past me as I placed flowers in Albie's memory. There was no telling if it had been the same man, come to see what was happening. A murderer returning to the scene of his crime. But if it had been the same man, he knew this towpath, access points, width, evenness of surface, everything. He was on home ground. I was playing his game.

So I obliged him further, stepping out on to

the path. When he'd had time to spot me, I turned to run back the way I'd come.

He spotted me. The engine roared triumphantly. The headlight, leaping back into life, flung its long white beam the length of the path as he charged down it towards me—and the rope, drawn tightly a few inches above the ground.

I don't know whether he saw it before he hit it or not. It wouldn't have made much difference the speed he was going. I didn't wait. Behind me a deafening crash shattered my ears, a final screaming roar from the engine, which was abruptly cut off and followed almost at once by a mini tidal wave as the surface of the canal lurched and splashed up over the towpath and my fleeing feet. I'd reached the steps leading back up to the road. I stopped briefly and looked back.

There was no sign of my pursuer on the towpath nor in the heaving water. Then a head popped up, an arm followed, waving frantically and he was splashing about in the canal shouting out for help. All at once, a light beamed out as the hatch of one of the houseboats was opened. A figure emerged and began flashing a torch around. It picked up the figure struggling in the water.

I heard the boat-owner shouting, 'What the devil is going on?' as I ran up the steps to the road.

I was scarcely aware how I managed the rest

of the way home. Only when I'd stumbled down the basement steps and got inside my own flat could I even begin to take stock and organise my thoughts.

First aid was a priority. I went into the bathroom and took a look at myself in the mirror. I'd cut my chin, and blood was trickling down. The palms of both hands were badly grazed and grit was embedded in the weeping flesh. I wriggled out of my jacket. Using my elbow, I turned on the cold tap and ran the water over the raw area of my palms until the grit had washed out. The injuries burned like a million wasp stings. I smeared on antiseptic cream, yelping and swearing, because I'm a total coward when it comes to medical treatment of any kind.

My jeans were torn but had largely saved my knees from being skinned as well. My toe was red and swelling badly where it had struck the mooring ring. I hoped it wasn't broken.

It all hardly mattered. I was alive.

So was he, my pursuer. I supposed they'd got him out of the canal by now. He'd lost his bike. Serve him right! I tried to be pleased he hadn't drowned and I hadn't his death on my conscience. But in truth my conscience was untroubled. He'd been luckier than Albie. If he was connected with Albie's death then justice *hadn't* been done. He ought to have drowned.

I hobbled into the kitchen and boiled the

kettle. I don't normally take sugar in drinks but it was supposed to be good for shock so I put two spoonfuls in my instant coffee. I retreated to my living room and settled on the sofa, the duvet pulled round my shoulders, and sipped the hot sweet brew. My toe pulsated painfully in the flip-flops I'd donned and my hands still felt as though they were on fire.

Who was he? And why the murderous assault? He might have been drunk or high. But he'd handled the machine too well. It might've been mistaken identity. He'd wanted to get someone else. But no, he'd been waiting outside Jimmie's, I remembered, and he'd moved the moment I'd left the cafe.

He'd been out to get me. It had to be someone to do with either Lauren's kidnapping or Albie's murder or both, supposing the two to be connected as I was sure they were. Had it been Merv? If Merv had torched his car the other night, he might have taken to a motorcycle.

Otherwise I'd only come across one motorcyclist lately. That had been the courier in the offices of Thais Fine Arts. The possibilities opened up by that were endless. I'd no way of knowing if it had been the same man, of course, and mustn't jump to conclusions.

'Well, anyway, you've got 'em worried,' I told myself aloud in a poor attempt at comfort.

And they had me worried. They were unlikely to give up. They'd try again.

Much as it went against the grain to appeal to the police, and little faith though I had in them, I knew I had to report this.

I finished the coffee, reluctantly got off the sofa, found another pair of jeans, and let myself out of the flat. I felt distinctly unsafe out here in the street but I knew Daphne went to bed fairly late and there was still a light at an upper window. I hobbled briskly up the steps and pressed the bell. Then I opened the letter box and called through it. The hall light went on within a couple of minutes.

'Fran?' She peered through the chained door. 'Just a sec!' The door was shut again, the chain rattled, and the door reopened, wide enough to let me in.

Daphne was wrapped in an ancient dressing gown and her grey fringe was secured in a row of pin curls. She cut short my apologies, took my arm and guided me straight to her warm, cheerful kitchen, where she switched on the coffee-maker for a proper brew, and produced a bottle of brandy.

'What happened, dear?' Her eyes crinkled up with concern and the low-level lighting from the worktop made the row of aluminium pins across her forehead gleam like a silver tiara.

I told her I'd had a near miss in a traffic accident. I thought I ought to phone the police.

'I'll phone them,' she said firmly. 'That's a nasty cut on your chin. Perhaps you ought to get it stitched.'

The very idea made me feel faint. 'It'll be fine,' I said hastily. 'And I'd better speak to the police myself. You know, for the details.'

She was giving me a look that clearly said she guessed there was a lot more to this 'traffic accident' than I was saying.

The deeply unimpressed police voice at the other end of the line promised that they'd look into it and would send someone round in the morning to get a statement. I told them I was working in the morning and suggested they get a message to Sergeant Parry tonight.

'He's gone off duty,' said the voice disapprovingly.

'Listen!' I snapped. 'Someone tried to kill me! Get hold of Parry! Tell him I want protection!'

*　　　*　　　*

If I hadn't had such a stressful evening I wouldn't have said that, the bit about protection. It was asking for trouble.

I'd sat with Daphne for a few minutes and then made my way back to my flat. It felt chilly and I lit the gas fire in the grate. I didn't feel much like going to bed. It hardly seemed likely I'd sleep. But I had to be at the Community

Hall first thing in the morning ready for a full day being a tree. I hoped I wouldn't fall asleep tomorrow, wedged in that frame Angus had constructed.

A car drew up outside, a door slammed, footsteps clattered down the steps and someone rang the doorbell.

I froze with fear. Was it my hunter? Now that he'd quitted the shadows for open attack, had he decided on the direct approach here, at my home?

'Fran?' A fist beat on the door. 'You all right in there?'

It was Parry, galloping over like a knight on a white horse at the first shriek from the damsel in distress. I told myself forcefully that I was an idiot and opened the door.

Parry bounded in clad in a sweat-stained tracksuit. 'You all right, Fran? Bloody hell, what happened to your face? What's been going on?'

'I didn't mean for you to come round here,' I told him.

'They said you'd asked for me to come. You asked for protection. I was over at the sports club. Lucky I had my mobile with me. You mightn't have got me otherwise.'

I should've been so lucky. He had found himself a chair as he spoke and now sat there, looking at me with concern.

'That's a nasty cut. You oughta get that stitched.'

I ignored that suggestion and told him what had happened that day. I told him about my night-time prowler too, and that I was sure he and my murderous biker were one and the same.

Parry's face got redder and redder as I spoke and when I finished, he threw both arms in the air. 'I can't understand you,' he bawled. 'You're not daft. You're bright enough. You just act thick. Didn't I tell you to leave well alone? Why didn't you tell me you had this herbert creeping about at night? Who did you think he was? Father Christmas? You think he was just going to be content with hanging around by moonlight? He was bound to move in on you sooner or later. He's a perishing psycho.'

I informed Parry I wasn't in the mood to be lectured. 'What's more,' I added, 'I arranged my visit to Copperfield with Szabo and if he didn't mind, you've got no reason to whinge on about it.'

Parry leaned forward, pale blue eyes protruding with a righteous anger. 'Oh, haven't I? Just to remind you, this is a police matter and highly sensitive. What do you want, you and Szabo? For that kid Lauren to turn up dead? Buried out in the country somewhere? Divided up between half a dozen black plastic sacks on a rubbish tip? Pulled out of the canal like old Albie?'

'Don't be stupid!' I snapped.

239

'Take a leaf out of your own book,' he retorted. 'Don't tell me your going round to see Copperfield didn't do any harm! Caused you plenty of trouble, didn't it? Chased all round the streets by a lunatic on a motorbike. Like dicing with death, do you?'

We sat scowling at one another. I decided there was nothing to be gained by pursuing this argument.

'What about Copperfield?' I asked. 'I didn't like him. He didn't strike me as the slightest bit upset about Lauren's disappearance.'

'What you mean,' Parry said offensively, 'is that he didn't choose to talk to you about it. Not the same thing.'

'But what about him?' I persisted. 'Is he on the level? Is it worth checking him out? What about that fine arts business of his? Does it make any money?'

He chewed the ends of his ragged ginger moustache as he worked out how much, if anything, he could tell me. He was sitting near the gas fire and the sweat patches on his clothing had dried out with a resultant lingering aroma of BO. He made a decision.

'As it happens,' he said, 'and strictly between us, he's on the PNC.'

'What?' He'd thrown the initials at me casually and in my blurred state, they became confused with PCC, the parochial church council. As a fact, it seemed possible but hardly relevant.

'The Police National Computer,' he explained kindly, putting me right. 'Out at Hendon.'

That made a lot more sense. 'You mean, he's got form?' I gasped, and jumped up, forgetting my sore foot and other aches and bruises. My whole body twanged in painful protest and I sat down quickly.

Parry coughed discreetly behind his hand as if I'd said something risqué.

'Well, hardly what you'd call real form. A few years back the Fine Art and Antiques Squad took a bit of interest in him. They broke a setup dealing in dodgy export licences. A lot of people were pulled in for questioning, Copperfield among them. He got a suspended sentence. He'd never committed an offence before—or not been found out if he had—and the court took the view he'd been the pawn of cleverer blokes than himself. Seeing as he's a first-class, grade A prat, that means just about the rest of the world! The worst you could say about the poor sod was that he'd been foolish in some of his business relationships. More sinned against than sinning, as the maiden said.'

He uttered a hawking sound that was probably intended as a chuckle. 'As for that firm of his, trade suffered what you'd call a temporary setback while he was under a cloud. He got into financial difficulties but he's pulled out of it. After all, a lot of businessmen these days have had the odd embarrassment with the law, and it don't do 'em no harm. Now he's dealing straight, although word is, he owes big money to the banks.'

I thought this over. 'How about Szabo?' I asked. 'Is he as rich as the kidnappers think he is?'

'You bet he is,' said Parry, and chuckled. 'And the kidnappers must know what he's worth because—' He broke off and looked momentarily embarrassed.

'Go on,' I encouraged him. 'You might as well. You've started.'

'Well...' He fidgeted. 'The first ransom demand was fairly modest—as ransoms go. Then, the next demand, the price had gone up stiffly. Szabo reckons it's because he didn't pay the first price. See, he's afraid it'll go on increasing the longer they hold her. We're having trouble keeping tabs on him, making sure he doesn't go behind our backs and try to make a deal with the villains.'

'Is that why you sent him to me?' A thought struck me, which, until now, would've seemed incredible but suddenly seemed quite likely. 'Hey!' I said indignantly. 'Did you think he might try to use me as a go-between?'

'He'd have to use someone.' Parry sounded defiant and truculent in equal parts. 'He might've thought you'd fit the role.'

'Well, he didn't—he hasn't suggested it!' I told him. 'And if he did, I'd tell him to forget

242

it!'

'What you do,' said Parry, 'if he does suggest it, is tell me, right? Me or someone else on the case. Straight away, no delays, no trying to be clever, no attempts at fancy footwork.'

'This is a really lovely setup,' I said. 'No one trusts anyone else. Szabo doesn't trust the police or the kidnappers. You don't trust him. I don't trust you or Vinnie or the kidnappers or Jeremy Copperfield or anyone! And by the way, have you found Merv and has he got a motorbike?'

'We found him.' Parry folded his arms and looked smug. 'He's got an alibi for the night the old man fell in the canal. He was watching telly with a bunch of his mates. Football, international match. They all swear to it. They'd stocked up with a few crates of beer and didn't leave the flat they were in. And what d'you mean, you don't trust *me*?'

'Alibi?' I couldn't believe my ears.

'That's right. And he can discuss the match. Not, I realise, that that means anything because edited highlights were repeated the following night. But four other blokes saying he was there does carry weight.'

'I saw him—Ganesh and I both saw him—try to snatch Albie off the street. Merv and another man!' I protested.

'Poor lighting, difficult circumstances—you can't swear it was him, Fran.'

'Who can't? And what about his car? Was it

his car torched up by the park that night?'

'Yes, it was. But he says it was taken earlier by joyriders. He'd had trouble with joyriders hanging around it before.' Parry's eyes gleamed. 'Seems one evening he was having a quiet drink in the pub when in comes a young woman and warns him that kids are hanging around the motor, and the alarm's gone off. He describes her as having short brown hair, skinny figure and a voice like a foghorn. She'd been hanging about outside talking to a couple of Asian guys by a junk food van. Anyone you know?'

'Can't imagine. Do you want me to give you a statement about the attack on me or what?'

'Fair enough. I've got nothing with me, coming here straight from the club. Got a bit of paper?'

I told him my story again. He wrote it down and I signed it.

'Thank you very much, madam,' he said formally.

'That's all right, officer. Thank you for coming round. You can go now. I'm all right.'

'I was going to offer,' he said, 'to doss down here on a chair tonight. Protect you, like you asked.'

'It won't be necessary!' I informed him.

He looked almost wistful. Even his moustache drooped. 'You did send for me.'

'Correction. I asked them to tell you. Not the same thing.'

'But you did request protection,' he insisted, clinging to his hopes.

I dashed them. 'Just to have the area patrol car include the house on their route a couple of times would do the trick. Or a uniformed officer calling in once a day to see if I'm all right.'

'How much spare manpower do you think we've got?' he retorted disagreeably. 'Not a chance.'

'How about moving me to a place of safety, then, a hotel?' I suggested.

'Who do you think you are?' he asked. 'Prime witness in a matter of national security? Forget it.'

In the end, he checked the safety catches on my windows and the lock and chain on the door and pronounced me secure.

'Only you ought to have a phone. I can't leave you my mobile. I need it. But that's what you ought to get, a mobile. Every woman on her own ought to have one.'

I promised I'd look into it. By this time it was nearly one in the morning and I finally persuaded him to go home.

At least his visit had dealt with my overwrought wakefulness. I collapsed on the sofa. Oblivious of my bruises, I slept, as they say, like the dead.

CHAPTER THIRTEEN

I arrived early at the Community Hall the following morning, as requested. I'd spent some time and my theatrical make-up skills disguising the cut on my chin. I'd washed my hair and knew I looked fine, not like someone who'd been fleeing for her life only hours before. Despite this, I was feeling highly nervous. A persuasive little Mephisto in the corner of my mind kept whispering, 'Hey! You'd rather be anywhere else than here! Why don't you just turn and run?'

But I'm not one to break a promise. Angus was depending on me. If I let him down, I'd feel bad about it, and I'd never be able to eat at Jimmie's again. Though the last thought was more an inducement to defect than to stay, I ordered the tempter to be silent and looked around.

At least I wasn't alone. People were arriving from all directions. Beneath a banner proclaiming 'Art for a Cleaner Safer World', artists working in every medium were struggling through the doors with exhibits. As I watched, a thin man with a neatly trimmed beard, and a red neckerchief knotted fancily around his scraggy throat, staggered past. His arms clasped a scrap-metal sculpture to his bosom as if it were a dancing partner.

'Fran! Fran, over here!' I heard Angus's voice as my eye caught a waving arm.

He was sitting between the open doors at the rear of an ancient rust-pitted Transit van, drinking milk from a carton. He put it down as I approached.

'Just having my breakfast,' he explained. 'Thanks for being on time. You know, we're really in with a chance. I've seen most of the other stuff. Talk about unimaginative, run-of-the-mill junk. We'll knock 'em into next week!'

Trying hard to share his enthusiasm, I peered past him into the van. 'Jimmie said something about vegetables,' I mumbled.

The interior of the van, as far as I could see, was littered with foliage of various sorts. A pineapple poked its fronds from a Tesco bag.

'Veg?' Angus looked puzzled. 'No, he's got it wrong. Fruit.'

'Oh.' I supposed that was better. 'Where's the thing, you know, the frame.'

'Already taken it in.' He stood up. 'Right, you take the bag there and this one . . .' he thrust another plastic carrier at me, 'I'll bring the lianas.'

Inside the hall, chaos reigned. A shrill woman in a long purple skirt and a patchwork jacket was shouting instructions at anyone who cared to listen, though most people were ignoring her. She clasped a sheaf of cards to her flat bosom.

'All the individual areas are marked in chalk on the floor!' she shrieked. 'Newcomers please get a number from me!' She held the sheaf of cards up in the air but no one took the slightest bit of notice.

'They're not doing it properly, Reg!' she wailed to a gloomy, middle-aged individual standing nearby.

'Let 'em sort themselves out,' advised Reg.

'But it'll be a dreadful mess. Do something, Reg!'

Two girls trotted past, bearing between them a lurid canvas splashed with lime green and red.

'Come and get your number!' begged the woman.

The girls, like everyone else, took no notice and carried straight on to the back of the hall.

The woman caught my eye. 'Have you got your number?' she asked dispiritedly.

I explained I was an exhibit, not an exhibitor.

'You've still got to have a number,' she said obstinately.

Reg edged over and peered into my Tesco bags. 'Blimey, brought your lunch with you, love?'

Hearing I was going to wear it, not eat it, he chuckled. 'Cor! Carmen bloomin' Miranda!'

I recalled that Angus had promised a couple of minders on the door to stop troublemakers disrupting our festival of culture. Apparently, all we had was Reg. He was in his fifties and overweight. He may once have been a fine figure of a man, but not since it had all settled round his midriff. I enquired tentatively about the door attendants.

'They cost money, do professional bouncers,' said Reg. 'Shouldn't need them. Not in broad daylight.'

'It's an arts festival,' put in the purple-skirted woman. 'One couldn't have a couple of heavyweights on the door, scowling at people. It would put the visitors off.'

Well, we mustn't frighten the horses. But the news did nothing for my already fragile nerves.

Angus appeared, his arms filled with strands of greenery. 'We're over on the right,' he informed me.

'Your number!' shrilled the woman.

'Don't worry, I've got it,' he told her.

'Then you're the only bloody one who has!' she snapped. She pushed the sheaf of cards into Reg's hand. 'You carry on, I'm going to find a coffee. My head is splitting!'

Angus and I progressed to a chalked area on the floor where the frame stood waiting for us, looking more than ever like something from a castle dungeon. The thin man had set up his scrap-metal sculpture alongside us in the next chalked area.

Its creator stood back and squinted at it. 'Does that look straight to you?'

Given the nature of the exhibit, it was hard

to tell. I said it looked more or less straight to me.

'We are reducing the world to a mountain of debris, the legacy of our life-style,' he informed me. 'And in doing so, we are reducing ourselves to mere accumulation of debris. Junk in. Junk out.'

Hence the scrap metal figure, I deduced. The thin man was staring fiercely at the frame created by Angus for my support. 'I see your friend is a minimalist,' he said. 'The pure spiral, representing man's spiritual search, guiding him to the heavens or dragging him inexorably earthwards, am I right?'

I was saved replying by one of the girls who had carried in the lurid canvas. She approached. 'Oy!' she hailed the thin man. 'You're in our square.' She brandished a numbered card at him.

'Find yourself another one,' he retorted.

'You find your own square!'

'I can't use my own square. Someone's already in it!'

'Reg!' screeched the girl down the hall. 'Come 'n' tell this silly sod he's in our square!'

Avoid other people's fights is my motto. The bystander always gets hurt. I returned to Angus. 'Where's my costume?'

He handed me yet another plastic bag. I peered into it. It was the body stocking, dyed a fetching sludge green. It did, however, look reassuringly robust.

'You'll have to change in the women's loo,' he said. 'But if you bring your clothes back here, I'll lock 'em in the van till it's over.'

*   *   *

A little later I emerged hesitantly from the washroom clad in the green body stocking. But I needn't have worried that anyone would take any notice of me. They were all too busy arguing over floor space and setting up their exhibits. The woman with the purple skirt was running up and down in increasing hysteria. Her cries of, 'No, no, you can't *do* that!' were alternated with appeals of, 'Reg, do *something*!' I had to admit there was a real air of excitement, just like the last minutes before a first night. I began to cheer up.

Nevertheless, things didn't start too well, with Angus and I having a serious disagreement over the pineapple. To my horror, he intended this to go on my head, fixed with a wire crown. I flatly refused to consider it.

'Look here,' he said, getting truculent, 'I'm the artist and you're the model, right? We'll get nowhere if you're going to carp at everything. You agreed.'

'I'll model the rest, but not that thing, certainly not on top of my head! I've already heard one Carmen Miranda joke. I mean it. You'll have no model at all if you insist.'

'But it finishes the whole thing off,' he protested.

'Too right, it'll finish it off. It'll finish me off for a start. It's naff, Angus. Forget it.'

He said crossly that it had cost a lot. I told him to take it over to Jimmie's and sell it on to him. 'He can chop it up, mix it with cottage cheese and stick it in the potatoes.'

He gave way with bad grace. Miraculously things sorted themselves out and we were all just about ready at ten thirty when the doors were opened to the public. The frame wasn't that comfortable but it wasn't actively uncomfortable. Angus, working from a diagram, had attached all the bits of greenery and some flowers, together with some large and beautifully painted paper butterflies and birds. Reg came along to watch. He looked impressed.

Angus positioned me facing the scrap-metal man next door and I felt it and I would be good friends by the end of the day.

The atmosphere, as Reg approached the doors, quivered with the vibrations from artistic nerves strung like violin strings. The first members of the public to drift in were clearly friends and supporters of the different artists. They clutched leaflets pressed on them by the organisers. In addition, they all had a private brief, which was to stand in front of their friend's chalk square and express loud admiration, before moving on to the other

252

squares and pronouncing all the other work rubbish.

Before our square they fell silent. I wasn't sure whether this was because they were struck with awe or because, with Angus being brawny and wearing his Scottish football shirt, they didn't feel it was wise to make the sort of sarcastic comments they were firing at other exhibits. They were rude about the scrap-metal man instead.

The thin man was soon pale with emotion. 'Philistines!' he howled. 'Cultural cretins!'

After a while, genuine punters began to arrive—only a few at first, some carrying bags of Saturday shopping, but all of them seemed strangely attracted to our square. Angus had been right about the living sculpture. It—I— exerted a weird fascination over observers.

Word must have got around because a lot of people began to arrive and they all made for our corner where it became very congested. I concentrated on keeping still and soon realised how the Buckingham Palace guards must suffer.

Comments floated towards me. 'She must be real, you can see her eyes blinking.' 'Poor girl, she'll get terrible cramp.' More mysteriously, I heard, 'I expect she's used to this sort of thing.'

Cameras began to flash. Angus was in seventh heaven and even the thin man brightened up, probably hoping that the

253

photographers would include his sculpture in the picture.

The show closed for a lunch break between one and two. Angus helped me out of the frame and removed some of the less firmly fixed greenery and artwork.

'You were right about the pineapple,' he said generously.

'Of course I was,' I said.

I nipped along to the loo to struggle out of the rest and answer Nature's call. There was a chair in the washroom. I sat on it in my bra and pants to drink a cup of coffee and eat a sandwich, which Angus had sent in care of the woman in the purple skirt.

'It's going awfully well,' she enthused. 'I do think you're terribly brave.' She hovered over me. 'You won't catch cold, will you? We have got the heating on.'

I promised her I wasn't cold. In fact, inside the body stocking and all the attachments, it had been very warm in the hall. She told me again that I was brave and she wouldn't have done it, not for the world.

I had to get back to my stand well before two so that Angus could reattach everything. The crowd was thinner after lunch. People had other ways of spending their Saturday afternoons. The exhibition was due to close at four thirty anyway, and by three fifteen I was beginning to think we might be able to knock off early. Even as I thought this, I became aware of fresh eyes staring at me.

I had quite got used to the gawpers, but this was a gaze so intent, it made my skin tingle. Worse than that, it sent out signals of recognition and of menace. It conjured up fear such as I'd felt in my underground bedroom. My night visitor—it had to be.

A bead of sweat trickled from my shoulders, down inside the clammy body stocking, running along my spine like the touch of a finger. I eased my head round just a little.

There were two of them, standing side by side: Merv and his mate. Merv, tall, pale and slab-like as ever, chewed gum impassively. I no longer cared about Merv. I was interested in the other. I was seeing him face to face for the first time. No smoky-visored biker's helmet, no curtained window, no thick piece of opaque glass veiled him from my sight. I saw my ogre, fair and square.

In appearance he was disappointing, short, squat, olive-complexioned and losing his hair. His build was that of the glimpsed silhouette against my curtains. I realised, too, that this was the man Ganesh and I had seen with Merv the fateful evening they'd tried to bundle Albie into Merv's car.

Hats or helmets, the man liked to cover his head. It could either be from vanity or because baldness is quickly identifiable, something even a confused witness would remember.

We'd foiled their attempt at a snatch that

night, but later they'd found their quarry. This man, I knew, had killed Albie.

I expected to feel a surge of hate yet somehow it eluded me. The baldness remained disconcerting, a mark of human frailty. I don't quite know what I'd expected of Merv's partner. Whatever it had been, it hadn't been ordinariness, even dullness. Yet everyone, they say, has one striking feature. With this man, it was the eyes. Enormous eyes, it seemed to me, like the eyes in an oil painting, and very slightly protuberant. In colour they were very dark brown, almost black, so that they seemed not to consist of iris and pupil, but just a large dark luminous disc in the surrounding whiteness of the eyeball.

I knew him and he knew I knew him. As I met his gaze of those unnaturally large dark eyes, they laughed at me, matching a mocking curve of his fleshy lips. My mind picked up his message clear as a bell. *I had you running scared, gal . . . Now you see me face to face. Still scared?*

You bet I was scared. Ordinary thugs are simple souls. This one was a nutter. Merv's interest in me, I supposed, was professional. I'd got in the way of a job and he would remove me as any other obstacle in his path, animate or inanimate. It made no difference.

This other one's interest was different, personal. To begin with, I'd cost him a valuable

256

motorbike and with it, I supposed, his employment as a courier. Even if I hadn't, his attitude would still be different to Merv's. He'd enjoyed prowling outside my flat, or chasing me on that bike, as he enjoyed staring at me here. He was doing it for kicks.

Well, I didn't for a moment suppose that either of them was an art lover. Nor did I think they'd give up an afternoon normally spent on the football terraces unless they had urgent business. The business, I was miserably certain, was finding me. Now they'd found me.

I didn't know how they'd tracked me down. Possibly Jimmie, meaning to advertise Angus's work, had put the word around and by bad luck, it had reached Merv's ear. Merv caught my eye and his chewing mouth stilled and then twitched nastily. My balding adversary continued to stare, eyes bulging with lewd interest, laughing himself sick inside as he watched me squirm there on my stand, dressed in my ridiculous costume, unable to escape. I must have looked like a butterfly impaled on a pin. It was an uncomfortable image. I could imagine this man as a child, pulling the wings off living insects, tying cans to dogs' tails, interfering with the neighbourhood's little girls. A really nice sort.

'Angus . . .' I hissed, as loudly as I dared.

But Angus was busy explaining what I represented to an interested audience of two middle-aged women and a girl with a baby in a buggy. The balding man shook his head at me chidingly. Merv was chewing again and studying me with puzzled care, as if he couldn't work out what the hell I was supposed to be or why I was dressed like it. I was wondering myself.

When his questioners had moved on to the scrap-metal man, I tried again to attract Angus.

This time he heard my hoarse whisper and came over. 'What's the matter, Fran? You don't need to go to the loo again? Can't you hang on till the end? It's only another three-quarters of an hour.'

'Ring the police . . .' I breathed huskily. My voice seemed clogged in my throat.

'What?' He put his ear closer. Merv and his chum began to move away.

'Ring the police. Ask for Sergeant Parry. Tell him Merv and—and another man are here and have seen me.'

'Can't it wait till four o'clock? It's going well and I don't want to leave the stand.'

'No!' I found my voice and it emerged in a strange squawk. The scrap-metal sculptor looked across at us in surprise and some concern. Perhaps he thought some part of my anatomy had been pierced by a pin securing a liana.

'Go and ring them now!' I urged. 'There must be a phone in this hall somewhere.'

Some more people had arrived and stopped

to study me. 'Excuse me . . .' one of them said diffidently to Angus.

'I'll ring in a minute, when I get a chance!' Angus promised me hurriedly.

There wasn't much I could do. I couldn't see either Merv or his pal. My field of vision was restricted so I had no way of knowing whether they had left the hall altogether. Perhaps they'd heard my request for the police and decided to make themselves scarce. I hoped so.

There was a flurry of new visitors in the last ten minutes. Angus was fully employed and didn't leave me, or not for long enough to have phoned. Then, miraculously, the public had gone and clearly weren't coming back. Merv and the other had also vanished to my great relief. At four thirty, or just after, Reg closed the doors.

The woman in the purple skirt clapped her hands and shrilled, 'Oh, well done, everybody!'

There was a huge combined sigh of relief from the various exhibitors. They turned to one another, offering congratulations or, in a few cases, recriminations. The two girls with the painting had fallen out over something. The thin man produced a hip flask and saluted his scrap-metal creation before taking a swig. I climbed down from the stand unaided.

'Gimme my clothes!' I gasped as I began to divest myself of paper birds and strings of greenery.

'Hey!' Angus yelped. 'You'll damage everything! Wait, let me do it!'

'You can untangle the bits later. I just want to get out of this suit. Look, fetch my gear, will you?'

'It's all right,' he said, realisation dawning on his face. 'Those two blokes have gone. They went ages ago. I don't know what they were doing in here. Just a couple of creeps, I suppose, hoping for a free boob show. I didn't ring the police, I'm afraid. I didn't get time. Reg was supposed to keep the weirdos out. But it didn't matter. They didn't cause any trouble. You didn't know them, did you?'

'Believe me,' I wailed, 'they were very bad news. I've got to get out of here, Angus!'

It finally dawned on him that this was a genuine emergency. His forehead crinkled in decent dismay. 'Sorry, Fran, didn't realise you were really worried about them. I thought you just thought they were kinky. I'll get your gear from the van,' he promised. 'Hang on.'

Back in the loo, I transferred myself into my own things in record time and emerged holding the body stocking, which was still festooned with birds and greenery. The corridor was empty. From the hall came noisy scraping and bumpings as the exhibits were dismantled. I started forward with the intention of returning the body stocking to Angus, who would be worried about it, and

260

then making for the nearest phone.

I was vaguely aware that the door of the men's washroom opposite was opening, but paid no attention. That was a big mistake but I was barely given time to realise it. There was a scuffling behind me and the next thing I knew, someone had enveloped my head and shoulders in a musty-smelling piece of cloth.

I dropped the body stocking and tried to shout for help and disentangle myself at the same time. My voice was muffled by the cloth and my arms were neatly pinned to my sides. I was trussed up as neatly as an oven-ready chicken with some kind of belt or rope, then hoisted by feet and shoulders. I was carried away full length and at a cracking pace, with no more control over what was happening than one of the exhibits in the hall might have had. (Amongst which, as I had time to reflect, I'd recently featured with such distinction.)

I was aware that we'd left the hall. We bumped down some steps and I could hear traffic. Without warning I was dropped, landing with a painful wallop that knocked the breath out of me. Doors slammed. An engine revved. My world, wherever it was, began to move around me, lurching and rattling. I'd been slung into the back of a van and was being driven away.

CHAPTER FOURTEEN

It wasn't easy to keep my wits about me in the circumstances, but I did my best.

I reasoned with glum realism that no one would have paid any attention to my plight, even if they'd seen me thrown in the van. Everyone was busy with their own valued works of art, intent on dismantling and moving them out of the hall without damage. Oddly shaped articles of every kind were being lugged into the car park and a body form wrapped in a cloth wouldn't attract even a cursory glance.

Angus would worry, though, if I didn't come back. He'd go looking for me and the body stocking. I'd dropped that on the floor when my captors grabbed me and unless they'd had the presence of mind to scoop it up, it still lay where it fell and Angus would find it.

He would be bright enough to connect this with my earlier plea to call the police and with luck, he'd belatedly do just that. Whether this would help me or not was debatable. Lauren Szabo had been missing two weeks with the police hunting high and low and no one had found her.

I considered trying to bump my way along to the rear doors of the van and kick them open. On telly, captives do that kind of thing all the time. Believe me, it's not so easy. I was being thrown around all over the place as it was, and organising myself to move in a controlled fashion quickly proved hopeless.

I was sweating profusely and my mouth was parched with thirst and fear. It was increasingly difficult to breathe. The cloth wrapped itself tightly over my face and loose fibres forced their way into my nose and mouth. It stank. Since there was no point in struggling and getting exhausted, I concentrated on not suffocating and conserving my strength for when we should arrive. Always assuming, of course, they didn't intend simply to wait till nightfall and drop me off the nearest bridge. They'd already shown a tendency to dispose of inconvenient individuals in water. I tried not to think about that option.

I couldn't judge time well. In my situation minutes had to feel like hours. I certainly seemed to be thrown around in my prison for some time, but in London traffic, that didn't necessarily mean we'd travelled a vast distance. As far as I could tell, we'd not spent more than a third of the journey time stuck in one spot. I was sure we were still in London and probably not more than a couple of miles or so from where we'd started. Merv and his mate had tribal instincts. They wouldn't move far off their own patch where they knew every alley and bolt hole. (And where a phone call to an obliging pal would fix up an alibi if need be, as they'd demonstrated on the night Albie died.)

263

At last we stopped altogether. Doors slammed again. Footsteps approached. Though I still couldn't see anything, the darkness had lifted. The van doors had been opened. Hands grabbed me and I was unceremoniously but highly efficiently carried, as before, into a building.

They were careless now, manhandling me with less regard than would've been shown by a couple of piano-shifters for a pub's beat-up set of ivories. They were talking to each other and in normal voices, arguing about where to put me. A voice I identified as Merv's suggested taking me upstairs. The other man was against this as getting me around the corners would be difficult. It wasn't as if the lifts were working, he grumbled. What's more, for such a skinny little cow I was beginning to weigh effing heavy. He refused point-blank to carry me any further. They put me down, upright this time, while they argued it out. The second-man, I'd been able to gather, went by the name of Baz.

To me all this meant they felt themselves secure wherever they were. There was no one to see or hear them and they had complete freedom of the place, choosing where to put me and able to bawl at one another to their hearts' delight. In the end, they decided I could walk up a flight of stairs if guided.

I was shoved along and then ordered to start climbing. I don't know if you've ever tried going upstairs with your arms pinned to your sides and a cloth over your head. Try it as a party game, if you want to get rid of your friends. I stumbled repeatedly and fell headlong twice, bruising my shins badly and cracking my forehead on the stairs above. Even Merv and Baz seemed relieved when we reached the next landing and there was no talk, even from Merv, of moving up another flight.

All this told me we were in some large, or at least tall, building. Their voices had an echoing quality suggesting emptiness, and together with their attitude indicated a deserted block of condemned flats, or possibly of office units that had failed to attract tenants. There were such places, and small industrial units sporting sun-faded 'To rent' signs, all over London.

We moved forward again on the level. A door was opened.

'In here,' said Merv, as if I could see.

I moved forward. A chair scraped and hit the back of my legs.

'Siddown!' he invited.

I sat down. There was movement and the door creaked. One of them went out. The other hesitated by my chair before stooping to whisper in my ear.

'I'll be back, darlin'.'

I had no doubt of it. But for the moment, blessedly, he left too. They muttered together some distance away, I guessed outside the room in a hall or corridor.

I strained my ears but they kept their voices

265

low and the cloth muffled their words. For a brief moment Baz raised his voice: 'The little cow cost me my bike!'

Merv swore at him.

'. . . got it coming to her.' That was Baz again. He sounded like a man looking forward to having fun. Not very pleasant fun for someone. Me.

More mumblings from Merv and Baz subsided like a grumbling volcano. It wasn't a nice thought that I depended on someone like Merv to protect me from Baz and whatever perverted ideas he might dream up by way of vengeance.

There was a rattle and scraping noise and my heart leaped in panic. Were they coming back? No, the door was slammed and a key turned. Faintly I caught the sound of retreating footsteps, then there was silence.

*   *   *

My relief at their departure was soon eclipsed by the grim knowledge that I had very little time to get out of here, wherever here was. Wrapped up as I was like Pharaoh's mummy, I couldn't do a thing, so my first task was to get out of my bindings. Apart from being unable to see, breathe properly or move my arms, the material smelled evil. God knew where it'd been.

I managed to wriggle one arm to the front

and by dint of breathing in and ignoring the pressure on my ribs, I dragged the arm up and free. That enabled me to grab the cloth from inside and heave it. I pulled it off my head with a sigh of relief, taking a deep breath. The air was marginally fresher but still whiffy.

The room I was in was gloomy but I was able to see that I'd been enveloped in an old curtain, blue and dirty, very dirty, cream. It had been held in place by a leather belt. I was soon able to deal with that and release my other arm. I stepped out of the whole lot, kicked it away across the floor, and looked around me.

Though I hadn't time to feel smug about it, I'd guessed remarkably accurately to what type of building I'd been taken: a disused office block. The walls were bare and pitted with holes where shelving had been dismantled. The only furniture consisted of my seat, which proved to be an ancient typist's chair with foam stuffing coming out of the padded back, and a metal filing cabinet with a massive dent caving in one side. The floor was covered with worn and filthy carpeting and scrap paper. The stale air was imprinted with traces of a lost way of life, of cigarette smoke, dispenser coffee, 3-In-One oil, and more recently, mouse droppings.

There were no external windows. Light filtered in through a glass transom above the door from the corridor outside. I went over to the light switch and flicked it but nothing happened. I rattled the door handle, despite having heard the key turned in the lock as they left. I didn't know for how long Merv and Baz would be gone, but I guessed not for long. They'd dumped me here while they worked out what to do with me, or went for orders from someone else. I wondered if the unknown controller was Copperfield.

Finding out could come later. In the meantime, I had to get out of here. I looked up at the dusty glass transom. It was hinged.

Standing on the chair didn't raise me high enough. My eye fell on the filing cabinet. It wasn't easy to move, too awkward and heavy to slide across the carpet. On the other hand, the carpet muffled the sound it made as I manhandled it clumsily toward the door. Sweating and puffing, I finally managed to get it into place and scrambled on top of it.

Now I could reach the transom catch which was on the inside and although it was stiff from disuse, I was able to twist it up. I pushed at the frame and it moved protestingly. I fixed it with its metal arm. The resultant space was narrow, but it was the only way out and fortunately, I was slim or, as Baz had opined, skinny.

I had to disconnect the arm and let the transom fall back again, because in the fixed position the arm barred my exit. Gripping the frame with both hands, I hauled myself up and swivelled over it on my stomach, pushing the glass open with my body and trying to anchor myself with my right leg while my left leg hung down on the other side of the door.

So far, so good. Painful and insecure, but progress. The next bit was worse. While teetering dangerously, I had to get my right leg over the frame and at the same time try to turn my body so that I could drop down straight into the corridor without being decapitated by the loose transom frame, which would fall back as soon as I released pressure on it.

I almost did it neatly. But at the last moment my sweaty hands slipped on the metal frame. I couldn't hold on and support my own weight and I plummeted to the corridor floor below. I hit my chin and nose on the frame edge as I went down and landed crunchingly on the unyielding floor tiles. Had I not been taught on the drama course to take a stage fall, I should almost certainly have broken something. As it was the breath was knocked out of my body and my jaw felt as though a mule had kicked it, taking in the bridge of my nose at the same time. The cut on my chin, which I'd received when fleeing from Baz the biker, had reopened and was bleeding. I discovered my nose was trickling blood, too. I hoped I hadn't broken it.

The transom had fallen back into place with a metallic clang that echoed down the corridor. I had no time to hang about here, although other office doors along either side stood ajar and revealed only empty rooms.

I rubbed the stream of gore away with my

sleeve and scurried along the corridor to the staircase at the far end. At some stage this place had been adapted from warehouse to office premises, I guessed in the late fifties or early sixties. Most of the internal walls were gimcrack, forming endless tiny airless rooms out of what had been an open floor. Hence the lack of windows. The outer shell appeared more solid and even older.

The surrounding air smelled foul, of damp, dust, crumbling plaster and vermin, a fetid miasma redolent of failure. The building was clearly redundant because it'd been built when the welfare of employees hadn't been considered important and even the later attempt at modernisation had fallen lamentably short of its goal. It was antiquated in every way, including the cobwebby exposed iron heating pipes that had been fixed along the base of the walls, probably at the time of the conversion to offices, and which were big enough to serve a power plant.

But here at least was a large window, one of the originals, through which light beamed down the passageway and illuminated the graffiti-decorated stairwell. Peering through the grimy glass, I saw that it overlooked a deserted yard and a chained and padlocked pair of high gates. There was a row of brick outhouses, which had lost their roofs and looked remarkably like old-fashioned privies. Visits to those had probably been rationed in the good old days.

I tried the window catch but it'd been painted over and stuck fast. Even if I'd been able to open it, I wouldn't have fancied another dead drop, this time from the upper floor where I was. Apart from its other many disadvantages, this place was a fire trap and certainly wouldn't conform to any modern regulations. No wonder it was abandoned.

I wondered how many floors were above me. There was at least one other, because the staircase ran upwards as well as down. I hesitated. Self-preservation indicated immediate descent to the ground floor and discovery of an exit. But I'd had an idea.

If this place was used by Merv and Baz as a sort of safe house to which they could bring me with no fear that I'd be discovered, then might they not have brought Lauren here, too? I'd never get another chance to find out. For an unspecified length of time I had the place to myself unless there was another prisoner.

I crept up the staircase and emerged on the floor above and as I did so, it seemed to me that the silence was broken by the muffled sound of voices. Was I not alone? I paused and half turned to run. Then the voices were interrupted by a burst of music and a squeal of car tyres. Somewhere in this apparently deserted pile was a television set.

I realised that if I investigated, I might simply walk in on Merv and Baz, taking a tea-break. But that was a risk I had to take. The initial floorplan up here was on the same pattern as below. The office doors to either side gaped open to reveal dismal abandoned interiors. But one opened on to a washroom and on the shelf above the basins stood a jumble of toiletry items, soap, handcream, toothpaste.

At the far end of the corridor and facing me was a door with a narrow panel of reinforced glass set in it. It was shut but there was no doubt that from behind that came the sound of the television.

I crept down the corridor towards it. Luckily whoever watched the telly was a fan of the noisier kind of car-chase movie. The squealing of tyres and the frantic music had both increased and now were interspersed with shots. The viewer or viewers wouldn't hear me.

I'd reached the door and there I stopped to work out my next move. I couldn't just open it, not knowing what lay beyond. I might not even be able to open it. There was no key in the lock.

I put my eye to the glass strip. The crisscross wire reinforcing and the grime obscured my view. I ventured to breath on it and rub. A clearer patch emerged.

The first thing I saw was the TV screen. It flickered wildly and the music was deafening. The film was coming to an end in a final pile-up of vehicles and lots of running bodies. The credits began to roll up the screen.

There was a scrape as of a chair and a shape moved across my spyhole. My view of the TV screen was blocked by a body as someone, jeans-clad, stooped to switch it off. The figure was neither Merv or Baz, of that I was sure. It was too small and slightly built.

The noise of the set silenced, the person in the room straightened up and turned towards the door. I ducked down in the nick of time before she saw my silhouette on the glass.

Because 'it' was definitely 'she'. I'd only had a brief glimpse but it was enough. I'd seen Lauren Szabo.

I stepped away from the door and wondered what to do. Escape from the building and contact Parry would make sense. But if Merv or Baz came back and found me gone, they'd move Lauren at once. I had to take her with me.

I could hear her moving about the room. I put my eye back against the clear patch. I couldn't see her now, but neither could I see anyone else. I was pretty sure she was on her own in there.

I raised my hand, tapped on the glass panel and called as loudly as I dared, 'Lauren?'

From inside the room came a quick intake of breath and a muttered exclamation. She came back into view, darting towards the door, long hair flying, and with an expression on her face that told me everything. Dismay, surprise, anger were there, but not relief, not hope or delight at being found, at the arrival of a friend.

I hadn't time to tell myself how stupid I'd been, but I knew it at once. The door was jerked open from inside. Yes, Fran, I thought miserably, it wasn't locked. You are a class-one idiot. You might at least have tried the handle before you starting calling out her name.

She stood in the doorway, red-faced and staring at me in fury. I stared back, no less angry.

She spoke first. 'How the hell did you get out?' she asked.

I wasn't here to answer her questions. I had questions of my own. I launched myself at her, catching her in the midriff and knocking her backwards. She sprawled on the floor, but rolled over and grabbed my ankle. I kicked out and she released me, swearing in a way no nice girl should.

Behind, the door had clicked shut and as I turned towards it, I saw the key was in the lock on the inside. I twisted it and snatched it out of the key hole. She dived for it, but I shoved it down my shirt where, in time-honoured fashion, it lodged in my bra.

'Right, Lauren,' I panted. 'I think we'd both better stay here so you can tell me exactly what's been going on!'

'You stupid cow!' she yelled. 'Give me the key! You don't know what you're doing!'

'I thought,' I said, 'that I was rescuing you. But I'm not, am I? Because you're not a prisoner?'

She hesitated before saying sulkily, 'Merv told me they'd picked up the girl who was hanging around, poking her nose in. He said you were tied up safe, downstairs.'

'That'll teach you,' I retorted, 'to believe everything you're told by someone like Merv. What's going on here?'

She blinked at me, reddening. 'You shouldn't have meddled and you can damn well stop doing it now. This is none of your business. You're not involved.'

'Excuse me,' I said. 'I've been grabbed, trussed up, chucked in a van and driven over here like a sack of spuds, slung in a filthy disused office and left there, locked in. I feel very involved.'

'It's your own fault!' she shouted, before she realised this wouldn't get her anywhere and it might be better to be reasonable with me. 'Your own fault,' she repeated more calmly. 'We had to do it, to keep you quiet for a bit. We weren't going to hurt you. We'd have let you go once—once everything was settled. Right now, you must stay here. You're going to spoil it all, don't you see?'

Her voice rose passionately. 'Look, I've gone through a hell of a lot here! You don't think it's been easy for me, do you? I mean, since they grabbed me off the street? You don't know what happened! You don't know the trouble I've had managing those two nutters, Merv and Baz! Getting them to do what I wanted. Even now, I still can't trust them! Apart from anything else, they're so bloody incompetent! Everything is—is just balanced on a knife edge! If it goes wrong, we're both in real trouble, you and me!'

This was all very well and interesting, but missing the point. 'If you're on the level at all, you'll walk out of here with me now,' I argued.

'But I can't!' she wailed, throwing out her hands despairingly. 'I'll explain it if you want, if it'll satisfy you. Once you see how it is, you'll understand why you mustn't interfere!'

She was genuinely distraught. I didn't know what all this was about, but there was enough agony in her voice to make me hesitate.

'You've got five minutes to convince me,' I told her sceptically. 'And then I'm getting out of here, with or without you. But talk fast. No playing for time until your two muscle-bounds chums come back!'

'All right, all right!' she promised breathlessly. 'It's like this . . .'

CHAPTER FIFTEEN

An expression of relief had crossed Lauren's face as she spoke and it irritated me. She'd made the offer to explain grudgingly, as if it were something on which I'd been insisting, suggesting I'd won a point. But I realised too late that, on the contrary, it was what she wanted. I'd been in full flow bawling her out. She'd got me to shut up and listen while she put her spin on whatever was going on here.

Ruefully I told myself that Vinnie's pride and joy wasn't the wide-eyed innocent he believed her to be. She was a quick-thinker and had certainly shown herself smarter than me. Now that rankled because, let's be honest, I fancied myself as fairly streetwise and not one to fall for a sob story or a neat line in manipulation. Yet here I was, taking the bait, hook, line and sinker.

Of course I knew I didn't have to do as she wanted. Especially as a sentence she'd let slip about getting Merv and Baz to do her bidding had lodged in my brain. The clear implication was that I was being lumped together with those two. This I did not like one bit.

My mulish expression must have warned her. 'Look,' she said persuasively, 'why don't we sit down? There's no point standing here shouting at each other.'

I've learned over the years to trust my instinct with people and it's kept me safe till now. Instinct warned me not to trust Lauren Szabo. Instinct said, run like the clappers out of there.

But there were so many questions I wanted

answered that I actually wanted to hear what she had to say. To begin with, there had to be some really strong reason why she was sitting here watching telly behind an unlocked door when all she had to do was walk out. Albie *had* seen her snatched. She'd been genuinely upset moments before. By not listening I could miss something vital. For the first time in my life, I told instinct to shut up for a minute and I sat down.

The chair she'd offered me was an old-fashioned wooden kitchen type. Lauren herself made a dive for a ropy armchair, which looked as if it'd come from a dump, but offered far more comfort. She sat well back in it with her hands resting on the scabby moquette arms. She looked as pleased with herself as a boxer who knows he's won the first round and anticipates finishing off his opponent easily before too long.

All the alarm bells were ringing frantically in my brain, telling me this supposed kidnap victim was actually a shrewd manipulator, one who always got her own way. But somehow, despite that, I still sat there, waiting for her to speak. Annoyed by my own unquenchable curiosity that kept me there, I was also struck by how very impolite it was of her to have grabbed the only comfortable chair like that.

Irritation stops you thinking. I stopped being irritated and kick-started my brain. When I did, I realised it wasn't her lack of manners that was bothering me.

There was something about that chair and her smug expression now she was sitting in it that was highly suspicious. She'd not only got me physically where she wanted me, she was also physically where *she* wanted to be, which was in that rickety old armchair. I couldn't understand its significance and my unease increased, if that were possible.

I took a quick look around the rest of the room. The window was like the one I'd looked out of before, large and old-fashioned. Juggling the geography of the place in my head, I worked out that if the window from which I'd seen the yard with the privies had overlooked the back of the building, this one overlooked the front.

The furnishings were spare. The portable telly on a wooden crate. A Put-u-up bed with a crumpled duvet and pillow thrown on it. The armchair and the chair I sat on. One of those tin trays on collapsible legs that come in handy if someone is bedridden, or to take on picnics. There were a paper plate and an emptied foil carton on the tray, both smeared with the remains of takeaway food, Chinese, by the look of the dried rice grains welded to the surface. A battered tin fork didn't looks as if it'd been washed through several meals. This place was the pits and I couldn't think what made her sit here, patiently waiting. For what?

'Is it for the money?' I asked the obvious

first. 'Doesn't your father give you enough of that without you have to try to cheat him out of more?'

Her face thinned with tension. She snapped, 'He's not my father. He's my stepfather. There's a world of difference.'

'But you've taken his name.'

'I got given it whether I wanted it or not. He adopted me after he married my mother. He didn't do that because he wanted me or loved me. He did that because it gave him a hold over Mummy.'

I said carefully, 'I've met Vincent Szabo. It seems he knew my father when they were kids.'

Surprise flashed into her eyes, which mirrored the mental gymnastics within as she adjusted to the new facts. She got them sorted out and filed away.

'Nice,' she said rudely, adding, 'What did you think of him, my *stepdaddy*, when you met him?'

I considered my reply. I recalled the little man in his too-big clothes, sitting in his outsize car, driven by a hulking chauffeur. It had been like watching a child trying on grown-up clothes in play, shuffling perilously in overlarge shoes while lugging a parent's briefcase along with both hands. Yet it would be foolish to dismiss such a successful man as a mere player. Whatever else he might be, he wasn't that. There was something about the little man that made one cautious. The truth was, I hadn't

280

known, and still didn't, what to make of Szabo. All I could remember was his pain at the thought of the torments he had imagined his daughter was suffering at this very moment. That same daughter, however, would appear to be cruelly indifferent to his feelings.

I said cautiously, 'He's really distressed about all this, Lauren. He's imagining all sorts. He thinks you're terrified, starved, locked in a cupboard or something. Even dead.'

'Good,' she said viciously. 'Let him sweat.'

'Why?' I asked her simply.

She took her hands from the moquette arms of the chair and rested them on her thighs. 'What you've got to know about Vinnie Szabo,' she said, 'is that he's just an old-fashioned wife beater. A plausible and clever one when it came to covering up the evidence. But a nasty, cruel, sadistic little monster all the same.'

'The women's refuge!' It suddenly dawned on me. 'That's why you helped out there.'

'Sure. Mummy and I even lived there for a couple of weeks when I was eight. She ran away and came down to London because she thought he wouldn't find us. But you don't shake off Vincent Szabo that easily. He tracked us down and persuaded Mummy to come home with him. He promised he was going to change, all that sort of crap. He didn't. He was OK for about a month and then it started again. It's a sex thing with him, you see. He can't do it unless he beats the woman

281

around first. It gives him a thrill, gets him going.'

'Did he hit you too?' I asked.

She shook her head, long hair falling around her face. She raised her right hand to push it back and when she let the hand fall again, it rested between her thigh and the side of the chair.

'He knew that would be the one thing Mummy wouldn't put up with. He didn't need to hit me, though. He could use me to frighten Mummy in quite a different way. He was paying for expensive schools, for ballet lessons, piano lessons. He bought me a pony. We had a nice big comfortable house. All he had to say to Mummy was that if she left and took me, I'd be the loser because I'd lose all that. My mother wanted the best for me and he'd persuaded her all those things added up to the best. That a house full of violence and fear went with them didn't make them seem less desirable.'

Aggressively, Lauren added, 'Don't get my mother wrong! She didn't want material advantages for herself, she wanted them for me. She'd been at a really low point when she met him. She'd lost everything and she was desperate. She'd even feared she might have to put me into care. He appeared like the answer to a prayer and he'd seemed all right. Not one to set the world on fire, but a nice man who'd offer a comfortable home and security to us both.

'She couldn't have been more wrong. He wasn't a nice man. There was no security—not from fear. Only the comfortable home was real. She clung to it, salvaging it, if you like, from the wreck of her dreams.'

Lauren's gaze had grown absent, staring back into memory. 'I tried to tell her that all I wanted was to see her free of him and happy. But she only told me I didn't understand how important it was for me to be well educated, to move in good company, make nice friends, meet nice boys. She was trying to make the best of a bad job. If I got something out of the whole rotten deal, then at least she hadn't failed completely.'

She sniffed in derision. 'Those nice boys and their nice parents would've run a mile if they'd known the truth. Mummy wasn't a fool but she was a sick woman and she worried about the future. She knew she was going to die and leave me. If she left me with Vinnie at least I'd be comfortable. "I'm not going to make old bones, Lauren," was how she put it.'

I ventured to interrupt: 'But she did run away at least once.'

'Yes. At the bottom of her heart she knew she ought to get out. She was confused, I suppose. She got into a situation which was bad but she didn't know how to change it. Vinnie had got the upper hand. She was sort of conditioned to accept whatever he dealt out. I can't explain it. It happens. It happens all the time.'

'I understand, believe it or not,' I said. 'But after your mother died, you could have left Szabo's house.'

She gave an odd tight little smile. 'Sure I could. I could have walked out and let Vinnie get away with it. Get away with all those years of misery my mother suffered. Well, I'd long ago made up my mind he wasn't going to do that! I'd make him pay somehow. I wasn't sure how, but I knew I'd do it one day. So I stayed around and watched for an opportunity.'

She shrugged. 'The funny thing is, I think that after Mummy died, Vinnie began to be scared of me. I definitely have the edge over him in our relationship. Perhaps he's got a guilty conscience over Mummy. I started doing voluntary work at the hostel, just to let him know I hadn't forgotten. I didn't need to say anything. All I had to do was keep going to that hostel, rubbing his nose in it. He hated it but he couldn't stop me. He's frightened to let me go and frightened of me when I stay. I think the roles have got reversed somehow. He can't do without me, even though he's on hot coals all the time I'm around.' She gave an unexpected giggle.

'What about Copperfield?' I asked, puncturing her self-congratulation.

'What about him?' She raised her eyebrows and stared straight at me. 'He's Vinnie's stooge. I played along, but you don't think for a minute I've ever seriously considered marrying Jeremy, do you?'

'I had my doubts,' I confessed. 'All right, suppose you tell me about the kidnap.'

'It wasn't my idea,' she said quickly. 'It's—it was—a real kidnap. Those two dumbclucks Merv and Baz thought it up. Baz works as a motorcycle messenger. Jeremy's business uses him. Baz saw me at Jeremy's office and I suppose he worked out, wrongly, that we were engaged. He nosed around and found out a bit more about me.'

I couldn't help interrupting at this point to remark that Baz seemed to like prowling around finding out about people. Lauren looked mildly puzzled so I explained that Baz had made a habit of hanging about outside my flat in the middle of the night. 'He's dangerous,' I said. 'He's not just hired muscle like Merv. Something else makes him tick.'

'He's a weirdo,' she said, as if that explained everything. 'They lurk about,' she continued, kindly explaining the nature of the animal to me. 'They get a kick out of the daftest things.' She tapped her forehead. 'It's all in here. Not that he's shown any interest in me.' She paused to survey me with a critical eye. 'I wonder why he took a fancy to you.'

I told her I appreciated the plain speaking and had no more idea than she did why Baz had taken an interest in me. She should think herself lucky he hadn't taken an interest in *her*. 'And please,' I begged, 'don't say I must be his type.'

Lauren wasn't really interested in Baz's sexual preferences. 'Does it matter?' She shrugged before briskly getting on with her story. 'He decided there was easy money to be got. So he and Merv hatched their little plan. They grabbed me off the street by St Agatha's church!' She started getting worked up as the insult of the snatch was relived in her mind. 'They doped me and brought me here, the bastards.'

'Yes, they're good at snatching people,' I said. 'I know. But at what point did the rules of the game change?'

'When they started talking money, boasting what they'd do when they got the paltry thousand or two they hoped to make.' Lauren's eyes opened wide. 'God, they hadn't a clue. They had no idea how much real money they could make out of this. They thought if they got enough—' here Lauren's voice changed, mimicking the two men's speech— '"*to buy a flash motor, some new gear, pull a few birds*—"' she resumed her normal tones and finished—'and drink themselves senseless too, I suppose. Well, that was it. That was living it up! Talk about pathetic. I said, "Look, fellers, we can play it your way. You keep me here against my will, which I guarantee will be a lot of hard work and cut into your drinking time, and if you're lucky you get a minuscule payoff at the end of it all. Or we all work together. You don't have to guard me because I'll stay put. We ask for a hell of a lot more, and we split it three ways." I worked out just how much I thought we could sting Vinnie for. You should've seen their faces, Merv's and the other one's. They were awe-struck. They stood here in this room, staring at me as if I was a holy vision, dispensing salvation. After that, it was easy. They did everything I suggested. They're simple souls.'

'Just in case you're under the impression,' I said coldly, 'I am not a simple soul.'

She leaned forward. 'I know that! Look, my share of the money will go to the women's refuge. They need the cash and I'll make it an anonymous donation, once Vinnie's paid up. You see why you mustn't rock the boat. Vinnie's got the money. He's got it piled up in offshore investment companies, numbered Swiss accounts, you name it.'

I looked at her while I thought about it. If all she'd told me was true, and I guessed it was, then Szabo certainly ought to pay up. I oughtn't to feel pity for him. But I still felt uneasy. I think it was Lauren herself, her intensity and the deep hatred she nursed for the man. It had been eating away at her for years, and somehow I didn't think this one act of vengeance would appease it. I began to wonder if she wasn't just a bit unhinged on this point. She certainly seemed focused on her immediate revenge to the exclusion of all else.

I began, 'Supposing it had worked, this scheme of yours—'

'It will work,' she interrupted. 'If you don't screw it up!'

'All right, let's assume it all goes according to your plans. What then?'

She goggled at me and then snapped, 'What do you mean, what then?'

I was right. She hadn't thought any of it through. 'What do you do next?' I asked. 'Do you just go home?'

She shrugged. 'It doesn't matter what I do next.'

'Of course it does!' I argued. 'Are you going to feel better about Szabo when this is over? Will you be ready to call it quits?'

She stared at me, her face showing something of the hatred infesting her. 'Call it quits? Are you out of your mind? Of course I'll never forgive him!'

'I didn't say forgive,' I pointed out. 'I wouldn't expect that. But are you going to just go on trying to get even with him, for years and years, the rest of your life? Because if you do, you're letting him win. You're throwing your life away worrying about Vincent Szabo. That doesn't seem very clever to me.'

She explained pithily that my opinion was of no value where she was concerned. She wasn't doing it for herself, she was doing it for her mother.

'Your mother's dead, Lauren. She went through all those years of hell for one reason—so that you could have what she saw as opportunity. You're throwing away all her sacrifice, aren't you?'

'Shut up!' she said in a low, cold voice.

I tried another tack. I told her how my mother had walked out on us when I was seven. It still hurt if I thought about it. So I'd learned not to think about it. 'You've got to put it behind you,' I argue, 'or you'll go nowhere.'

She told me to stop preaching. Right, I would. What did I care whether she messed up the rest of her life? Besides, who was I to tell people how to live? My life hadn't been a spectacular success to date. But at least I wasn't carrying the burden of old resentments around with me. I'd be kidding myself if I pretended I wasn't carrying any left-over baggage from the past. We all do that to some extent or other. But I was doing my level best not to let it screw up my future.

It occurred to me that she'd succeeded, through the intensity of this single obsession of hers, in excluding everything but herself from the situation. She'd even hijacked me into addressing her personal problems. It meant there was something I'd been in danger of forgetting, and which she was overlooking completely. I wasn't there just because of her.

There was someone else and I was his advocate. If he didn't speak through me, he had no voice.

'What about Albie?' I asked.

My question appeared to puzzle her. Her face went blank and then her eyebrows rose. 'Who's he?'

'He's the down-and-out who saw you snatched. Only he's dead now, which is convenient. The one and only witness.'

She looked at me as if I were mad. 'There wasn't anyone to see. The street was empty.'

I told her Albie had been in the church porch.

She thought about it, shrugged and dismissed it. 'I didn't see anyone. I don't know anything about him. Does it matter? I mean, if he's dead now?'

I lost my temper. 'Matter? Of course it matters! If he's dead, it's because of you, because of what he saw!'

Her features tightened again. She was a pretty girl but when she looked like that, she appeared shrewish. She was wearing jeans, a pullover and a jeans jacket, basically the same gear she'd been wearing the night Albie saw her grabbed off the street. Missing was the Alice band.

The accusation in my voice made her restless. She blurted out, 'Look, I'm sorry if he's dead, and if what you say is true. But I don't know that it is true, and I don't know a

290

damn thing about any old drunk!'

'You didn't send Merv and Baz out to take care of him, by any chance?' I asked. I was so angry with her by now, I was ready to accuse her of anything.

'Of course I bloody didn't!' she shouted. She leaned forward in the chair in emotion but fell back again into place immediately.

'Right!' I snapped. 'Out of that chair, now!'

She stayed put, pushing herself right back into the well of the chair and grabbing the arms defensively. 'Why?'

'Because I say so!' I dived at her and grabbed her.

We were about evenly matched in build but she'd never had to take care of herself physically as I had. She was no street-fighter. I got her out of the chair and down on the floor, and planted a boot on her neck.

'Let me go!' she gurgled, threshing about. She seized my leg but pressure on her throat soon changed her mind.

'All I want to see,' I said, 'is what's hidden in this chair that you're so keen I don't find.'

Well, would you know? It was a mobile phone, pushed down between the cushioned seat and the arm. I picked it up and waved it at her.

'Control line to your heavies?'

She spluttered and swore at me from the floor. I pulled out the aerial and punched in 999.

Lauren twisted beneath my foot and threw me off balance. I staggered and fell backwards into the armchair. She launched herself at me and I kicked out. She stumbled and landed on her backside on the floor. Her eyes blazed through the tumbled mess of her long fair hair. If she could have done it, she'd have torn me limb from limb. I jumped out of the chair and got clear of her.

I was through to the operator. I asked for the police, but as soon as I was connected Lauren took advantage of my momentary distraction and threw herself at me, screeching, 'No!'

We were by the tin table and her wild lunge tipped it over. The paper plate fell on the floor and with it, the fork. I snatched it up a split second before she did and darted back with it held out ready to jab her.

'This is about the Szabo kidnapping!' I panted into the phone. 'I'm Fran Varady and I've found Lauren Szabo. We're in an empty office block.'

Hell's teeth, I didn't know where the block was! I scurried to the window at the end of the room, still holding the fork as a weapon, and keeping my eye on Lauren, who stood, panting and waiting her chance. I took the briefest possible glance out of the window.

What I saw gave me a shock. A road, railings, bushes and—the canal. My God, I thought, I ran past this place the night Baz chased me on his bike. Perhaps Lauren had even been standing here at this window, in a darkened room, watching me run for my life. Any lingering feeling I might have had that she and I were basically on the same side was scotched by the thought.

'It's a disused warehouse opposite the Grand Union Canal. Converted into offices inside but Victorian-looking outside. It's about two or three blocks from—'

Lauren flew at me screaming like a banshee. She struck the fork from my hand and grabbed at the phone. I was forced to release the mobile. It shot up in the air, crashed through the window pane and disappeared down into the street below.

We glared at each other.

'You stupid bitch!' Lauren hissed. Her face was twisted in anger and all her prettiness vanished. 'You've spoiled everything!'

'You should've left Albie alone!' I riposted. 'I don't give a tinker's cuss about Szabo, or you, come to that. But someone has to care about Albie and it seems it has to be me.'

'I don't know anything about your blasted Albie!' she yelled. 'You keep yammering on about him but I don't give a damn, whoever he is! All I know is I'm getting out of here! Hand over that key!' She held out her hand. 'If you don't,' she added nastily, 'you're holding me against my will.'

She had brass neck, give her that. But she

had convinced me she really didn't know about Albie. Perhaps the two men had taken care of that little business all by themselves. I scrabbled in my bra for the key and handed it to her in silence.

She grabbed it with smirk of triumph and made for the door. But as she turned the key in the lock, I asked, 'Where are you going, Lauren? You don't have anywhere to go. The police have kept all this quiet until now because you were presumed an innocent victim of kidnap. Now they'll go public, pull out all the stops looking for you. Your face will be flashed on the nation's television screens. How long do you think you can last out there?' I indicated the window. 'Someone will recognise you and turn you in within twenty-four hours. I dare say there'll be a reward.'

She froze, then turned back to face me and I had to give her credit for nimbleness of mind. 'Right,' she said. 'You're right. So I'll stay here and when the police get here, it'll be my word against yours. All I need to say is, you found the key on the outside of the door. I was locked in here.'

'Don't be too sure of yourself,' I snapped. 'Not only will I tell them the key was on the inside and you were free to walk out, but Merv and Baz, when they pick them up—which they will do—will say the same.'

'They can say what they like.' She smiled at me serenely. 'So can you. Tell them about the

294

key, it doesn't matter. You forget, I know about victims conspiring with their tormentors in their own oppression. Vinnie showed me how it was done, with Mummy. Anyway, it's a classic hostage situation. Stockholm syndrome. The prisoner ends up doing voluntarily whatever the captor wants, even to outright helping, in a weird partnership. As for me, I'll claim I was too scared to try to escape, and later, too brain-washed to try anything independent.'

Crazy as it seemed, I wasn't sure she couldn't make that work for her. She was clever, manipulative, and I was certain she'd prove no mean actress. No one would take Merv's word, or Baz's. Parry might take mine, but in a witness box, a clever lawyer would destroy my credibility with the jury in minutes. It was all so neat and credible, except for one thing—something we'd both overlooked.

Merv and Baz. That's what couldn't be made to make sense. They didn't have an original thought between them. Look how easily they'd been swayed by Lauren's arguments and had handed over all the advantages so meekly to her, putting themselves under her control. Could that pair really have worked out the original kidnap plan? Just to abandon it? Why had they been expecting so little money from the deal? Was it because they were not in charge of the haggling? Not prime movers, in fact, but mere hired heavies?

It was so obvious, I almost smiled. They had been paid cash to seize and hold Lauren. They had not been intended to share in any ransom. Not until Lauren came up with her own deal. Yes, that made a lot more sense.

'Lauren,' I said, 'it's not going to be that easy.'

'Oh, why?' she sneered.

I explained briefly how I reasoned it. 'You thought you were running things because the only people you saw were Merv and Baz, and you had that pair of lowlifes eating out of your hand. But if you think it through, there has to be someone else behind all this.'

She began to look uncertain. I pressed home my argument.

'For goodness' sake, Lauren! The only thing you can be sure about with Merv and Baz is that they're foot soldiers. They take orders from people they perceive as having brains. They even took orders from you. The one thing that motivates them is the thought of money. When they snatched you, they were following the orders of someone who planned it. That person was paying them what looked like a lot to them at the time. It was a flat rate for their services, not a cut of the ransom money. You said yourself, they had no idea how high a ransom could be asked.

'But when you offered them a three-way split in a new deal, they decided to double-cross whoever was employing them. Whoever masterminded the kidnap still thinks they have you tied up here with a bag over your head. Because the organiser daren't risk coming here himself to check. It's far too dangerous. He has to accept Merv or Baz's reports. Merv says you're a prisoner here and Mr Unknown can only accept it.'

Lauren's confidence was evaporating visibly as I spoke. 'But who could it be?' she asked.

'How about Copperfield?' I suggested. 'He owes money to the banks.'

She shook her head vehemently. 'Forget it. No way is Jeremy behind this. He's terrified of blotting his copybook again. He had some trouble a couple of years ago when he got involved in some dodgy deals. He got off with a suspended sentence but it scared the wits out of him. He wants to continue in the art and antiques business. He can't afford any more damage to his reputation. He wouldn't touch anything crooked. He breaks out in a sweat whenever he sees a police uniform. Anyway,' she concluded firmly, 'not only hasn't he got the nerve to organise anything like this, he hasn't got the brains. It has to be someone else.'

Before I could answer, the sound of approaching motor vehicles became audible. We both hurried to peer out of the window.

'The police have found us already!' Lauren exclaimed disbelievingly.

I wish she'd been right. But it wasn't the police. It was a private car, one I didn't recognise, and following it an old van.

Both vehicles stopped. The van doors opened and Merv and Baz jumped down into the street. They went to the driver's side of the car. At their approach, the window was wound down. Then two men stooped and put their heads close to it. An animated conversation began.

'What are they all talking about?' Lauren whispered, and for the first time she seemed scared.

'Your pals are getting their final orders,' I said. Merv and Baz were still huddled over the car window. 'Getting the details right.'

'What do you mean?' Now she'd lost all her self-assurance. She looked at me helplessly.

'Triple-cross,' I explained. 'Now they're double-crossing you, Lauren. You had them seeing pound signs with your offer, but it's all getting too complicated and they can't handle it themselves. Suddenly a flat payment and no strings looks awfully attractive to them. Let someone else sweat over extorting a ransom, arranging the drop and all the rest of it. It's way out of their league. Maybe it's just occurred to them that, even if they did get their hands on a really large sum of money, they'd have no way of laundering it. Word would get round in hours and reach the police.'

She blinked at me. 'How?' she argued, but

without her former spirit.

This was not the time for me to give her a detailed rundown on the criminal world. I said irritably, 'It's called informing, Lauren, in case you haven't heard of it. Merv and Baz know that if they show up with more than the average windfall in used notes, someone will grass. So they've gone to their original employer with a highly edited version of recent events. They're ditching you and your grand scheme, and taking orders from their former boss.'

Lauren was staring down in morbid fascination at the car below and the huddled figures. She put a finger to her mouth and chewed nervously at the nail.

'Down there?' she mumbled. 'He's really down there in that car?'

'You bet he is!' I told her heartlessly. 'He's been under the impression he's been giving them orders all along, of course! But now he's smelled a rat, or in this case, two rats. He's not sure how far he can trust them any longer. He's down there, in that car, come to see for himself what's going on here and to make sure Merv and Baz do the job they've been sent to do.'

'What's that?' she faltered.

There was no point in hiding the truth from her. 'This whole thing's got in such a mess, I don't think any of them can let either of us leave here alive,' I said. 'They've come here on a damage-limitation exercise. Remember, they all think I'm locked in a room on the floor below. The big chief thinks you're locked up here. None of them has any way of knowing I've called the police.

'The man in the car is badly rattled by being told he's now got two prisoners, but he still believes he can shake the money out of Szabo. He doesn't realise that his two henchmen have tried to cut a deal with you and—' I allowed myself a nasty smile—'provided you and he never meet face to face, there's no reason he'll find out. So Merv and Baz will make sure you never do meet him.

'From Mr Unknown's point of view, you and I are just too much of a nuisance. All three of them, for different reasons, want us permanently out of the way. On that they're well agreed.'

Merv and Baz straightened up and began to walk towards the building where we were. Lauren gripped my arm.

'But who is he?' she whispered desperately. 'He can't just order them to kill us!'

'Why not? They killed Albie.'

Below us, without warning, the car door opened. There was a flash of long blonde hair as the driver leaned out and called to Merv and Baz. They went back to the car and there was another brief exchange. The two men eventually nodded and started off again towards the building. The driver got out of the car and stood by the door, watching them go.

'There you are,' I said. 'Not a he but a she after all.'

Beside me, Lauren gasped, 'That's Jane Stratton, Jeremy's receptionist.'

CHAPTER SIXTEEN

Recognising Jane Stratton effectively disposed of Lauren's temporary nervousness. In a flash she was back to her old dictatorial self.

'Bitch!' she yelled at the window panes. 'Wait till I get my hands on you!'

'You're not going to get the chance,' I reminded her crisply. 'Because the way things are going, Merv and Baz'll reach us first if we don't get out of here! Baz, for one, will be looking forward to it! Come on!'

I made for the door, but she stayed by the window. Would you believe it? She was still intent on yelling abuse at the blissfully unaware Ice Queen below. I ran back to her, glancing out to see how things were going below. Stratton stood elegantly by her motor, waiting for her two thugs to return and report they'd dealt with us.

'She can't hear you, you idiot!' I snarled and grabbed Lauren's wrist. I could've left her there, but I'd come this far in finding her, and losing her now made little sense. I hauled her away from the scene, with me through the door and down the corridor.

She was still spluttering with rage as she ran, obsessed, even at a moment like this, with the wrongs done her.

'Would you believe it? I should've known—I should've guessed! She fancied her chances with Jeremy before I came on the scene, you know. She thought she'd be Mrs Copperfield, heaven help us! Not that she had the hots for him—but she always thought she could run that business better than he could . . .'

We'd reached the end of the corridor and the stairwell. From the floor below came a hoarse yell and a burst of profanity as Merv and Baz discovered I wasn't where they'd left me. Baz sounded particularly enraged, cheated of whatever fun he'd promised himself. I needed no further encouragement to make myself scarce. We couldn't go down so we had to go up. Stairs indicated another floor and we took them.

'He dumped her for me because he thought he could get his hands on Szabo money!' Lauren panted as she pounded up the staircase beside me. 'So I suppose she thought she'd get her own back on him *and* get her own hands on Szabo money—'

'Will you shut up for a minute!' I gasped as we stumbled out on to the next landing. 'Just concentrate on finding somewhere to hide!'

Fat chance, was what was I was thinking.

This floor mirrored the ones below, a corridor of stripped rabbit hutches. It offered no hiding place safe from the vengeful Merv and Baz who, from the sound of it, had reached the floor we'd just quit and any minute now, would find that Lauren was also missing.

A painted sign on the wall read 'FIRE EXIT' and an arrow pointed upwards. This staircase was unlike the others, narrow and dimly lit. It was Hobson's choice. I raced up it, Lauren on my heels.

At the top our way was barred by a steel emergency door. 'Give me a hand!' I gasped.

We wrestled with the bar and managed to release it. The door scraped open outwards and a blast of fresh air hit us as we stumbled through to find ourselves on the roof.

I hadn't realised, until we came out into the open, how late it had got. The daylight was fading fast and a grey pall hung over the skyline. The roof itself was flat, with a surrounding waist-high parapet. We'd exited through a square concrete hut-like affair. It was the only thing up here apart from a similar locked hut which was probably the housing for the immobilised lift machinery. Dotted around were some metal hoods crowning ventilation shafts. In the gloom, they looked eerily like giant mushrooms. The wind gusted around freely up here and it was very cold. There had to be a way down. It wasn't a fire exit otherwise.

I raced round the parapet and finally spotted a short flight of metal rungs running up the inside of the low wall to a pair of hooped handgrips bolted to the rim. I looked over.

The malicious wind grabbed my hair and blew it across my face. The world swam unpleasantly from side to side. I shut my eyes and opened them again. Over the parapet was a straightforward metal rung ladder leading down to the floor below. An encircling metal cage offered the escapee some protection from falling as he/she climbed out on to the ladder and negotiated the top rungs. The cage looked anything but reliable. Its effect would be purely psychological. The lower rungs lacked even this nominal safety device. The ladder terminated at a metal platform opposite a window on the floor below. From there on downwards there was an iron staircase, running in sections from floor to floor, window landing to window landing, to touch down in a deserted shadowy alley at the side of the building.

I felt sick at the thought of clambering down there, but sicker still at the idea of falling into Baz's hands. The bolts fastening the top of the ladder to the parapet had leached orange stain into the concrete, but when I shook the handgrips they seemed firm enough. We had to chance it. I showed it to Lauren.

'Shit,' she said. 'I'm not going down there,'

'Please yourself,' I told her. I was more than fed up with her by now. 'Stay here and let Merv throw you over the edge, why don't you?'

'I might just as well,' she retorted. 'Look,' she pointed at the cage, 'if a cat climbed out on to that rickety old thing the whole lot would fall off the wall.'

'That's dodgy, but the ladder's OK. All you've got to do is climb down to that platform, see? From there on down it's a proper iron staircase.'

'I don't much like the look of that either,' she grumbled.

Nor did I, to be honest, and the longer I stood here arguing with her, the less I liked it. It was either climb down there now, straight away, or lose my nerve.

I grabbed the handles, fixed my eyes resolutely on the concrete wall and climbed over. My toes felt for the rungs. They were thin and insubstantial and my feet teetered on them, seesawing as I attempted to find balance. The wind whipped past me fiercer and even colder than up on the roof. It took my breath away, snatching it from my nostrils and mouth. I had a terrible sensation of being suspended in space and for a split second I froze, unable to move at all. I didn't want to look down, but I couldn't avoid looking sideways.

I wished I hadn't. What I saw made things worse. There in the gap, where the alley met

305

the road, was Jane Stratton, pacing up and down in the twilight beneath a flickering streetlamp. She kept looking at her wristwatch, perhaps wondering why her two goons were taking so long. If she looked down the alley and up, it was likely that even in the poor light, she'd see me clinging to the side of the building.

'Sst!' That was Lauren. I looked up and she was leaning over, glaring at me. 'Well, go on, then,' she said. 'I can't climb down till you get going.'

I managed to avoid pointing out she'd only just said she wasn't going to try. Instead I told her I could see Jane Stratton.

'So we'll have to keep it as quiet as possible!' I warned, hoping I could count on her to control her desire to shout insults. I wouldn't put it past her.

I left her to make up her mind and got my feet moving, creeping downwards. My heart was pounding, I felt sick, and my hands sweated, but somehow my foot touched the landing at last.

The ladder quivered and creaked ominously. Lauren was scrambling down. She managed pretty well. That girl just liked making the maximum fuss.

'Now what?' she said, as she joined me.

'We carry on down,' I said. 'And do shut up and try not to make the metal treads rattle. The Stratton woman will hear us.'

Jane had her back to the alley at the moment, which was all to the good. This slight plus was immediately wiped out by the sound of voices from above. Merv and Baz had found their way out on to the roof.

They would certainly see the top of the fire escape ladder and take a look over the parapet. I made a quick inspection of the window alongside the landing, but it only opened from the inside.

'For God's sake, get going!' Lauren poked me painfully in the back. 'Why're you hesitating?'

With Lauren so close behind me that she threatened to dislodge me and send me plummeting down, I began to descent of the metal stair to the landing below.

We reached that all right but then such luck as we'd had ran out. What hadn't been discernible in the dull light was that a complete section of the next staircase down was missing, about four treads in all, leaving a space too big to bridge with an outstretched leg.

'We'll have to let ourselves drop down,' I said. 'From here, down through the gap to the landing below.'

'You first,' she said, running true to form. Somehow, even if we succeeded in getting out of this, I was never going to be able to take a shine to this girl.

I lowered myself to the landing and sat there with my legs dangling through the hole left by the missing treads as I tried to judge it. The absence of good light made it tricky. The gap seemed to fluctuate in width and the metal platform below alternatively rose towards me and fell away. I couldn't see what kind of condition it was in, and what worried me most—always supposing I didn't fall off the side of the platform when I hit it—was that the sudden impact of my weight on a long-unmaintained structure might be enough to shake the whole thing loose.

The exercise would, moreover, make a heck of a noise and was likely to attract attention.

I glanced over my shoulder towards the spot where the alley below debouched into the road, looking for Jane Stratton. She was still there, wandering up and down in a fidgety manner. Her blonde hair gleaming in the lamplight, she suggested a sort of latter-day Lili Marlene. But then I saw something very odd.

Without warning she turned and ran past the alley entrance in an attitude of complete panic, blonde mane flying.

Seconds later an engine roared and headlights swept the street. Her car lurched past but the moment it went out of sight, there was a screech of brakes, then more engine noise and more protesting metal. Something had caused her get out of her car again, because she reappeared, racing back towards the building. Hard on her stiletto heels came several uniformed figures, pounding along on their size twelves.

'We haven't got to jump it,' I told Lauren in relief. 'The police are here. Thank God for that!'

And it's not often you hear me say that when the boys in blue pop into view.

'About time too,' she grumbled, always the happy little soul.

From our windswept perch where we crouched like a pair of dispossessed eagles, we watched figures scurry back and forth. Two brawny uniformed figures emerged, holding Baz between them. He glanced back and up as they shoved him into the police van, and even at that distance and in twilight, I felt the stare of those bulbous dark eyes.

'They've got Baz,' I said to Lauren, unable to disguise the relief in my voice. 'I hope they put him away for a long time.'

I didn't add that if they failed to do that, and the law does funny things sometimes, I would have to quit the flat. Probably quit the country. I fully expected to see two more coppers frogmarching Merv away in similar fashion, but although there seemed to be a good deal of activity within the building, no one came out for several minutes. Then a movement caught my eye in the dusk away to my right. Here the wall around the building's rear yard bordered the alley. To my surprise, a man had appeared, perched astride the top with one leg dangling down on the alley side, the other still on the yard side. Even as I watched in dismay, he completed the movement he'd begun, slipping over the wall and dropping down into the alley.

'Hey,' I yelled desperately. 'Hey! Stop him!' I rattled the nearest iron stanchion in an attempt to attract attention. 'Hey, you lot in there, he's getting away!'

'What do you think you're doing?' Lauren's fingers gripped my arm like a vice. 'Leave it alone, look, the bolts are coming out of the brickwork! Are you crazy or something?'

'Merv!' I gasped, pointing.

She released me and peered in the direction I indicated. He hadn't run down the alley, but crossed it to the buildings on the other side and we were just in time to see him squeeze his bulk into a narrow gap between them. Rats know their bolt-holes and Merv had found his.

I cursed fruitlessly while Lauren wittered about the danger I had put us in by shaking the rickety stair.

'It's all right, we don't have to stay here now!' I snapped back in exasperation. 'We can go on back up.'

'I can't,' she objected. 'It was bad enough coming down that wretched rung affair. Now you've loosened it even more. It's got too dark now and I can't see.'

'We haven't got any choice!' I yelled at her. 'Start climbing!'

'Don't shout at me!' she snapped, hoity-toity.

'Shout at you? If you don't watch it, I'll push you off!' I bellowed.

'Oy! You down there!' a male voice shouted from above.

Torchlight bathed us. We looked up. A familiar head had appeared over the parapet, festooned with hair that looked colourless in the torchbeam and a mangy moustache.

'For Gawd's sake, Fran,' Parry called. 'How did you get down there?'

*   *   *

If it'd been only me stuck down there they'd have told me to start climbing. But then they realised the kidnapped Szabo heiress, as they probably thought of her, was with me. They started talking about sending for the fire brigade and a turntable ladder.

I'd no intention of sitting there for another fifteen minutes waiting for Captain Flack. I told Lauren she could wait on her own. I was climbing back up the ladder.

'I'm not staying here on my own,' she snivelled. With that, she shoved me out of the way and shinned up the ladder like the boy in the Indian rope trick. Metropolitan Police arms lifted her the last part of the way and over the parapet to safety.

Then they all disappeared, taking their torches with them, leaving me to struggle up the vertical rungs in semidarkness, under my own steam.

'Oy!' I called up. 'What about me?'

Parry reappeared. He handed the torch to a uniformed man who directed it at me in a haphazard way as I crawled upwards. Parry seized my arms and dragged me unceremoniously the last few inches over the concrete wall.

'You've let Merv get away!' I gasped as my feet touched the flat roof. 'He ran over there, between those buildings!' I pointed out the crack into which Merv had scurried, hardly visible now in the dusk.

Parry swore, abandoned me and went to yell instructions to others. Reaction had set in. My legs began to quiver and nausea swept over me. I sat down on the roof with my back against the parapet and rested my head on my bent knees.

A few minutes later heavy footsteps crunched towards me. 'All right, there, Fran? Not going to throw up, are you?'

I looked up into Parry's face, looming over me. 'No, I'll be fine,' I managed to say weakly. 'How did you manage to lose him?'

'He must have got down into the basement here and hid up among the pipes. Slipped out behind our backs, but we'll pick him, don't worry.' He dropped on to his heels before me and went on. 'By the way, your Jock boyfriend rang us up, the artist. He said he thought you'd been kidnapped.'

'I was kidnapped,' I told him. 'I've been tied up, hooded, driven around, dumped in a locked room . . .'

'Well, you're all right now,' he interrupted. 'No harm done, eh? You've even got your clothes on.'

Not for the first time, Parry's reasoning eluded me. As it stood, his remark sounded highly insulting but at least it cured my temporary weakness. 'Clothes?' I snarled. 'Why not?'

'Rabbie Burns said he found your costume on the floor. He thought you might be in your frillies.' He grinned. 'Oh well, next time, eh?'

'Just turn it in, will you?' I groaned. 'I've suffered enough.'

He frowned at me. 'Yeah. Someone smash your face again?'

I'd forgotten the blood smears. 'I hit a door,' I said, 'climbing through a transom window.'

'Sounds like you,' he said. 'You don't ever learn, do you?'

I looked over his shoulder to where a sympathetic group was still gathered around Lauren. They were dispensing TLC by the bucketful and I wondered why no one, not even Parry, ever gave me so much as a reassuring pat on the shoulder.

'About her,' I said. 'About Lauren Szabo. There are one or two things you ought to know . . .'

313

Lauren looked up at that point and saw me and Parry huddled together by the parapet. She met my eye, swayed, and crumpled realistically to the ground in a dead faint.

Immediate pandemonium, of course, and summoning of an ambulance with paramedics and all the rest of it.

'Poor kid,' said Parry, jumping to his feet. 'Gawd knows what's been happening to her.'

I let it go for the time being. I've seen some stage faints and Lauren's was a good one. But she was going to have to put on a better act than that to get out of this.

CHAPTER SEVENTEEN

Lauren was borne away in the ambulance for a hospital checkup. I was taken to the nick and asked to make a statement.

An inspector appeared, a thin, pale man. He looked resentful, as though he'd been called in on his day off, probably in the middle of a dinner party, if the smudge of tomato on his tie was anything to go by. If so, he clearly blamed me for his bad luck and incipient indigestion. I had foolishly imagined he—all of them—would be crowding around, vying for the chance to congratulate me and thank me grovellingly for doing their job for them.

Instead I was seated on a hard chair,

presented with a mug of tarry tea, and invited to relate my adventures into a tape recorder.

In the less than comfortable surrounds of the interview room, I told them everything. I didn't leave anything out. A policewoman had joined us. The inspector took a packet of indigestion tablets from his pocket and chewed on them. Apart from that, he sighed a few times in an irritable way but he didn't say anything. Even Parry didn't interrupt more than twice. The policewoman began to show signs of restiveness as my account progressed but Parry silenced her with a look. By the time I'd finished, they all looked thoroughly glum and it was dawning on me that far from being the heroine of the hour, I'd upset the police applecart well and truly.

I'd done what they hate most. I'd introduced a whole new aspect to things and it would result in paperwork.

The inspector rose to his feet, put his tube of pastilles in his pocket, dusted himself down and announced that he would leave everything in the hands of the sergeant. He nodded to me as he left but avoided my eyes in a decidedly shifty manner.

With his departure, the atmosphere changed but not for the better. I wondered whether the senior man had left because if anything irregular was going to take place here, he didn't want to know about it. Perhaps he was just hurrying off in hopes of getting back in time for the pudding.

Parry looked up at the fly-speckled neon strip in the ceiling and chewed the ends of his moustache. The policewoman found her voice and asked if I wanted to add to or change anything in my statement. I said no, I didn't, that was it.

'Play the tape back,' Parry ordered.

She played it back. I thought I sounded coherent enough. In fact, all things considered, I thought I sounded pretty good.

'You're sure about all that, then?' Parry asked.

'Sergeant,' I said, 'I am absolutely sure. I will, if necessary, go into a witness box and swear to it.'

They still looked down in the mouth—more so, if anything. They offered me another cup of tea and said, perhaps we could go through it again later?

I was awash with tea by now, tired and just wanted to go home. In considerable bad temper, I told them all this and added that if they would just get the statement typed up, I'd sign it.

The pair of them exchanged glances. The policewoman switched off the tape recorder. Parry leaned forward earnestly.

'Look, Fran,' he said. 'You're making a serious accusation here. For God's sake, unless you're absolutely one hundred per cent sure, tone it down now, before anything's signed.

You don't want to go on record with some wild tale you can't back up.'

'The point is,' the policewoman chimed in, 'that you can hardly expect Miss Szabo to support what you've told us about her part in things. You've accused her of plotting to extort money from her own father.'

'I'm not accusing her,' I pointed out. 'She told me.'

The policewoman gave me a gargoyle grimace. 'Was there any witness to this confession of hers?'

'It wasn't a confession. She told me because she was trying to get me on her side. He's her stepfather, incidentally, not her father, and I told you what she told me, about how he used to knock her mother around and she and her mother ran away to the refuge. Actually, you can check all that. The refuge must have records.' I knew I was beginning to sound exasperated but that always happens when I deal with the police.

'We'll check,' Parry said grimly. 'But Szabo's not going to take kindly to this.'

It seemed to me it didn't matter whether Szabo took kindly to it or went into a red rage. If that's the way it had been, then his misdeeds had caught up with him, and he oughtn't to grumble about it. Chickens come home to roost and all the rest of it.

'You're making a lot of trouble for the girl, you know,' said the policewoman accusingly.

'And for us,' said Parry, who had his priorities in strict order with himself first.

I felt the tiniest twinge of compunction. Why drop Lauren in it? Hadn't she and her late mother suffered enough? It wouldn't take much. Hints were being dropped here with resounding thuds. I couldn't ignore them so why not listen?

All I had to do was murmur apologetically that perhaps I'd misunderstood and they'd all be happy. It was what Parry and his steely-eyed female partner here wanted. The dyspeptic DI would be mightily relieved. In Lauren's place, wouldn't I have done as she did? Hadn't she some right to try to make Szabo suffer a little in his turn? I owed him nothing.

But neither, I told my overcharitable conscience, did I owe Lauren anything. If she could have got the better of me in our scrap for the mobile phone, it was unlikely we'd be here now. Come to that, she had known Merv and Baz had locked me in a room on the floor below and hadn't even had the decency to come down and check whether I was still breathing. Self-centred little madam. She had wanted to play dirty and she had to take the consequences.

Nor was I going to oblige the police, who were playing their own dirty game, pressuring me to change my story while I was tired and shocked. Justice was in danger in slipping out of the window here, just to save everyone

318

inconvenience.

But I had justice firmly by the coat-tails and wasn't letting go. There was another issue, one that mattered an awful lot more to me than anything we'd discussed here so far. I hadn't forgotten how casually Lauren had dismissed Albie's death. I wasn't dismissing it and neither was I going to allow the police to sweep it aside.

'Look,' I said, 'I'm fed up with the entire Szabo family. I've told you all I know and you can sort it out. You've got her back all in one piece. No ransom paid. You can take the credit for all of that. I suppose you'll do that anyway and not think to share any of it with me! But I don't care about that. What concerns me is that we're in danger of forgetting Albie.'

Parry glowered and the policewoman looked vague. She shuffled some papers in the hope of her memory being jogged. That annoyed me more than anything. As I feared, they'd just forgotten the poor old blighter.

'Albert Antony Smith, deceased!' I said loudly. 'The murder victim you fished out of the canal.'

'Alkie Albie?' Parry's sparse ginger eyelashes fluttered in alarm. 'You're not going to accuse Lauren Szabo of sending a couple of killers after a witness?'

'No, not her,' I said wearily. 'Stratton did that. Lauren Szabo didn't know about Alkie Albie and had no reason to tell the men to get rid of him. Stratton is the efficient type. She'd eliminate any loose ends. You want to know what I think happened?'

Neither of them looked as though they did, but they were going to hear it anyhow. 'I think you told Szabo there was a witness to the kidnap, a homeless man. The witness had spoken to me. Szabo hurried off to find out what I knew. But he also told Copperfield the police were looking for the vagrant, as I expect you called him. Copperfield, in turn, confided in his receptionist. She had probably been holding his hand and making soothing noises during this stressful time, and he'd obligingly kept her up to date on the progress the police were making, or lack of it.'

Parry glowered, but he was on weak ground where setting Szabo on to me was concerned, so he didn't interrupt.

'Mind you,' I added, 'Merv and Baz might have decided off their own bat to eliminate Albie. But for my money, Stratton told them to do it.'

Parry thought it over. 'Leave it with us, Fran,' he said. 'We're not overlooking the old man's death, whatever you think. But we need more to go on than your theories. Right now we can't prove either of the two men was ever in that church porch.'

'They're going to get away with it, aren't they?' I asked, exasperated. 'They killed poor Albie and are going to get clean away with it.'

'Have a bit of faith in us,' coaxed the woman officer.

But I'd lost faith in them. I said, 'I want to go home.'

*   *   *

They drove me home in a police car. Although by now it was very late, both Daphne and Ganesh were waiting for me. They'd been sitting in Daphne's warm, comfortable kitchen, which smelled strongly of coffee.

They greeted me with relief tinged, on Ganesh's part, with disapprobation.

'If you had told me,' he said, 'that you were going to accept to be a model for that crazy artist, I should have advised you very strongly against it.'

'I know,' I said. 'That's why I didn't tell you.'

I collapsed on to a chair. Daphne took charge.

'Don't scold her now,' she ordered Ganesh. 'She needs some hot food and lots of rest.'

She proceeded to feed me homemade soup and crusty bread, and brewed up a hot toddy to finish it—and me—off.

In between mouthfuls of soup, I told them all about everything, what had happened to me at the community hall, at the office block, on the fire escape, and at the police station.

Daphne clicked her tongue disapprovingly. 'That girl's certainly caused a lot of people a

321

lot of trouble, much of it unnecessary by the sound of it. To think she could simply have walked out of there! If you ask me . . .'

Daphne was fair-minded. She searched for some form of condemnation which would make allowance for Lauren's unhappy childhood and well-intentioned if warped scheme for raising money for the refuge, all of which I'd explained.

'If you ask me,' she concluded, 'that young woman needs straightening out.'

I thought, good luck to anyone rash enough to try.

Ganesh said unexpectedly, 'You can't expect her, Lauren, to be a nice person.'

We stared at him.

'Where would she learn about niceness?' he asked. 'She was a young child when her mother married Szabo. From then on, all she saw was violence and betrayal, not only in her own home, but at the refuge, listening to the stories of the other women there.'

'And yet,' I said unwillingly, because it was hard to speak up on behalf of anyone in this whole business, 'and yet Szabo did seem so fond of her when he talked to me. When he spoke of her being in the hands of criminals, he was nearly in tears.'

'People cry for all sorts of reasons,' was Ganesh's response to this. 'Half the time, they're crying for themselves. How do you know Szabo wasn't just feeling sorry for himself?'

Daphne cleared her throat delicately. 'I've always been fascinated by the story of Elizabeth Barrett,' she said. 'You know, the Barretts of Wimpole Street? She was a poetess and ran away with Robert Browning?'

'I know it,' I said. 'But sorry, Daphne, I don't see the connection. I don't see Lauren lying on a sofa writing verse.'

Daphne leaned forward. 'But there was no need for Elizabeth to lie on her sofa, day in and day out, in Wimpole Street, was there? She wasn't an invalid. Her father had persuaded her that she was, to keep her there. By all accounts he treated his children abominably, yet had he been asked to defend his actions, he would have insisted he'd acted out of love.'

'I don't know these Barretts,' said Ganesh. 'But I do know that when something's really badly wrong in a family, you often find that every member of it swears blind everything is just fine. You read it in the papers every day. Women married to murderers swear the bloke was a perfect husband and father. Families,' added Ganesh with some emotion, 'no one understands them, only the family members.'

This was all getting beyond me. I wasn't in the mood for subtle argument. I'd had a very packed day, and the toddy and the soup combined were making me drowsy. The kitchen was very warm. Exhaustion took over.

'You know,' I mumbled. 'I told Parry no one trusted anyone else in this business. I was right. Even Stratton didn't know her two goons were cutting a separate deal with the kidnap victim.'

'You need to go to bed,' Daphne said firmly. 'A good night's sleep will set you right.'

'Is that the time?' Ganesh looked at his watch and leaped up with a hunted expression. 'I've got to go! Hari will have locked up the place and I'll have to get him out of bed to let me in. I'll never hear the last of it.'

'You can doss down in my place till morning,' I mumbled, 'and go back when he opens the shop.'

'Or I've got a spare bed,' offered Daphne.

'Thanks but no,' he said. 'Hari will've been on the phone to High Wycombe by then. Dad'll be on the first train up to town.'

Let him sort it out. Not for the first time, I appreciated the fact that I had no one. I propped my head in my hands. I knew I ought to go but was too tired to move.

'Don't be depressed, dear,' Daphne said, returning from showing Ganesh out. 'I think you've been a heroine.'

I thanked her, but said I felt a failure. 'All I wanted to do was get justice for Albie. I also wanted to find the missing girl and I did find her. But justice for Albie seems as far away as ever. On top of all that, they've lost Merv.'

Daphne sighed and joined me at the table. 'Things will work out, Fran. Give the police a chance. They've only just got the girl back. They'll go into it all very thoroughly, I'm sure.' With slightly less assurance she added, 'They'll find out the truth about your friend, Albie.'

'Truth is no good without evidence,' I told her. I hauled myself to my feet, because I was going to fall asleep where I sat if I didn't make a move right there and then. I apologised for keeping her and thanked her for the soup.

'Nonsense,' she said. 'I'm just so glad you're safe. You're sure you wouldn't like to sleep here tonight? I can make up a bed in a jiff.'

'Thanks, but I've only got to go down to the basement, after all,' I told her.

She led me down the hall and opened the front door. A blast of cool air swept in, shaking me out of the mist of tiredness. The street was bathed in murky lamplight and empty—no!

It wasn't empty. Coming towards us along the pavement was an extraordinary sight.

Two figures lurched along in a disorganised fashion as if arguing with one another. The taller one, who urged the other on, I recognised at once as Ganesh. The smaller one, who was protesting and grumbling as he scurried spider-fashion alongside, was invisible beneath a motley assortment of old clothes bound round with string. One of those old-fashioned Balaclava knitted hoods covered his head and in his arms he was clasping some sort of bundle. The pair of them reached the bottom of the steps to Daphne's door.

'Fran!' Ganesh called up excitedly. 'I've found him! I mean, he found me! He was waiting for me at the shop!'

The mobile pile of rags emerged from behind Ganesh into the light flooding down the steps from Daphne's hall.

'Good gracious!' muttered Daphne as a powerful odour enveloped us.

Only one person smelled that bad.

'Jonty!' I cried. 'I—we—thought you were dead!'

'Dead?' He snorted, coughed and wheezed, then spat to one side.

Ganesh leaped back. 'Hey!'

'If I ain't dead,' Jonty croaked, 'it's because I was bloody lucky. I got out, I did. I run like I never run before or since! They was busy nabbing poor old Albie and they hadn't time to grab me. I got away and I've kept away till now.'

He moved up a step, closer to us, still clasping the sack with his assorted possessions. Daphne retreated hastily.

Jonty peered up at me. I hadn't seen his face before. Framed in the filthy knitted hood, it resembled some sort of monkey's, creased in deep lines and sprinkled with grey whiskers. His eyes were small and bloodshot and fixed me with a ferocious expression. Spittle dribbled from his mouth as he spoke and he appeared to have very few teeth.

'Go on, tell her!' urged Ganesh from behind

him. 'Tell her why you came back.'

Jonty cast him a look of mixed surprise and disapproval. 'Course I come back, soon as it was safe. He was my mate, was Albie. I couldn't have helped him. I couldn't have done nothing to save him, but I want ter see right done by Albie. By his memory, like.' He took one hand from the bundle and poked a yellowed forefinger at me. 'You're a do-gooder, you are. Well, do a bit of good, then. Go and tell the coppers what I told him!' Jonty jerked his thumb over his shoulder at Ganesh.

'Yes, I know you've told me!' Ganesh said testily. 'But I want you to tell Fran!'

'All right, then.' Jonty cleared his throat again and I waited apprehensively for him to spit. But after taking a brief look round, he seemed to decide this wasn't the place, and just began, 'When you come and found me that night in the porch, I told you, didn't I, I was waiting for old Albie to turn up? Expected him, I did. Sure enough, a bit later he come along. He brought a bottle of whisky. Half-bottle of Bell's it was. He said, he'd seen you two and you wanted to take him along to talk to the police the next day. You wanted him to tell 'em what he saw, about that girl being snatched. He said, he'd fixed to meet the young lady there at Marylebone Station. He said that he—' Jonty's blackened thumbnail hooked towards Ganesh again—'that feller there worked in that newsagent's, up near the traffic lights, a bit down from that spud caff. So when I reckoned things might've quietened down a bit and those two fellers weren't looking for me no more, that's where I went.'

'He was waiting for me,' said Ganesh. 'In a doorway near the shop. He jumped out as I went past. I couldn't believe my eyes.'

'Jonty,' I whispered, all trace of tiredness gone, 'are you saying you saw the two men take Albie away? That you can remember what they looked like and can identify them?'

'That's what I'm telling you, isn't it?' Jonty was getting irritated at my obtuseness. 'I saw them two blokes. I was there when they grabbed old Albie. One was a big slab of a feller, all pale, pale hair, eyes, like a walkin' stick of lard. The other was a little dark feller wearing one of them leather motorcyclist's jackets. They drove up in an old Cortina. They hadn't reckoned on finding me there too, and they'd have taken me along with Albie, I reckon, only Albie was putting up a good scrap and it took the two of 'em to drag him away. So that's when I scarpered. Remember 'em? I'll never forget 'em.'

I could've kissed him. I didn't because of the smell. But I could've done.

We weren't going to make the mistake with Jonty we'd made with Albie. Now we'd got him, we weren't going to lose him. We marched him down to the police station right away.

They weren't too pleased to see us. They complained about the smell. But when we got them to understand what it was all about, they changed their minds.

When I finally got home again, it was one in the morning. I fell on the sofa and slept through till noon the following day.

CHAPTER EIGHTEEN

I was woken by the ringing of my doorbell. It gave me quite a start and for a moment I was disorientated, then I pushed my head out of the duvet, squinted at the alarm clock and saw it was one in the afternoon.

Someone was outside the window and tapping on the pane. I hoped it wasn't Parry. I couldn't face the police in any form just at the moment, even if they'd come to tell me they'd caught Merv. For a nasty moment I wondered whether it could be Merv, bent on revenge. But he was unlikely to tap politely at the window. Chuck a brick through it, more likely. I trailed over there and saw Ganesh gesturing at me.

I let him in. He was carrying a plastic bag filled with something that clinked as he set it down.

'I just dashed round to see how you are today,' he said. 'In my lunch-break,' he added sounding martyred.

I said I was fine. I had a slight headache and was also hungry.

Ganesh fished a large block of milk chocolate from inside his jacket. 'Hari sends this and is glad you're safe.' He pushed the plastic carrier with his foot. 'And I've brought these from the chilled cupboard. Half a dozen iced teas. Good for you. I'll put 'em in your fridge.'

I could hear him rattling around in the fridge and in my kitchen generally. He came back to announce. 'All you've got is a tin of tomato soup and some stale sliced bread. I can make toast and heat the soup, if you like.'

I told him to carry on while I went to shower. A little later, sharing the soup, accompanied by iced tea, with milk chocolate squares for dessert, I listened while he told me that word of my heroism had spread locally.

'Hari's telling everyone,' he said. 'You're famous.'

'That'll please Parry,' I said. 'You haven't heard whether they've picked up Merv, I suppose?'

'No, but they'll find him. He's a local villain. He won't go far. Off his home turf he'd be lost.' He nodded confidently and broke off another square of chocolate. 'They'll pick him up in no time.'

I was glad Ganesh was so certain, but had I been in Merv's boots, I'd be putting as much distance as I could between London and myself. Lost in the grey underworld of any large city, Merv could be at liberty indefinitely, not a pleasant thought.

'To think I handed the whole gang to them on a plate,' I said bitterly, 'and still the coppers managed to lose one of them.'

'They ought to give you a reward,' Ganesh insisted indistinctly through the chocolate. 'They owe everything to you.'

I put down my spoon. 'Listen, I just want to forget it for a few hours, right? It's going to be bad enough reliving it when the case gets to court. I only ever wanted to achieve two things and I managed both. I wanted to find Lauren and I found her. I wanted to see justice done by Albie. With luck we'll get that now Jonty's turned up again.'

Ganesh looked as if he'd just remembered something. 'That Scotsman's been into the shop,' he said. 'The artist. He left this for you.' He delved into his pocket again and produced a grubby envelope.

It contained twenty quid and a note promising to pay me the remaining ten pounds when Angus should have it.

'That's legal,' said Ganesh, who had read the note upside-down. 'That's an IOU. Make him pay you. You earned it.'

'He'll pay me,' I said. 'He's the honest type.'

'And you're too trusting,' he said sententiously.

'Me? I'll never trust anyone again. Not after all I've been through. But Angus will pay me. I'll keep nagging Reekie Jimmie if he doesn't and Jimmie will make him pay.'

'You know,' Ganesh said, 'I really don't think you ought to do anything like that again. That modelling business, it wasn't decent.'

I told him it had been more than decent. But I wouldn't be offering my services to Angus again. Not because I was suddenly prudish or was having to wait for the balance of my money—I was sure Angus would pay me—but because I didn't dare think what Angus's next project might be.

* * *

It was all very well talking airily to Ganesh of my resolve to keep well away from the aftermath of the whole business. I knew I'd have to give evidence at some future point when Stratton and her henchmen came to trial. I also knew in my bones that I hadn't seen the last of Vinnie Szabo. I'd come across him eventually in court, but he wouldn't wait that long. By the time it got to court, it'd be too late. He'd be round before that. Even so, I didn't expect him to turn up quite so soon as he did.

He came that very day. Ganesh hadn't been gone long. It was about two thirty and I was in the kitchenette, washing up the soup bowls.

The doorbell rang again. When I looked out of the window, fearing this time it would be Parry, I saw Szabo, standing in the basement well. I think I'd have preferred Parry.

I couldn't see the chauffeur. I supposed he was waiting with the car nearby. I opened the door.

Szabo bustled in, rubbing his hands together, his fringe of hair standing up like a halo round his bald crown.

'My dear,' he said with patently false solicitude, 'are you all right?'

I told him I was fine.

He shifted about from foot to foot and looked uneasily around the room. 'You're alone? I was hoping to have a confidential word . . .'

I said I was alone and asked him if he wanted to sit down. He was making me nervous fidgeting about like that.

He sat on the edge of my blue rep sofa and it was a bad choice because being a little fellow, the big old sofa dwarfed him. His feet, I noticed for the first time, were as tiny as a woman's and neatly shod in highly polished black shoes with pointed toes and built-up heels. Handmade at a guess and very expensive. He looked so ill at ease that I had to start the conversation off.

'How's Lauren?' I asked, trying to sound neutral.

'Oh, recovering. It was a terrible ordeal . . .'

He blinked. 'About the circumstances in which she was held—in which you found her. I am, of course, more than grateful that you did! I can't express my thanks enough. But there, er, there does seem to have been some misunderstanding, about the *exact* circumstances, I mean . . .'

'Oh?' I asked coolly, and waited for what I knew was coming.

'It's quite understandable,' he said quickly, 'that you were unable to think clearly by the time the police arrived last night at that dreadful warehouse. You may be misremembering some things as a result.'

'Me not thinking clearly?' I interrupted indignantly. 'I got your precious Lauren out of there!'

He held up both hands palms outward to stem my protest. 'My dear, my dear! I'm not accusing you of anything! I'm not blaming you, please believe me! In no way at all am I criticising, not in the slightest! Without you, I wouldn't have my girl back again. Forgive me if I've phrased this badly. I'll start again. Let me put it another way. Perhaps you didn't lack presence of mind. But Lauren had been imprisoned in that place at the mercy of those thugs and as a result, she was confused and frightened. She may have said things to you which—well, which were not quite correct.'

'About her time at the refuge with her mother, you mean?' I asked.

The muscles round his mouth twitched and the skin turned white. 'She was rambling, almost delirious. She'd been held prisoner, mistreated, starved. You should pay no attention either to that story or anything else she may have said regarding her relationship with the two scoundrels who held her captive.'

'Look,' I told him, 'you've got to sort this out with her, not with me.'

'But you are the only reason the police have heard these—these ramblings. They've been asking questions. It's highly embarrassing for a man in my position. You really shouldn't have repeated what my poor girl said. Not without checking it with me first. Most importantly, you obviously made a mistake in one significant detail, a very significant detail. There is one clear mistake in the story you told the police and it must be put right without delay.'

'What's that, then?' I asked.

'The key. You said the key to the room in which my daughter was held prisoner was in the lock on the inside. But obviously it was on the outside and you turned it to open the door—and found her.'

'No,' I said. 'She opened the door, from the inside, and found me, if you like.'

Szabo stopped fidgeting and in a cold little voice said, 'That is impossible.'

'I'm sorry,' I said, because after all, it was hard for him to accept the humiliation he must be suffering, now that the whole story had come out. Not that I had any real reason to be sorry for him, but we all do things we're ashamed of from time to time. Supposing Vinnie to be ashamed, which I'd no reason to believe he was. But I gave him the benefit of the doubt.

'You were mistaken,' he repeated in the same cold little voice. 'You had hit your head. Lauren said you were covered in blood when she first set eyes on you.'

'I hit my nose and chin,' I said. 'I wasn't concussed, if that's what you're suggesting. I know what I saw, what I did, and what Lauren told me.'

He sat back in his chair and fixing his grey pebble eyes on me, said flatly, 'I want you to change your story.'

I pointed out I couldn't if I wanted to. I'd already made a statement to the police.

'The police were remiss,' he said. 'They should have asked a doctor to examine you. Despite what you say, I believe you were concussed and confused. Indeed, you still are. So much is obvious. No blame will attach to you if you go back to the police and say you've thought it all through, and you want to amend your statement. If necessary, I can get a doctor to certify that you are suffering from a head injury received last night and no statement made by you can be taken as it stands. It was wrong of the police even to question you at that time, before—'

'Before you'd had this chat with me?' I suggested.

'Before,' he said coldly, 'before you'd had a good night's rest and time to think things over.'

His voice grew louder. 'It is unthinkable,' he said, 'that a foolish rumour should be allowed to take root and grow. It is, at the very least, highly speculative, fanciful. At the worst, it is slanderous. I cannot allow it. I'm a well-known businessman. I have friends, not only in Manchester but throughout the soft-furnishing trade. They respect me. I've got influence, connections in local government who are important men. This story you've told, if it became public knowledge, would be damaging, very damaging. It could ruin my standing, lose me their respect, I'd be finished!' He was breathing heavily, his voice shaking. Tears filled his eyes and he blinked them away and he leaned towards me, 'It must be stopped. I've come here to stop it and I shall stop it.' Behind the tears his eyes gleamed with frightening intensity.

I forced back the instinct to flinch and managed to hold that almost maniacal gaze. I wondered why, a few minutes before, I'd been feeling sorry for him. Here he was asking me to swear to lies. Not to protect Lauren from any charge of conspiracy to impede police enquiries or to extort money, or whatever she might be guilty of. No, he feared for himself, for his reputation socially, his business contacts, the cosy little deals with his influential friends and his personal self-esteem.

'Forget it,' I told him. 'Ganesh was right. You don't care about Lauren, you only care about yourself. You want to keep her under your thumb, at home where you can keep an eye on her or married to Copperfield which would be the next best thing, because you don't trust her not to blab out the truth. You're just a control freak, that's what you are, and a nasty little sadistic one!'

His mouth twitched. The tears had dried. For a moment I almost thought he might hit me. Instead, he turned to another method of settling opposition, one which he'd probably found effective in the past.

He put a hand to his inside coat pocket and said silkily, 'If it's a question of money . . .'

'It's not a question of money!' I snapped.

He hastened to rephrase the offer he'd been about to make. 'I mean, I had been intending to offer a reward to anyone leading us to Lauren. I would have done so if the police hadn't insisted on a media ban. It's quite allowable in the circumstances and you are more than entitled to that reward. It's a considerable amount.'

He might be able to buy a doctor's certificate, but he wasn't going to buy me.

'There are other things beside money,' I told

him.

His hand dropped from his lapel. 'Such as?' He stared at me with his mouth twisted scornfully. 'I'd have thought that in your situation money was of prime importance. What else could there be?'

'Honour,' I said. 'Honour, Mr Szabo. My father understood honour. He was an honourable man. Which is why, although you may have known him as a boy, I don't believe you and he were ever friends.'

His mouth opened and closed soundlessly. For a moment there was such fury in his eyes that this time I really thought he was going to attack me and I cast my eye round for some sort of weapon with which I could fend him off. But instead he got to his feet.

'I see you are indeed your father's daughter,' he said nastily. 'Bondi could also be very stupid.'

I watched him leave. I'd made an enemy, but it couldn't be helped. You can't go through life without treading on a few toes. I hoped I'd trodden hard on Vinnie Szabo's polished handmades.

*   *   *

The next few days passed off uneventfully, for which I was grateful. They were busy, however. Some kind of family crisis blew up in High Wycombe which meant Ganesh had to go there and stay over to help settle it. So I went to help out Hari in the shop. I was still basking in glory in Hari's eyes so he was over the moon to have me there and kept pointing me out to customers, which was embarrassing. It was also good business, of course. They hung around to gawp at me and generally bought some extra item to excuse their curiosity.

Hari appeared quite sorry when the last day of my temporary employment came. When he shut up shop at eight, he invited me into his back parlour for a cup of tea and told me his medical history in amazing detail. Hari cheers up when he talks about illness. I've come to the conclusion it's a sort of hobby with him. He probably got little encouragement from Ganesh, but in me he had a fresh audience, so I got the complete works including the time he fell off a ladder while stacking the top shelf and chipped two vertebrae. Poor Hari does seem accident-prone.

It was nearly nine when I left. It was that moment before dusk settles properly when your eyes play tricks because it seems as if it ought to be light enough to distinguish objects, but it isn't. As I turned into the street where I lived, I thought I glimpsed something whisk into a doorway a little down from my place. People came and went all the time and it was an hour at which quite a lot of people are about so I didn't pay too much attention. Nevertheless, some little warning signal must have rung in my brain because I paused at the top of the basement steps to look up and down the street.

Had I done what I usually did, which was just swing round the railing post and clatter down into the basement well, I'd have had a bad accident. Perhaps, too, I had Hari's story of his fall from the ladder still ringing in my head. So as it turned out, when I moved forward again, I did so more cautiously than usual.

Even so I almost fell. My ankle snagged some resistance and I stumbled and for a dreadful moment I thought I would plunge headfirst down the stone steps to the concreted floor below. I just managed to clasp the railings and hang on desperately until I found my footing. It was very gloomy now, even though the street lighting had come on. I reached down and felt around and my fingers found the wire. It was stretched across the second step down. That was clever. It was also the trick I'd played on Baz on the tow-path so I didn't need to guess who'd played it on me now. Merv was still around all right. Ganesh was again proved right. Even hunted, Merv still felt safer on his own territory. I glanced down the street. Was he still in the doorway, waiting to see if I fell? Or had he slipped out while I was disengaging the wire?

I went back up again and rang Daphne's doorbell.

I told her not to worry but I needed to ring the police. They came quickly this time. Parry wasn't with them, off-shift it seemed, but the two who came knew about me and about Merv. They searched up and down the street but he'd made off. One of them went back to their car and radioed in while the other checked my flat before I was allowed to return to it.

As it proved, letting us know he was around and active was Merv's big mistake. It established that he was holed up locally somewhere. The radio message the copper had sent resulted in an immediate raid on Merv's mother's house.

It was hard to think of Merv with a devoted mum but apparently he'd been known to hide up at her place before. They had checked it out right after he'd given them the slip at the office building, but now they went back there in force and sure enough, he'd scuttled there with the intention of packing up a few things and clearing out. But the police arrived before he could leave and he was trapped.

Dear old Mum barricaded the front door against the forces of law and order and hurled abuse and kitchenware at them from an upper window, while her darling boy tried to escape out the back. But the police were waiting for him so Mum had sacrificed her nonstick saucepans in vain.

Jonty later picked out Merv and Baz at an

identity parade. Faced with a witness, they started gabbing. They blamed each other and both of them blamed Stratton.

Parry came round and told me the police had searched Stratton's flat, which he described admiringly as 'a real tart's boo-dwar, all satin sheets and white fur rugs'.

The police also checked out Baz's home. I wasn't surprised to learn he'd been living in a single filthy room stacked high with mouldy junk food cartons and women's underwear.

'Knickers,' said Parry with relish. 'Hundreds of pairs. He must've pinched them off washing-lines. We had to bring 'em away in umpteen boxes, filled a squad car. We can't charge him because we can't prove he stole them. No one's been down to complain they lost any and I don't suppose anyone will come in to identify 'em. You've not lost anything off your washing-line, have you?' He raised his foxy eyebrows hopefully.

I told him I hadn't got a washing line, not outdoors. 'What does he do with them all?' I asked naively.

'He collects them,' said Parry. 'You know, like people collect dolls in national costumes or old football programmes. He collects ladies' panties.'

He seemed to think this was a logical explanation, which not only told me something about Baz, but quite a lot about Parry.

In the end, and not surprising anyone, no

charges were brought against Lauren Szabo. Vinnie got a top medical man to give his highly paid opinion that she'd been brainwashed during her time in that deserted block. As the official version went, the two men had put ideas in her head and she'd gone along with what they'd suggested. She'd been living a kind of fantasy whilst in captivity. Szabo sent her off to an expensive Swiss nursing home to recuperate and get her side of the story right before she met the general public again. I hoped she remembered to take her skis along.

As far as I know, she and her stepfather are still together as a family unit. I imagine them, Szabo trying to buy her goodwill and silence with endless presents, terrified of what she might do if she leaves and frightened of her when she's there: she circling round him like a shark waiting for a chance to dive in and destroy him, and all the time letting bitterness eat away at her. There's a name for that sort of relationship. Mutually destructive.

I bought two Alice bands, one in black velvet and one in pink satin, put them in a Jiffy bag, addressed it to Samantha and took it over to the refuge. I approached the place with some caution in view of my ignominious exit on the last occasion I was there. But this time it was all smiles because news of my part in Lauren's rescue had given me something akin to celebrity status. This couldn't last, but I might as well enjoy it while it did. Miriam even made me a cup of coffee and showed me the newspaper clipping recounting my exploits.

'It's nice to have some good news for a change,' she said. 'Generally we hear nothing but bad news here.'

She told me Samantha and her mum weren't there at the moment, but they would keep my gift safe until they returned. 'Because they're bound to be back,' Miriam added with depressed certainty.

Angus paid me the ten pounds two weeks later. I'd been sure he would and so made a point of telling Ganesh and reminding him of my confidence. Ganesh retorted that Angus was the type who would happily give you his last fiver, if he wasn't trying to borrow your last tenner.

'Spend it before he asks for it back!' he advised.

Thanks to all the excitement and being involved in a front-page rescue story, the photos taken of me at the community hall art show not only got into the local press, but into the *Standard* and two of the national tabloids.

But it hasn't led to any more offers of modelling work for me. Nor, as far as I know, has anyone expressed any interest in any other work by Angus. He's still swabbing out Reekie Jimmie's spud bar of a morning.

The world just isn't ready for either of us.

We hope you have enjoyed this Large Print book. Other Chivers Press or Thorndike Press Large Print books are available at your library or directly from the publishers.

For more information about current and forthcoming titles, please call or write, without obligation, to:

Chivers Press Limited
Windsor Bridge Road
Bath BA2 3AX
England
Tel. (01225) 335336

OR

Thorndike Press
P.O. Box 159
Thorndike, Maine 04986
USA
Tel. (800) 223-2336

All our Large Print titles are designed for easy reading, and all our books are made to last.